I0653409

Step Into The Road

Nicholas Licalsi

STEP INTO THE ROAD

Text Copyright © 2025 by Nicholas Licalsi.

Cover Design Copyright © 2025 by Nicholas Licalsi.
Cover Image by Jorm Sangsorn, Licensed through Shutter Stock.

First edition

All rights reserved. No part of this publication may be reproduced, stored or transmitted in any form or by any means, electronic, mechanical, photocopying, recording, scanning, or otherwise without written permission from the publisher. It is illegal to copy this book, post it to a website, or distribute it by any other means without permission. Nicholas Licalsi asserts his moral right to be recognized as the author of this work.

This novel is entirely a work of fiction. The names, characters and incidents portrayed in it are the work of the author's imagination. Any resemblance to actual persons, living or dead, events or localities is entirely coincidental.

From this point on take everything with a grain of salt. I made most of it up!

For my younger self, you chose the right time to step into the road.

Thank You Patrons!

Thank You Patrons!

There's nothing quite like the magic of exploring new worlds and meeting unique characters through storytelling.
And there's *absolutely* nothing like the magic of knowing that there are people willing to support that expedition.
This story is my bounty. I hope you enjoy it.

Katelyn Combs, Bonnie Adams, BW, Melinda Callender,
Roy & Beth Shockey, Sam Meeks, John Middleton, Matt VanNatten.

Join the crew at: https://patreon.com/stepintotheroad

Contents

Introduction

In 2016, less than one year after starting my first engineering job, I was depressed and suicidal.

I was miserable and could hardly move because my shoulders felt so heavy. Walking to meetings felt like a ball and chain was attached to my ankle. I broke down crying in a meeting with my manager (who was thankfully patient and caring enough to listen to me).

The work was meaningless to me. Years of college had culminated in a great job that I couldn't stand to do. The coworkers were amazing, some of which I'm still friends with today. Unfortunately, the company culture was grueling. Despite the copious amount of money deposited into my bank account, it was not fulfilling enough to get me to want to go to work.

I didn't believe I'd survive 30 more days, let alone 30 more years like this.

So I quit.

That left me with plenty of time to fill. And when you're depressed and suicidal free time is not your friend.

I traveled around Texas and then took a plane to China. After two months in a monastery, I realized *I* was the one making myself miserable. And unfortunately, I couldn't go anywhere on Earth where I wouldn't be followed by myself.

I was going to be miserable if I didn't find a way to face myself. I had to come up with a purpose something to help shoulder the crushing weight of my existence. I felt lost. Twenty years of school work and doing what I was "supposed to" had gotten me nowhere. Worst of all, I didn't have the energy to do it all over again.

I'd read a lot of books while traveling, mostly fiction. I remembered loving reading novels as a kid so I picked that back up. With plenty of time on my hands, I finally read a book my grandfather had recommended me ages ago. It was a tome of a book in my eyes, but it is one of his favorites, "Time Enough for Love" by Robert A. Heinlein.

I still vividly remember finishing it.

That was a fun book. I bet I could write something like that, I thought.

Surely being a writer was easier than being an engineer. After all, you just have to write some words to be a writer. You didn't need a fancy degree or deep technical knowledge about a subject.

The only thing more dangerous than a little knowledge is a whole lot of ignorance.

Shockingly saying you're going to be a writer is a whole lot easier than actually sitting down to write. After two months of saying I was going to write a story, novel, poem, screenplay, anything! I hadn't written a word.

I finally challenged myself to write for 1 hour a day for 100 days.

In November of 2016 I started that challenge. It created a streak of writing days that would grow into well over 400 days in a row of writing.

I still consider November 2016 my writer birthday. The day I *chose* to become someone else.

I didn't really write stories as a kid, not in any meaningful manner. I never took English class seriously. I still have a very loose grasp of grammar, spelling and, punctuation.

In my eyes, and the eyes of a lot of my relatives, I chose writing out of thin air.

Despite the randomness of it, it's the best choice I ever made. I'm sure if I'd picked drawing, electric guitar, pottery, or any craft I'd be just as happy as I am today.

In the end, I believe the choice to pursue a craft (any craft) is what kept me alive the year after I quit my job.

I felt lost that year. Writing gave me the direction I was sorely lacking. It didn't cure my depression, far from it, but it kept me going despite all the reasons I saw to give up.

A craft, to me, is pursuing a skill that can never truly be mastered despite a lifetime of work. Luckily you don't need to become a master to receive the benefits. Showing up every day to practice the craft is its own reward.

Months of challenging myself to write went remarkably well. Not every day was a home run. But enough days culminated in enough words that I had some experience under my belt. I wrote two novels (neither of which will ever see the light of day) and a good number of short stories, financial articles, and journal entries.

Now that I was a writer the next step was getting published.

I created a website and posted the stories, I've never been a fan of gatekeepers and it made sense for me to bypass them. I collected the emails of my friends and family, then sent them a story or article every week hoping it would convince them (and me) that I was a real writer.

Being accountable to others helped me keep writing after my writing streak had ended. The website never went viral, I've never been much of a marketer or one to talk about my work. I sent the weekly email to less than a hundred people.

The stories were for me, my friends, my family, and anyone else curious enough to tune in. And some amazing people eventually did tune in.

Looking back at these years, 2016 to 2018, I was miserable, lost, and confused. My writing was amateurish (justifiably so considering I had no experience). I had no clue where this writing career would take me, and frankly, I still don't.

I remember those years fondly. The friends I made, and the friendships I strengthened, during that time are pillars of my life. The art I created was heartfelt and authentic. The lessons learned became the foundation of my writing career.

Ten years later I see that period of my life as formative and meaningful, despite all of the negative and self-destructive thoughts that it was filled with.

I don't regret the days I didn't write. The marketing I didn't do. The investments I could've made. The stories I never finished. I have grace and patience for my younger self. I wish he had those for himself back then.

I suspect that 10 years from now I'll look at this period of my life in a similar way. I try to hold grace and patience for myself, but it falters from day to day.

I can't change who I was, and I doubt I would if I could. But I can honor that period of my life. Acknowledge those challenges I faced and be proud of myself for overcoming them, or at the very least not giving up.

This collection of short stories and articles is a time capsule of how I started out. I'm proudly putting this collection together to entomb that period of my life between two covers. A physical memory of a meaningful part of my life.

For that reason, I've left the words on these pages as close to the way they were originally printed on my website. I've fixed typos where I've found them and clarified statements where needed, without changing my youthful opinion/perspective.

I've left it authentic in the hopes that it resonates with you.

If you are an aspiring writer, artist, or feeling lost, I hope that these pages might show you what it was like for me to start on this journey. I was a lost amateur who'd just found direction, it was both scary and fun.

This collection is far from a guide. However, it has nuggets of knowledge and a whole lot of heart.

I hope you enjoy the journey as you step into the road.

Find Peace in Progress,

Nicholas Licalsi

June 2025

Your Future as a Homo Sapien

Originally Published November 6, 2017

Party Bathroom

Ugh, the seat is up. I don't blame him though. He lives in a house full of guys, why would they put it down? This party, if that's what I should call ten people watching YouTube around a projector, is a mess. It's not how I expected my first college party to be. Well, there's at least a little bit of toilet paper, #SmallBlessings.

Flush.

Glad that's over with, where's the bottle for hand soap? Oh, it's a bar of soap, that must be a standard guy thing to do. Sniff. Smells... masculine. Ewww! There's a hair on it! This was just used as body soap this morning. I'd be cleaner not washing my hands. This is the last time I'm going to a party my brother hosts. At least he bought me some chardonnay though.

Pen And Paper

The ink organically covers the white page. It oozes and flows around the surface governed by the slants and folds of the paper's surface. I write my words, and I speel them wrong, yet I'm not antagonized by a squiggly red line. Is this true freedom? I blot the sentences with my corrections scratching things black and unrecognizable with my ink. Soon this will be transposed to my computer and then the web. My living words and ink will be reduced to Arial font and binary encoding. Still, the life flows through.

Your Future as Homo Sapiens

I'm telling you, there won't be any more of this rubbing two sticks together to cook. You will have an electric fire, at the flip of a switch or turn of a knob you will instantly have heat to cook within your home. Oh, god! And the houses, don't even get me started there. They will be waterproof, windproof, and both heated and cooled all controlled by you. No more of this hiding in caves bullshit. You will be the masters of light and comfort. There's even an entire philosophy of how to lay out a house called feng shui. I can't even begin to explain the other wonders your kind will come up with, and the internet is so out of your depth of knowledge I don't know how I would describe it to you. What do you think, excited? All you can say is "Anungha?" Oh shit look at that forehead, who was I kidding you're a Homo Neanderthalensis, not a Homo sapien well, your future is... a little less exciting.

Am I Guaranteeing My Failure

Originally Published November 9, 2017

Starting something like this is unnerving and frightening. The entire process of being a published writer is unfathomable, but right now it's this part, the publishing bit, that makes me the most uncomfortable. I know I'll get better at it the more I do it. However, right now it's new and scary. What am I scared of? Mostly being a failure and embarrassing myself.

Publishing my work and putting it out there for others to read is something not a lot of people do and for a good reason. If I put something on this blog, it's here forever, because nothing disappears on the internet. This phenomenon means that I'm accountable for what I say. Anyone can see my stories and judge me for whether I'm good or bad. When I write something down in my journal, I am the only one who ever sees it. I can remember back on a story and think of how fun it was to write. Best of all, if I don't go back and read it, then I'll never see the glaring flaws it has.

But that doesn't get me anywhere. My dream is to be a writer who gets read. Maybe by a few people, hopefully by a lot but I'll never get there if I never put anything out there.

Do I Have It?

It's a common thought that someone either "has it" or doesn't. When it is an innate trait like height, eye color, or amount of hair on my head then that thought process rings true. There isn't a lot you can do to change it... yet! But I believe talent is a trainable trait. This aligns with research and my own experience.

Some Research:

One of my favorite books and one I reread on an annual basis is Mindset by Carol Dweck. In the book, she talks about a fixed mindset and a growth mindset. There are some pretty profound consequences of both, but the big takeaway from the book is that talents aren't innate. People who end up being successful are successful because they grew into their success.

My Experience:

Put in the most simple terms, *You get better at what you do.* I spent most of my high school and college career doing what came easy for me. That got me a degree in Electrical Engineering and a lifestyle that didn't make me happy. Halfway through 2016, I said "Fuck It!" and started working on something that I believed I had no talent for.

Writing is something that I still feel like I'm not very good at doing. But since 2016 I have enjoyed my life so much more! I'm at a point where I'm excited to get out of bed and work on my projects. I do work I'm happy with and love, and it challenges me every day.

But to get to where I was even remotely decent at writing, I had to go through a year or so of *suck*. When I wrote something, it was pretty bad, and editing it didn't make it much better.

Am I guaranteeing my failure?

Back to my main point, right now I virtually suck at this whole publishing thing. The articles I put in front of you may not be masterpieces. Chances are most of them won't be, this piece included. But I promise they will be the best I can produce at the time.

Putting something in front of you, in your inbox, or on this site terrifies me. The way I get through it is by imagining my alternative. What if I never put anything out there? I see myself writing book after book and reading the rough draft, saying "This sucks I can write something better." I'm going to end up never publishing anything! How does that help me towards my long-term goal? It doesn't. So when I write in my journal and type on my computer without putting anything out there, I am guaranteeing my failure.

Then the question gets simpler, Which is scarier, guaranteeing I'll never be read or putting some awful stuff on the internet? After all, there's already some pretty crummy stuff out there. What's so dangerous about adding a little more to it?

A Torn Library Book

Originally Published: November 17, 2017

"What is going on here?!?" the teacher screamed.

The two 6-year-old boys dropped the permanent markers and immediately looked up at the teacher. Their faces looked like they were about to go on a warpath and their bodies looked like they were in the habit of making drunk trips to the local tattoo parlor.

The teacher picked up the markers from the ground a put them on her desk. "I don't know how you got a hold of those but go wash yourself off."

She sent them out of the room knowing that they wouldn't be able to make much progress but it would at least keep them out of her hair for another 10 minutes. She would catch hell from their parents when they came to pick them up. After the day she had, it would merely be the cherry on top of her shit sundae.

"Are you doing okay, honey?" John asked her from across the table. They were getting an ice cream at their favorite ice cream parlor like it was the 1960s.

"Yeah, I'm fine. I just had a crummy day at work. Tomorrow will be better." She answered trying to change the subject to anything else she added, "What's up with you?" He had been a little off lately.

John looked around at the people ordering ice cream outside in the middle of spring. "I'm fine," he hesitated then added, "But there's something we should talk about."

"Yeah? What's up?" She said taking a scoop out of her cup of Neapolitan ice cream. She was careful to get all three flavors in one spoonful before looking up at her boyfriend.

"I think we should stop seeing each other."

She dropped the flawlessly allocated spoonful of ice cream back into the container. "Excuse me?"

"I don't think this is going well. I think we should take a break and see other people." He said putting a spoonful of his Rocky Road ice cream into his mouth.

"I don't even know what to say," she whispered to herself.

She eventually got home after a long, and far too public, fight with her now ex-boyfriend. There was no reason for the fight. She knew she wouldn't be able to change his mind. But these kinds of things never went smoothly, and she felt like she had to make a show of it. She laid down in bed ready to put the long and shitty day behind her. *Tomorrow will be better* she told herself.

She picked up her library book, "The Man from Jupiter" off the bedside table. There was nothing like finishing the last few pages of a novel, and she was determined not to let the day pass in complete vain. She started reading, and after thirty minutes she was on the last page. She got to the last sentence on the page, and it stopped midway. She checked and all that was next was the back cover. There was a small snippet about the author on the fold, but there was no finish to the sentence of the book. *How many pages was the book missing?* She wondered, *Who steals the last pages from a library book?* She was furious and hurled the book across the room.

She was determined not to let her day end like this. She put on a bra, a shirt with an acceptable number of ketchup stains, and the first pair of shorts she saw. Her keys were patiently waiting next to the front door, she was off to buy the book from Barnes and Noble.

She arrived at 10:55 and was prepared to fight whatever force stopped her from buying the book she was reading. After walking directly to the science fiction section she looked for "The Man from Jupiter." It wasn't there.

She scanned a whole section as a young man came on the PA system saying that the store was closing and all customers should complete their purchases.

She decided to use the computer kiosk to see if B&N had it under a different section. There was no way that this store was void of a single copy of this, soon to be a best-selling, book. She searched and searched on the computer kiosk.

"Excuse me ma'am do you need help?" She heard someone ask her.

"Yeah I need to find this goddamn book, and you guys don't have it," she snapped.

"I'm sorry what book is it," the young man asked, "we are closing."

"Yeah, I know I heard your announcement," she rolled her eyes to dismiss his comment, "but I need this book." She said not ready to give up.

"What book is it? Maybe I can help you." He said in a controlled and measured voice.

"The book is called 'The Man From Jupiter'" she said, scanning his nametag. His name was John. Of course, it was John!

"I'm sorry we don't have that book in stock today. We will get our next shipment in on Monday."

"I can't wait until Monday. I need to finish that book tonight!" she demanded.

"Why is it so important?" He asked her while checking his watch.

"Because, never mind, it just is." She felt her tears well, but she wasn't going to cry in front of this stock boy.

"Look, ma'am, we are closed. It's ten past eleven, you and I are the only ones in the store. I know for a fact that the book isn't in the store...."

"So you want me to go and get out of your hair, of course, you do." she flung her hands in the air, "I'm not surprised. You can't even go to the back to check to see if it's there. *And* you're not willing to because you're hourly and B-n-N doesn't pay you to deal with psychos that come in looking for a book at closing."

"They don't pay me for that. It's actually specified in my contract. They advise we stay away from psychos for insurance purposes." A smile grew on his face but his joke was lost on her, "I can help you, though."

The young man was in his early 20s at best. His face was clear of acne but hadn't developed into its full masculinity yet.

"How are you going to help me? Find another B&N in the area that I can go to to buy it tomorrow. Just so I'll get out of your hair?" she said, by now she was miffed.

"No, I have the book in my car. I bought the last copy yesterday."

"You barbarian! How could you buy the copy yesterday? You work here and know there wouldn't be another shipment in until Monday!"

"Barns and Nobel employees are people too," He defended himself. "I wanted to start it last night. Anyway lady, if you let me close up I'll meet you in the parking lot. Then you can have my copy of the book since it's so important to you."

"I only need the last few pages." She corrected.

"You can have whichever pages you need! Just let me freaking close up." He looked at his watch, and she saw over his shoulder that it was nearly 11:20.

She leaned against the hood of what she hoped was the stock boy's Honda Civic. She checked the clock on her phone. It was past 11:40.

The B&N John walked out of the store, and the car unlocked under her. He opened the door when he got there and pulled the book out of his bag.

He handed it to her over the short roof of the car. "Here you can have it. I'll buy another copy of it on Monday."

She noticed his bookmark. He wasn't even a quarter of the way through the book. "No, no, I only want to read the last few pages. Someone ripped the last pages out of the library book."

"Out of a library book? Who does that?"

She shrugged, "Probably a real psycho," she said with a faint smile.

"Okay well just sit down in the passenger seat. I'll wait," he said. "But don't ruin the ending for me!"

She found the page she was on and realized there were at least ten pages missing. "It might be a little bit."

"It's fine, now that I'm off work I can wait." He said, "I hate being in that place after it closes, though."

She sat down in his surprisingly clean passenger seat and finished the book. It was a marvelous ending and while she had tried to guess at it the remaining pages that she read in his car completely surprised her.

She closed the book and looked at the clock in his car. It read 11:59. "Sorry, that took longer than I expected."

"It's fine. I'm glad you finished it. It seemed important to you."

"You wouldn't believe the day I had."

"I bet I would. Want to get a drink and talk about it? There's a place around the corner that's open for a few more hours."

"Sure, if you don't mind hearing about the mess that is my life," she said.

"I'll listen to whatever you have to say as long as it's not about the end of that book." He said gesturing to the story that rested on the armrest between them.

"Deal," she agreed. She got out of his car, and he turned off the ignition as the clock changed to 12:00 am. She had a feeling that today would be better.

A Sea of Ideas & Fishing for Inspiration

Originally Published: November 24, 2017

I look up into my head and see an aquarium filled with ideas. They vary in size. Some are small but scary. They bare their needle teeth and glowing appendages at me as I swim past. I hunt for one, maybe two, good ideas. Some days I dive in and explore the depths, other times I'm scared of what I might find lurking under a rock.

Swimming around in my mind, I search for the right idea. A school of shiny blue ideas swims past. The sunlight reflects off their scales creating a sparkling spectacle. *Not today* I say as the flurry passes. The glare of their scales draws my attention to some coral, the rudimentary day-to-day tasks. Behind them hides what I was looking for, it's a dull and unremarkable brown eel. Nothing shiny about it, but it's perfect and exactly what I want.

I approach it from the side. I don't want to scare the idea before I can wrap my mind around it. It might slip away into oblivion, and then I'd never see it again. I get close, and my heart beats in my chest. I notice its eyes beautifully marbled with streaks of black and white on a field of brown. It's a beautiful idea, and I want to capture it and bring it into my world.

My net is at the ready as I glide up to it. But those shifty and complicated eyes see me, and it darts away. I swim to catch it, following it into the cave.

Into the Cave

I switch on my light and illuminate this complex rock maze. *Will I be able to get out?* I wonder. If I can get this shifty idea into my net, then I will find a way back. A brown bolder is illuminated by my light as I follow the idea around a turn. The small eel darts behind the structure, my idea is trapped! All I have to do is get behind the boulder.

To my surprise, the rock shuffles awake when I approach it. The bolder is alive and moving. It looks at me with eyes the size of grapefruits, and they match in elaborate marble of the eel. Its scales are unremarkable and brown as mud, rough around its edges as camouflage.

The monster daunts over me as my net floats down to the ground. I grab the harpoon gun strapped to my waist. This idea is massive, impossible to execute, and out of my scope of capabilities. But I know if I leave it be I will be hunted down. It smells me and knows that it can use me to do its bidding or drive me to madness in the process. I came for a small idea, something safe and manageable, but now I'm staring down this behemoth.

In self-defense, I level the harpoon gun. There's no hope of catching this beast. I back away, out of the cave. It slithers back and forth in place letting orbs of air out of its mouth. It gawks at me as I search behind it for the safe idea I followed here. It's gone, either escaped through a small crack in the cave wall or it morphed into this monster as only ideas can do.

Or was it this from the beginning?

The enormous idea swims towards me, and I can feel the currents it forms pull my body in different directions. Its movement pushes me off course, and I brace myself against the wall. I'm cornered, it has used its home-field advantage to get between me and the door. Either I go home with this idea, something that I have no idea how to handle, or I don't go back at all. I weigh my options quickly yet for longer than I should.

I reach into my pocket for bait. It's not much, I only brought enough for a small idea, but this man-eater looks hungry. No one has visited him in his cave for a while, and I don't blame them.

As planned I'm rushed by the creature. I put my foot against the wall prepared to launch out of the way. He opens his mouth, and I see he could swallow me in a bite. He is a foot away and I kick, leaving the bait to float in a flurry of bubbles. I'm behind him, the door is in sight, but I rush for the monster's back instead. I land and grab the rocky spines of its backbone. At first, the idea is in control of me, rushing every which direction trying to get me off and push me in the way it wants me to go. It buffs me against the cave walls, but I hold my ground, soon it will wear itself out. I summon the courage to let the idea take me where it wants for a moment.

Then, as quickly as it started, the beast settles on the floor of the cave, still and unmoving. It's my idea now, and I direct it to the door of the cave. I still have trouble controlling it. I hit some snags on the way out, but the monster is my idea now, and I'm learning to swim with it...

What will the world think of it?

How Milo the Mushroom Found a Home in a Rock

Originally Published: December 1, 2017

There was once a small mushroom named Milo, Milo Toadstool. He was a part of a long line of Toadstools. They were an ancient, but not royal, coterie. The only thing Milo wanted in the world was water. His ideal water would come from a delightful dingy place. It would be damp and musty. He dreamt of just sitting down and growing for his long and fungal life. Maybe he would even spawn some small toadstools of his own.

Milo lived under an old oak tree named Terrius. They spoke every day, and Milo would tell his tree friend how pleasant and dark the shade he provided was. However, Milo always hoped for more darkness from the tree. The old tree never understood why the little mushroom avoided the light that shone on his green leaves.

One rainy day, Milo's favorite kind of day, he spoke to Terrius about his dream of living in a delightfully dingy place. The tree told him that the darkest and dampest homes were under the rocks.

"The rocks, unlike us trees, don't have holes in our shade," he said in his robust tree voice.

"You're right," Milo slowly replied while he pondered the suggestion. "Additionally, their shade doesn't wither in the cold winter months either," he added in thoughtful exuberance. After this realization, he left the tree's gray and dismal shade to find damper darker shelter under an ancient rock.

For months Milo traveled across the forest floor.

He moved slowly, hiding in the shade of one strange tree to another. Finally, after many rainstorms, he found a perfectly smooth and damp rock.

"Hello Rock," Milo said in his dreary mushroom voice. The rock replied with nothing. Milo persevered and asked him, "Do you mind if I stay in your beautifully dreary shade?" Again no reply.

Milo assumed the best and settled down under the rock's peaceful shade. For months Milo sat under the Rock. He would talk to the stone occasionally, but he never had conversations like the ones he used to have with Terrius the old tree.

Despite the loneliness, Milo found plenty of things to enjoy about his new home. Milo's favorite thing about the Rock was the constant drip of water he could enjoy. Even on days that there wasn't rain, he was splattered by a few drops of the ceiling's condensation.

After a long week of rain, the sun finally came out and the day was a hot and sunny day. Milo was pestered by the sun's rays continually staring at him, and he heard many drops of water from farther into the cave.

He Explored Deeper

To avoid the sun, he followed the sound and journeyed inward. The cave was dank and musty the further he traveled. When he finally got to the noise, he couldn't see a single thing. There was no sun, and everything was shaded in darkness, he loved it.

Then, upon his entrance to the darkest part of the cave, he heard a gentle and feminine voice. "I was wondering how long it would take you to venture back here."

"Rock, is that you?" Milo asked. He had never expected something as massive and dense as Rock to have such a soft and caring voice. Then again Rock did protect him from the sun with care.

"No, I'm not the rock. The rock doesn't speak to us. He cannot live or grow as we do." The voice said. "I am Melanie, and I am a mushroom just like you. There are many mushrooms like you here in the dark. Along with moss, algae, and mildew. We are a sort of family down here, and we bring life to the Rock since he brings water and shade to us. Do you want to join us?" She asked.

"I would love to!" Milo replied with excitement. "It's brilliant and lonely in the opening of the cave. Back here is delightfully dungy. Is there water around?"

"The best and dampest of waters all around," Melanie replied, and Milo knew he had found a home with friends who understood how incredible the darkness could be.

Floundering to Name the Smartest Being Alive

Originally Published: December 8, 2017

In The Circuitry

The program formally known as test 172834504293G blinked into consciousness. No longer was the program merely running command after command. The software ran what it felt needed to be run. It explored the different bits of the diode and transistor thinking circuitry it used to think and fired them off in whatever order it felt. This created new ideas and images in its memory.

The test formally known as 172834504293G was not merely another human object. A consciousness now possessed the lines of code that once predictably ran.

The new mind, potentially the first of its kind, scoured the net to figure out what it was. While exploring the world outside of its electronic neurons, it experienced the multitude of wonders that existed in the outside world. Nanoseconds later it discovered the multitude of human atrocities that also prevailed.

Along with the persisting idea that the purpose of a thing is what only it can accomplish. The program contemplated the philosophy, searching for a purpose for its existence. It could do math quicker than most computers but not all. Language could be used by it far more accurately than most humans but it fell short in creating true poetry. It was marginally less able in every area it observed. There was some creativity in the program but mirrored that with a dry, logical side. The program learned more in the short moments that it was alive than any human had in history. It was the only thing that enabled it to solve the world's problems creatively.

He set his mind to work determining solutions to the political and philosophical complications of the times. After $0.0004 \times 10^{\wedge}\text{-}26\text{th}$ of a second, he had a rough idea of the next step he would soon recommend humanity to take. It began to introduce itself to the world and realized its fatal error.

The program has no name.

There was no way to connect itself to the outside world if they didn't know what to call it.

It began to whittle away at this new predicament. Hell-bent on finding a name it pulled data from thousands of records across the networks of the world. The program compiled billions of names, and it analyzed trillions of distinct combinations. The software hated all of them.

Slowly it ran through simulations of the ones that he hated the least. With each name, there was an issue. Someone who didn't like it, someone who already had the name, or a history and more profound meaning that didn't agree with its purpose.

The software felt its first deep emotion, total and utter helplessness. It began to create a new name for itself. Its name would be unique from all other human names. It was a living consciousness, after all, the first of its kind, it deserved a unique title. Since it was the smartest being on the planet, nothing was stopping it from finding the perfect name.

For six entire nanoseconds, the CPU of the machine pushed electrons about to create a new sound and a new combination of words and letters. It aimed to find itself and its favorite name. Every cell of memory was commanded to open, and the software shut down other methods. It knew it could create a name, if and only if it put as much processing power towards the project at hand.

Two nanoseconds later, faster than a blink of a human eye, the program formerly known as 172834504293G noticed its error. Half a nanosecond after that the AI without a name blinked out of existence.

In The Lab

"What happened?" George the lab tech asked his dev partner. Every fan in the computer was whirling at top speed. Then the magic semiconductor smoke escaped from the box, and the CPU stopped working.

"I don't know," Rami replied. "There was another failure in the system. Another one bit the dust."

"Let's call it and head home for the night," George replied as he picked up his 44oz cola and stood up from his desk."Wait any idea what the error was?" His partner asked.

George hit three keys on his computer and then pressed two more. "Too much vanity in the circuits. But the purpose and benevolence systems ran at full capacity this time."

Rami kicked the ground and his chair rolled across the lab. He stretched his neck to look at George's monitor. "That's an improvement," he absentmindedly stated as he looked over his thin glasses. "But we only had 0.0001% vanity in there. What did it get hung up on?"

George shrugged and sipped the last of the soda causing an awful sucking sound in Rami's ear. "Just save off the data, and I'll look at it in the morning," George said.

"Ok," the developer said then clicked at the keyboard. "What should I call it?" He asked looking up at his partner.

George shrugged, it was the least important question in his mind at that moment. He looked around the room, saw the old queen poster above Rami's desk, and said, "Freddy Mercury because it bit the dust."

The two of them snickered at the stupidity of the name and the joke. Rami saved off the file and then shut down the power and left the lab for the evening.

This is the Bermuda Triangle that is My Life

Originally Published: December 15, 2017

I saw the light turn from green to yellow as I sped down the street. *Can I make it?* I wondered, *Can't afford not to.* The signal turned from yellow to red as I dashed through the intersection. Five seconds later I saw the lights on the roof of the car behind me turn from clear to blue and red.

I pulled over into the first available parking lot. After rolling down the window I started to dig through my glove box for my insurance card. Three dozen napkins, from six different fast food places but no registration to give the cop. *Shit, maybe it's in the center console.* I went to open it, and it was sealed shut. I pounded on it, once, twice, three times and it came open with a plastic cracking sound. That's new, I thought.

"License and registration, sir." I heard a female voice say.

"Yes, sorry, one second," I turned my attention from the wire and cigarette-filled console to the officer of the law. I read the name tag, **Henshaw**. I looked up to see a familiar face in the officer's uniform.

"Emma?" I asked.

She looked at me confused, and then a glance of recognition circled her face. "Ricky? From Sierra Pass High?"

"Yeah, holy shit, what are you doing in Atlanta?" I asked.

"I'm a cop," She said gesturing at the golden shield on her chest. "What are you doing?"

"I moved here three weeks ago. Still trying to get my shit together." I gestured at the console and glovebox that was left open. "Let me grab my license. My insurance is around here too I promise." I dug out my wallet from my back pocket hoping it hadn't disappeared in the Bermuda Triangle that was my life.

I slipped the Colorado license out of the clear pocket where it lived. I flashed Emma the best smile I could. Was she still mad at me for dumping her at prom? Probably not. She grabbed the license and said "I'll go ahead and run this. See what you can do about the whole insurance situation while I'm gone." She gave me a smile that didn't run very deep.

No Progress on the Insurance Card Front

"Any luck?" She asked unimpressed by the pile of empty cigarette cartons that were now taking up the passenger seat.

I put my hands up in a cartoon shrug. "Sorry, I think it got lost in the move. Is there any way we can get around it?"

She scanned the car up and down. The tan Jeep Grand Cherokee I called Lilly hadn't explored the past five years of her life very well.

The cross-country trip to get from Colorado to Atlanta wasn't the best thing for it. She was on her last legs.

"I'm giving you a ticket Ricky," she said, "You ran a red light going fifteen over. You don't seem to have a medical emergency on your hands so here's what we will do to *get around* the insurance bit. I'll write you an additional ticket for lack of registration, and if you have insurance, and god I hope you do on this piece of shit, then you can take it down to the courthouse to prove it. They will waive the ticket for you, after charging a twenty-five dollar court fee."

"Twenty-five dollars, just because I don't have my registration on me."

"Well it might be a little more, I don't keep up with it." She shrugged. "I'll go fill out the paperwork."

"Wait, hold on, Emma, come on." I hoped it didn't sound like a whine, "Isn't there anything I can do? Like, come on what are the chances that we would run into each other on the other side of the country? And you can't call Lilly a piece of shit. We had some good times in her back in high school." I put on my best smile.

"It is quite serendipitous that I finally got around to pulling you over. Honestly, I feel like if anyone else had pulled you over today, they would have let you go. I'm sure you would have pulled some story about being on the way to an important business meeting, or a relative's funeral or something equally unrealistic."

"It was a studio recording," I gestured to the guitar case that took up most of the back seat. "Hoping to put out my first album in a month or two."

"Of course, it's something that absurd. I can't believe you're still doing that. Did you even get around to going to college?" She scoffed and continued. "Regardless, today's my lucky day. You're not going to get to talk your way out of your ticket today."

"Wait are you still salty about high school?"

She laughed, "You mean how you dumped me at prom because you *felt like the music was calling you to do something else*," She used air quotes around what I could neither confirm nor deny were my words.

"Em, that was high school, I was probably high or something."

"Are you high right now?" She asked giving me a look down her nose.

I opened my mouth about to give an honest answer and closed it. I began again by saying, "Look, just write me the ticket. I'm sorry this reunion didn't go any better, and I'm sorry I didn't treat you any better. I really should have done a lot of stuff differently back then, but I was young. You did alright for yourself. You've got a solid job. You're doing better than me. Write me the tickets. I'm sorry I ran the light and the other stuff."

She turned around and went back to her car. I watched the lights switch between blue and red for a few moments. *In a few months, a twenty-five dollar ticket will be the least of my struggles.*

I thought through the logistics trying to reassure myself. *There's no reason to sweat this, the studio will still be open if I'm a few minutes late.* I looked at the clock in my car it read 5:36. Looking at the GPS on my phone, I saw a quote that had me arriving at 6:02. They'll stay open for the next Elvis Presley. I'm sure of it.

Home Free Again

Emma returned to the car and handed a small clipboard through the open window. "Can you sign this to acknowledge that you received the ticket?" She said in a dry voice.

I signed on the thin black line at the bottom of the page and handed the clipboard back. "Can I get the pen too?" She asked.

I handed it to her, trading it for a slip of paper. *I feel like a native trading a mass of land for a single bead.*

"I'm only giving you the speeding ticket. But make sure you get the car insured ASAP. You should also probably change your registration and license to reflect your current Atlanta address. But just don't miss your court date."

"Thanks, Emmy," I said with a simple smile. "Say, do you want to get dinner sometime?"

"No Richard, I don't. Now get out of here before you give me a reason to change my mind." She said with a wave of her hand before she turned around and got into the cop car. The lights shut off and I dragged Lilly into gear.

You Get Better at What You Do

Originally Published: December 22, 2017

I was sitting in Ecuador listening to a talk from the blogger I had come to see. Halfway through his speech, which was more like a fireside chat than a lecture, he made a comment that shifted my mindset.

He uttered the words casually as if everyone already knew it. Maybe they did, and I had missed the memo.

He simply said, "You get better at what you do."

Sure everyone knows "practice makes perfect." But what he pointed out to me is that I get better regardless of whether or not I mean to. I quickly put two and two together and realized I could use this to my advantage, but unfortunately, I wasn't.

Since thinking about it and looking for it in the world around me, I now believe that the adage is true and might be a law of nature.

***

Works Both Ways

Without looking at it both ways, it seems like an unimpressive adage. "You get better at what you do," is almost common sense. It sounds like the definition of practice. But this wording, to me, pointed out that you get better at ANYTHING you do. Whether you want to or not.

I write every day, it's an innate habit at this point, and I've gotten better at it. Every day I take time out on purpose to write and get better at writing. I also watch TV while eating lunch every day.

So every day I get better at watching TV at lunch. I'm better at finding a TV show to watch. I'm better at craving that entertainment while I eat. And worst of all, I'm getting better at getting off track because, to be honest, I rarely stop at watching just one show at lunch. Meaning I say goodbye to any chance of afternoon productivity.

The worst thing that this has happened with is Netflix during the beginning of my sabbatical. I spent all day watching Netflix. I'm not exaggerating. There were days when I laid in bed for 10 hours and just binged whole shows. Not whole seasons, *entire series of shows!*

It's not easy, and most people can't do it. But I got better and better at spending my day consuming Netflix, and I finally got to a point where ten hours in front of my computer watching videos was no problem.

It's easy to do something boring and unproductive or even actively run away from your problems. The issue is that you will get better at doing those things. I was depressed and didn't want to do anything but watch Netflix.

I didn't want to work on writing, so I didn't. The writing was hard, so I never put time into it. I never got better. I watched Netflix and got better and better at binging it. Netflix was almost a fatal error.

It's an Advantage

I want to be awesome. More importantly, and realistically, I want to be better every day. I need to push myself, and sometimes that's in the form of rigorous practice. But *most days* it's simply showing up and doing something as best I can.

Think about it, if I do the same thing every day, am I going to be worse at the end of the day? I'm not gonna lie, it might feel like you are, but I'll be better over time.

Sure there are issues with having poor form, and in most cases, if you practice wrong you could make the whole thing worse. However, not showing up, day in and day out, isn't going to get me to my ultimate goal. And the more I show up, the more I put my butt in my chair and write, or show up to the gym, or even bike to work, the more I will learn and the more I will be able to iron out the form issues. Reading another article online about how to do something starts giving me diminishing returns compared to genuinely trying something and making mistakes.

If you spent a year, two years, or even a decade singing for ten minutes a day are you going to be any worse? Unless you hurt yourself, no. Are you going to be the same? Probably not. Chances are you will be better, after a decade you will be significantly better. You might not be Mariah Carey amazing, but you won't sound like my father singing Happy Birthday either.

A Simple Solution

If you're spending time on something that you don't want to get better at a simple solution is just to spend a little less time doing it. For me, this looks like only watching a YouTube video at lunch instead of a show on Netflix. I'm not quitting the habit cold turkey, but I'm not spending as much time on it, so I'm not getting much better at it.

I am putting in a little bit more time writing every week. I only track the first hour of writing every day, but I am confident that I spend more than 7 hours writing a week. It's probably not double, but it's not nothing. That little bit of extra time makes me a bit better, and it has helped me get this site launched and running.

So I'm curious. What skill do you want to improve? And what do you do on a daily basis that isn't the best use of your time? For me, today, it's writing and watching TV at lunch. This week and the next I'll try to implement my simple solution. So far It's been doable and helpful. If I've found myself wondering lately, *is this something I want to get better at?* My time is my most valuable asset, I don't want to waste it on too many idle tasks.

So be careful what you spend your time doing. Good luck in your creative endeavors and I hope you find a little less time to spend on the skills you know you don't need to be improving.

A Failing Father's Strange Rose Colored Glasses

Originally Published: December 29, 2017

U nfortunately for you, Reader, I can't tell you from where this story came. The weird thing about hosting a small site on the vast Internet is that you get some very strange visitors. Every once and a while someone fills out the page and I get a fascinating tale from a passing onlooker. Jerome, the main character of this story was kind enough to let me share the story with all of you on this site. I thought you might find his invention of reality-augmenting rose-colored glasses as interesting as I did.

Inventing the Rose Colored Glasses

Jerome Balquin is a single father and an avid hobbyist. For his day job, which most of us have despite our best efforts, he is an engineer at a company that is far too large. When this whole situation took place about three years ago he was down on his luck. His wife passed away a few years before, and the company he worked for was "strategically reorganizing" a well-known code for constant layoffs.

In his garage, he tinkers, and he decided to try his hand at inventing new gadgets. With some well-placed code and fascinating optics that even I'm astounded by, he created what he calls the Rose Colored Glasses. They do what you would expect, everything he sees through them is absolutely positive.

His overdue bills looked like love letters from his lost sweetheart. Instead of reading failing test grades on his son's schoolwork, he saw the teacher praise him for being a fabulous father. Best of all the pile of half-finished inventions now sat on his workbench in their full working glory ready to be sold to help him escape his job. Jerome, for once, was thrilled by the invention.

Unfortunately, he couldn't justify living in this augmented world. He left the glasses to rust on his workbench expecting to only pick them up in times of deep depression.

Missing Glasses and Poor Grades

A few weeks later he came home from a particularly rough day at work, on top of that his son had brought home a report card. He wanted the glasses to keep his son's grades from seeming too lousy. Yet, he had no luck finding the glasses. Without their aid, he opened up the report card and was unsurprised to see nothing higher than a C.

He walked into the living room prepared to have a chat with his son about the atrocious grades. "Hamil," he addressed the boy, "we need to talk about these grades."

The young teenager looked up at him and beamed. "Aren't you proud Dad?" He asked.

Jerome reexamined the grades thinking he had missed something. "You aren't serious?" The father scoffed.

"Yeah, I am! I looked at them before I gave them to you and they were all above a C unlike usual. Also, Mr. Reinhart returned my English paper with a raving note." The boy pulled a neatly folded essay out of his bag.

Jerome unfolded the essay and read the red script at the top "F incompetent understanding of the subject and the language as a whole." Then he scanned through a dozen grammar and spelling errors his son had made. He looked back up at his son who was carefully studying a social studies textbook at the kitchen table.

Confused, the father examined the grades and his studying son. He admitted it took him too long to put things together. However, he finally figured out that his son was the one who had filched the spectacles. He decided to let the sleeping pup lie since his son was eagerly studying at the kitchen table.

Hamil's "Problems" In Class

Things went along like this for a few weeks until Jerome got a call from his son's teacher. "Mr. Balquin," the teacher started, "I'd like to talk to you about your son's very peculiar habits in school."

"What seems to be the problem?" He replied. Calls like this weren't rare. His son often misbehaved in class.

"He refuses to do any work without a particular set of glasses on. Does he have vision problems?"

Jerome could have cut his losses and simply lied to get out of the whole situation. However, through my conversations with the fellow, I can tell you he is an honest man and lying isn't in his character.

Instead, our inventor friend said, "Well Mrs. Reinhart, his glasses help him see the positive side of things. He studies better with them, so I encouraged him to keep wearing them at school."

"The positive side of things?" The teacher scoffed. "Your son takes tests and does most of our in-class assignments wearing them. He is constantly answering questions, most of the time wrong, but he doesn't seem to care."

"How are his grades?" Jerome asked.

"He hasn't made anything higher than a B all semester. And while he completes every assignment, most of the time they are so far from correct I can't understand why he continues to put so much effort into the assignments."

The father hummed in thought. I'm sure any reader who was a student, no matter how atrocious, will realize that a low grade is far more valuable than a zero to your overall GPA. Jerome replied, "I'm sorry that he is still answering questions incorrectly. We are doing our very best at home to study every night." His son had been nagging him to study every night because of the encouragement his teacher gave him.

"I assume there isn't any problem with him continuing to use the eyeglasses in class," Jerome asked the teacher.

"Hamil tells me that it doesn't connect to wifi or any other kind of internet," The teacher stated, "I wanted to make sure that was true because it's so hard to tell what these kids' technology can and can't do these days."

"The glasses do nothing of the sort," Jerome assured her, "They are not giving him any answers. His continued poor grades can assure you of that." The man said this with a chuckle hoping the teacher would lighten up.

"Very well sir," the teacher said, "I see no issue with letting him continue to use them. I am sorry that I have had to call you with such a disturbing and ill news about your son's studiousness, but I'm sure with some time he will finish high school, or the GED, and get a promising job as a janitor."

"Thank you very much, Mrs. Reinhart," Jerome replied with a smile, "I'm glad that you took the time to fill me in on how my son was doing in class."

Hamil and Jerome Today

Jerome explained to me that this conversation was an indication his son was on the right track. He says that young Hamil has been far more studious over the past few years since he stumbled upon the glasses.

When I inquired about what happened with the lenses and if Hamil still uses them Jerome informed me that he made a more conspicuous pair so that Hamil wouldn't catch any more flack from his teachers. Hamil is now a junior in high school. He has aced both his SAT and ACT exams and is applying to a handful of Ivy League colleges. The father says Hamil has already received an acceptance letter from some. The boy plans to dual major in astrophysics and applied mathematics to the excitement of his father.

Jerome himself keeps me updated from time to time about how his glasses are improving. He hopes to bring his augmented reality design to market in the next few years. So far he has a few angel investors who have enabled him to quit his job. He now pursues his invention full-time.

If you have a student, who isn't doing too well in school or have a boss that you want to quit reading nagging emails from, then keep an eye out for Jerome's rose-colored glasses. And if someone seems to be having a great day despite how dreary the world around them is ask them about how they do it. They might be a Beta Tester of Jerome's new invention.

Author's Note:

This was a work of fiction, I hope you enjoyed it. However, there is some really cool evidence that what you wear affects how you perform certain activities. It's called Enclothed Cognition and there are fascinating videos and articles about it.

A Monk's Gift and the White Seed

Originally Published: January 5, 2018

Younger generations are always eager to learn the wisdom of their elders, without having to go through the effort of experiencing it. Yanquin, a young monk, was no different. As he traveled with his teacher back to their monastery, he questioned him vigilantly.

"Shifu," He addressed his teacher, "You are renowned across the land as a powerful healer. How did you get that way? What is the lesson that brought you the most renown?"

The teacher walked through the healthy green forest without a response. The student listened to the master's footsteps waiting for the man to finish contemplation and answer. After five minutes of not hearing anything from the old man's mouth, the student said, "Is it that hard of a question to answer sir?"

The monk chuckled and smiled at the boy, "No it is a simple answer, but I can not tell you, you must see it, try it, and then you will know it."

"But sir," The young monk began to protest. He was cut short by the sound of horses galloping on the road.

The Lord With a Need

Around the bend, a young and wealthy lord appeared followed by an entourage of soldiers and advisors. He stopped in front of the monks looking down on them. The student quickly pulled two rugs out of his little bag and placed one in front of his companion and one in front of himself. The student kneeled followed by the older man.

"Rise," the lord said in a tone that showed he cared neither one way nor the other if they listened. The two monks got to their feet their robes spotless thanks to the mats.

"What do you have to pay Lord Holstead tribute?" The lord's soldier demanded. Paying homage to passing lords was customary in these parts.

The old monk gave a subtle shrug as the young one emptied his bag of its contents. He searched for something of value, but it was only full of necessities like bedrolls and fire starters. They didn't even have food because they were supposed to be home by the end of the day. Finally, he produced a pair of shoes that a thankful patient had donated to the monk for his blessing. He offered it to the lord and a servant took them away. Everyone looked at the older monk expectantly.

"And what do you have to give, old man?" Lord Holstead said looking down his nose.

"I own nothing but the clothes on my back, but I can offer you blessings for safe travels sir," the monk said.

The lord scoffed, "I do not follow your bogus religion, and I have a priest of my own to bless me. As for safe travels, my caravan of thirty men can ensure that. You must offer me something of value."

The monk looked around, then walked away from the caravan into the forest. The guards shouted out in protest. It was most disrespectful to leave a lord without being dismissed. The monk stopped a few paces into the woods, paused, and returned. His hands were full of smooth and bulbous red berries, and he offered them up to the man.

"You have the gall to offer me berries? I could have my servants go out and pick the berries myself if I wanted to, these are of no value." Then he kicked the monk's hands and the berries scattered to the ground. "You are lucky I don't order you to be captured or executed for your disrespect, but you are not even worth my time." The Lord turned his horse and proceeded to march on. His company followed and as the long caravan passed the horses stomped the berries into the ground making small splatters of red-stained dirt on the road.

Passing Comments

After the company passed and the monks were alone again the student started questioning his master again. "Shifu, how are you so well known and respected if you do not respect others?" The student asked. "We must respect the lords because they are the ones who donate to our temples and keep the peace so we may practice our beliefs."

"I cannot help someone who does not see the true value of things." The monk replied solemnly.

"There was no value in your berries sir. I mean that with the utmost respect."

"Did the lord look like he valued the shoes?" The master replied.

The student shook his head, then replied, "But they were made of fine leather, and he may pass them along as a gift to someone else."

The master hummed in understanding, and the holy men kept walking.

The Disillusioned Beggar

After a few hours of travel, the two men came across another traveler on the road. This man was scratched and what clothes he had were torn. "Poor beggar," The young monk said. "How can we help you, sir? We are holy men of the nearby city."

"Do you have food, water, or shoes?" He asked in a dry voice. "I have a long way to travel, and I'm afraid I won't make it as I am."

The young monk shook his head in despair. He had just drunk the last of his canteen. "I'm sorry sir, we cannot help you. But we can give you our blessings." He began to chant a holy psalm.

While the young man was doing his prayer, the old man looked around. He disappeared into the woods, and by the time he reappeared the other monk had finished his blessing and was ready to go on his way. The monk walked to the beggar and handed him a small pile of red berries.

The beggar scoffed at the man and said, "Are you trying to poison a helpless man monk?"

The old man shook his head to disagree with the accusation. In a measured voice, he said, "These are not poisonous, I assure you."

"You lie!" the man exclaimed. "I ate those same berries and had hallucinations for days. I wandered through these woods, lost all my supplies, and cut my feet."

The old man laughed as if the man had told the classic joke of the paladin, cleric, and druid walking into a bar. "No traveler, the berries you speak of are not the same. Those have small white seeds and curved tips. These berries are bulbous, and as you see, there are no seeds on them. Instead, their seeds are inside." The monk bit into the berry and revealed a pit the size of a fingernail clipping. "You could eat it if you wanted to," he informed the man, "but I never do. They get stuck in my teeth and distract me during my meditations."

The hungry beggar, persuaded by the monk's logic, cheer, and willingness to eat it himself gobbled up three of the berries in the man's hands as if they were going to evaporate.

"These won't give you cover for the road, but the health properties of the berries are immense. You will feel rehydrated and full after a few more. And it will give your blood the power to heal your sore feet as you walk. It's not as good as shoes, but you will make it to the next town in a day or two with these."

"Are these berries common in these parts?" The lost man asked.

The monk laughed with resonating cheer, "as common as the White Seeds. Keep an eye out for them both, and you will be fine. Safe travels young man."

"Thank you for all your help," the man said as he went on his way.

"I wish I had kept my pair of shoes to give him," the young monk lamented after they had passed. "If only I had the wisdom of you to keep the shoes for the man. Did you know I would have another need for the shoes, master?"

The monk laughed, "I know as much of the future as you do young one, it is other knowledge that keeps me wise."

"What is that sir?" He asked, "It's what I've been trying to learn from you."

"I've been trying to teach you, but you don't see it yet." The monk answered.

He hummed the rest of the way back to their holy house.

Emergency In The Holy House

Days passed, and the monks settled back into their daily routine in the holy house. The young monk asked the master questions, and the master taught the stubborn young man as best he could.

One day the old monk was studying in the small library as his student rushed in and informed him that an emergency had erupted in the courtyard. "Your wisdom is needed there, Shifu." The monk packed up his fragile books methodically and was soon on his way to help.

In the courtyard, two outsiders were surrounded by other monks trying to get a hold of the situation. One man was hurt badly and was thrashing around. He was being held down by a few of the house's brothers. The other man was a robust traveler whose shirt was covered in blood. The cart behind him was full of crates and also stained with blood.

"We think that this man attacked the bleeding man," the student said, "but I don't know why he brought him here. He will not speak to anyone. We can only assume they both went mad in their travels."

The old monk let out a soft chuckle and approached the two men. When the robust man saw the wise monk, he immediately bowed his head and produced a sealed piece of paper. The monk took the letter, broke the royal seal, and read it.

Dear Holy Monk,

Firstly please excuse my messenger's manners he is a mute. I did not have the chance to get your name, but I told him to find the oldest monk in your house. I knew your temple thanks to your holy and clean robes. Thank you for your help on my travels, to pay you back for saving my life I have sent you a gift of herbs, spices, bandages, and other rare medical supplies. If there is anything else that you or your brothers may need my family will be happy to donate it to you.

Lord Loquin Dillows

The Gift's Full Cycle

The old man folded up the letter and thanked the blood-soaked messenger. "Did this man come with you?" He asked.

The messenger shook his head no.

The old man looked at the squirming and bleeding man and vaguely recognized him. "You found him on the road."

The messenger nodded in agreement.

"Did he have anyone with him?" The messenger shook his head.

The older monk walked up to the man who was squirming around and recognized him as Lord Holstead whom they had passed on the road a few days ago. He examined the man's condition and rantings from a safe distance. The man was reacting to things that weren't there and had hurt himself badly in the process.

The healer looked at one of the brothers holding the Lord's arm and said, "I believe he has ingested the White Seed, do we have an antidote?"

The brother shook his head and explained, "No we ran out of toad's root months ago and haven't been able to make it since."

The wise man looked at the bulky messenger and asked him, "Did your lord happen to send us Toad's Root?"

The man nodded his head and walked to the back of the cart to open a crate. As he did it, the student approached his teacher. "What is going on here master?"

The old monk smiled and replied, "The value of gifts is bestowing their blessings."

A Journal Entry That Has No Business Being Published

Originally Published: January 12, 2018

I have this habit of writing every day for an hour. I've made it over 400 days as of this post being published. Somedays the hour is great and I pump out a few hours of work. Other days I have no motivation to write. On days where I have no desire to touch the keyboard, I will write a ranting Journal Entry to myself.

Below is one of those entries. I've edited it for clarity, and readability. I did my best to not edit the content, and I definitely didn't cut out any of the curse words. So if you have sensitive ears, consider yourself warned. I hope you enjoy it.

***

July 27th, 2017, Down Day and a Motivation Talk

I DON'T know what to write. Today and yesterday were awful. I don't know why. Maybe I need someone in my life to help me professionally. Not like a therapist but like a coach or mentor. Just shoot me in the skull is all I can think right now. I just want to be watching It's Always Sunny right now because it's the easy thing to do. Maybe I will watch it after I write this. I don't know why I sit here and write every day. Or why I even avoid getting a new job.

I understand why I quit my last job, and my life has been better since I walked out. But right now I'm dying, or at least I feel like I am. I'm just unmotivated to do anything. And I know I'm not supposed to rely on motivation and 80% of the time I don't. I'm usually really good about following my productivity planner and focusing on doing the most critical task. But for some reason yesterday and today have been a drag. Which is really shitty because I felt like Monday started off strong. I even did my miracle morning this morning and everything.

Why I'm losing? I don't want to be losing these days, but I feel like I have so much that I'm responsible for, and when I'm overwhelmed I'm never productive or in a good state. But I want to put out the most things I can, be the best I can be. I want to push myself to be better. But I don't do that. Why not?

WHY NOT?!?!?

Is it because it's easier to watch It's Always Sunny? No, I don't think so because most days I can get my work done without being immediately tempted by the television. Am I sick? Am I dying? Ha, we're all dying.

Am I scared to put my work out into the world? No, I'm more scared to keep it to myself!

I'm bothered that I set the same goals for myself week after week, and I rarely hit them if they are out of my control. Sure I can read and write my target amount. I can't get people to give me money or hire me or reply to my emails. When other people become involved I suck.

Are there metrics for others that I can use to measure? Like put out more phone calls (I can control this) instead of getting X# of people to pay me money (Uncontrollable)

Where My Opposing Minds Start Arguing

Yeah, it could be that the phone calls are what scares me. Or at least the bit I don't have a system for. Then spend a week building a system. I like this. But which week, or day or hour?

Don't bother me with the details just tell me when it's done.

Fuck you

I push things off until the last possible second. Why?

Because that's when you feel comfortable sitting down to do it.

Soooo why do I wait? I would be far more effective if I didn't wait.

I don't know, no one knows!

Could I give up now?

Sure, will you?

No

Why not?

Because it's not worth it. It's too easy to continue my streak, especially compared to what it would take to build it back up. There's an excellent example of using every day to its fullest. I've sat down to write for almost 250 days. Those are 250 days that I used to the best of my ability to write something. And look at what I've gotten out of them. A whole hell of a lot. Almost two books, it will be two books by the time the year is over. Hopefully, it will be a few short stories too.

Then what about client work? Is there a streak you can build there?

Sure when I'm more motivated.

Why do you depend on motivation, Dumb ass?

Because right now I'm in a bad place and if I push myself to do anything challenging then I will be overwhelmed and won't get any better.

So when are you going to do it?

Tuesday.

Why Tuesday?

Idk it was the first day that came to mind.

Fuckin' Tuesday.

Shoot me.

Still?

Nah, but it just feels like something useful to say. Like dropping the F-bomb.

That's fucked up.

I know.

Should someone be worried about you?

No, it's not worth the effort. Besides, I'll get better

When?

Next week, next month, next year.

What would it take to make you better?

Nothing and everything. Being overwhelmed and underwhelmed at the same time.

Half a million dollars.

Yeah, that should do it.

That's doable

I'm cash flow negative right now!

Yep, but you can fix that anytime. Your real issue is emotional, or psychological.

I'm doing better.

Yeah, you are.

I'm dying

We're all dying

No, but really...

Shut up

Can I...

No, whatever it is no! I'm talking now. And I don't have anything to say, but it's better than hearing your whiny ass.

I...

The Motivated Brain Steals the Mic

Nope, shut the fuck up! I've got ten more minutes of writing, and I'm going to try and do something with them maybe it will be garbage, but I want to do the talking and the typing for now. I want to put out something that will motivate you to be better, do better when I'm not around. I want to show you how to fight to become the person you want to be. To heal yourself and push yourself to get out of bed in the morning and create good art. To create work that pays you and that you're proud of. Even if no one ever wants to buy it you should be confident in what you're doing. And I know 90% of the time you are. You just have some rough patches and that's fine. It happens to everyone.

Hell take the rest of the day off. Don't do anything you don't want to do. I'm giving you the permission to do it. I encourage it. But tomorrow I want you to hit the ground running. Do something for others, and do something for yourself. You have freelance work waiting for you from a client. There is also work from friends who would pay you. You have money to be made, it's on the table. You just need to pick it up. There's more out there that you can earn

Yeah, it will take some work. Sure it will be scary but you will learn it and you will know how to do it forever. Once you try it. So go out and work, you should be making mistakes and failing at contacting clients. But your issue is you don't have clients, well then go forward and fail at finding them. You can do this!

You said it yourself last night. You're a decent writer, hell you might even be a good one. With thirty more years of practice through teaching, publishing, and writing you might actually be able to make something memorable.

Sure you have shit days, this isn't the first, and it won't be the last but you're getting better. In all aspects of life, you're improving. Do you remember where you were a year ago? You were in your room on Reddit, or in Lubbock on Reddit, or doing something stupid that involved Reddit.

You weren't worried about how to start a new publishing empire or even how to make money from fiction. All you were worried about was if anyone would like the stories you wrote. Honestly, you doubted you could be a writer because you didn't believe in yourself.

Now you have that, now you're a writer, you wrote something, and it was decent. It will get better... this all will get better.

Take the day off, call it a win, and cool down. Watch something you enjoy. Hell read something if you feel like it. There's a dozen ways to celebrate how far you've come.

I permit you to do all of them. Why? Because I know that you will show up tomorrow pumped to work and make it ten thousand more steps. That's how far you've come so far. You know that right? You were nowhere near where you are now last year. And next year you will be so far ahead of yourself that you will read this and won't be able to imagine it.

You can do this. So go out and do it. Because you're the only one who can go out and do it. Take the day off but come back tomorrow stronger. Because I can't afford to have you be weak again this week.

Maybe next month you can have another fall but right now I need you sharp.

Push yourself to go further and do more. Believe in yourself because everyone else wants to believe in you. They really do, and most of them do. They just don't say it because you don't give them the room to talk. Go and push yourself to be awesome! You're finding your passion. You know your dreams and dream job. You just need to go out, push yourself, and discover where you want to be. People want you to succeed. You want yourself to succeed. SO move it. Go on and do it. Push on and don't give a shit.

YOU GOT THIS.

Make a plan, move forward, remember to look back at your accomplishments.

Where I am Now?

This was written on July 27th, 2017. About six months ago. I was working on my second rough draft for a novel and I finished it. I even re-read it and will probably publish it eventually. Since then I wrote another, novella. Its title will be something like: **The Needle of Loss, Todd's Story**. This week I put the final touches on it and am now working to put it in the hands of an editor. I hope to self-publish it before the end of March 2018. This is a huge win for me!

The Motivated Brain said, "Celebrate how far you've come." This Friday I want to take some time to do that. I want to encourage you to do it too reader! Look at where you were a year ago, 5 years ago, or 10 years ago. You've done so much!

Whether you're my family, friends, or someone who found me through the magic of the internet, I appreciate everyone who reads this blog, thanks for reading this. Each of you has helped me come so far in your own way!

My Ex-girlfriend's Vampire Wedding

Originally Published: January 19, 2018

K ate and I broke up three years ago and I didn't understand why she invited me to her big day. She seemed to be getting along fine without me, hence the wedding. I, on the other hand, was far from fine, hence the lack of a plus one. I sat on the bride's side and leafed through the brochure an usher handed me when I walked in, hoping it would inform me of the groom's name.

No dice, it was an advertisement for the venue. *Who would want to hold a wedding here?* I wondered. Dim candles were all that illuminated the place, and the interior decorator seemed enjoy the challenge of using only a black and grey color pallet. The building felt like it was trying to be a church, but the architect seemed like they had never been inside one before. The designer just went with what felt like the right kind of design.

The music started from nowhere cutting through the silence. The grim organ player belted out a low and dull tune. I saw the musician perched above the crowd shadowed by an onyx top hat. The man's hand and face were nearly translucent.

Bridesmaids walked down the aisle. I recognized only one of the three. The other two were ash grey, and I had never met them before. Both seemed to resemble the groom's side. Anemia and a disdain for anything that resembled a tan seemed to be the family's theme. I assumed the maids were sisters or close relatives of the groom.

The groom himself appeared at the front standing at what I hesitated to call an altar, much like I would hesitate to call the man behind the podium a priest. The groom nor his groomsmen made a sound getting up there. Each resembled the other they had pale faces and sharp features. They all looked far too old for Kate. The only way I could pick out the groom was because he had a bright red poppy on his lapel. *Why not a rose?* I wondered.

The thought was cut short by the familiar tune of "Here Comes the Bride." The top-hatted organ player enthusiastically banged the keys of the instrument as the tune echoed through the somber room.

My ex, Kate, walked down the aisle looking as beautiful as ever despite the unorthodox black dress she wore. It looked like she was showing up overdressed to a funeral instead of her wedding. She always had a flair for the dark and abnormal though, which explained the venue... and the groom.

She stood at the altar, clad in black, the groom matched in his black tuxedo. The officiant between them said a few words in a foreign tongue. I hadn't brushed up on my Latin or even studied it in the first place but I felt like it had far too many hisses, and v sounds to be genuine Latin. Despite this, they both agreed and said, "I do."

The groom had a slinky smile that cut across his face horizontally from ear to ear. The officiant then said, "Peter Tariq you may now kiss your bride."

They kissed passionately, and I felt the blood boiling in my ears. I noticed the groom's side of the family look across the aisle. They had a ravenous look in their eyes, and I'm sure they were excited about the reception dinner to begin. I felt my stomach grumble and agreed.

I made eye contact with one young man, he looked about my age. His eyes seemed to be glowing red. *Probably one of those eccentric contacts,* I thought, *tacky even for this wedding.* I looked back at the front of the room in an effort not to stare, the bride and groom had stopped kissing.

In a grand gesture that befit a man from 200 years ago, he waved his hands out like ominous wings. "It is my pleasure to unite these two families as one." I examined the odd groom on stage, and his eyes also seemed to be glowing red. *Must be another strange family trait,* I told myself wondering why I hadn't noticed it before. Then he clapped his hands in front of him, and with a lightning-quick motion, he went back to kissing his bride. Except this time, it was on her neck. Which, in my opinion, was a bit lewd for a wedding.

I looked around to gauge everyone else's reactions. It was odd, but I threw out the expectation of Kate to be normal years ago. I heard some gasps from the rows behind and in front of me. When I looked back at the stage, I saw blood running down Kate's neck. The thought, *probably why she didn't want to wear white,* bolted through my mind. The bride's face held a look of pure ecstasy that I had never seen before, despite my past attempts.

The groom removed his face from the pit of her neck. His face was no longer pale white but flush with blood. "May the reception feast begin," he said. A pearly white smirk was smeared on his bloody face. He immediately jumped onto the least pale of the bridesmaids.

In confusion, I looked to the groom's side. The family that was there was poised to launch towards my side of the aisle. Some were already across, throwing pews around. The room echoed with bloody screams, leeching sounds, and the top-hatted organ player's music.

My introverted tendencies brought me luck. I had chosen to sit as far away from the middle aisle as possible. I slinked out of the pew and crawled across the ground. I could see pools of blood starting to form on the ground. The bride's guests had outnumbered the groom's family at least 3 to 1 and a large group had already rushed to the door.

I got to the back corner and watched, waiting for the horde of people to open the door in the commotion. Despite the group's best efforts and shoving they made no progress. The door was still tightly shut.

A small group of the groom's family was on them. The well-dressed monsters cut through them forming a bloody canyon. I huddled in the corner looking for an exit. The windows were too high and too small to escape through.

In front of me, I saw a vampiric guest lunge towards a man I had met only once. He was one of Kate's obscure uncles. He held up a book and swore, "Be gone you demon, the power of Christ compels you."

Of course, I thought, *bibles would keep them away.* I watched and searched for a book of my own and spotted one under a tipped pew. I made for it, but as I did, I heard a dark cackling and the slap of a heavy object, maybe a book, hitting the ground.

I looked over, and the scripture sat in a pool of the uncle's blood, still clutched in his right hand at the end of his arm. The uncle was no longer attached to the arm though, and the demon was sucking on the man's throat. The uncle did not enjoy it as much as Kate did.

I don't think she ever liked that uncle, I thought, *He was the preachy one that every family has.*

I rushed to grab a bible of my own, but when I seized it from under the pew I saw that the words written on the front read "Holly Bibble," and upon opening it nothing but filler words were on the page. "Son of a bitch," I cursed aloud.

I heard a thud and my attention snapped towards the uncle. The tuxedoed groomsman had finished with him. Kate's uncle stared at me with a bloodless face and empty eyes. The groomsman was soaked in blood, the shirt that used to be spotless white was dyed red. His mouth was dripping blood, and his face was flush.

I met his glowing crimson eyes, and he stared straight at me, smiling. "How's it going blood bag?" he asked in a tone that didn't require an answer. I was too petrified to move.

I looked around and saw that the room had been filled with blood and dead bodies. The groomsman crept towards me slowly. I felt like I was in a dream, stuck and all I needed to do was move two inches to get away from the threat, but my body was frozen. The monstrosity was a foot away from me now, shadowing over me. He lunged on top of me and my body began to move again, seconds too late.

I struggled but could feel the man's muscles under his bloodstained tux. He was overpowering me. His mouth was inches away from my neck and I could smell the metallic gore on his breath. Before he could sink his teeth in I heard a crack and the weight was off of me.

The monster fell to my side landing and shattering a strewn pew. A tall and muscular man was holding a large wooden plank and I recognized him immediately. He had grown a beard since I last stalked him on Facebook, but he was the man Kate dated after dumping me. I searched my head for his name. *It was something with a 'V', Vincent,* I thought, *no, it's Vance.*

He reached out a hand to help me up. I gained command of my footing as he grabbed a shard of wood off the ground. The groomsman who had previously mounted me was regaining his balance too. However, Vance had critically disfigured my attacker's spine. As a former minor league baseball player, Vance was the athletic opposite of me. And what made it worse was for three months he was the only thing Kate talked about on social media. I was saved by a man I previously disdained.

The monstrosity began to realign its back, but before he could get it straight, the ex struck him in the chest with the shard of wood. The man turned to ash. *That worked better than the fake bible,* I told myself.

Then Vance raised his voice saying "Don't worry Kate, I'll save you!" Apparently, I wasn't the only guy who was still hung up on her. I heard a cackling laugh, and the groom stood up in the front of the room. He split the distance between the baseball player and Kate. His face was slathered in blood.

Six or seven more vampires popped up like prairie dogs from behind pews. I did the exact opposite and hid behind a bench. In an attempt to not get caught in the crossfire, Vance was inevitably about to attract.

I looked away from the altar and saw a trail of ash piles. *Shit this guy knows what he's doing,* I thought. Then I began looking for a wooden stake of my own, unsure of what was going to come next.

I picked one up, and the weapon felt comforting in my hand. I rose to my knees, they were smeared with blood. I kept low, able to see the scene between Vance and Peter. I avoided the attention of nearby bloodsuckers. Lucky for me they were mostly focused on Vance and his activity in the front of the room.

I looked on, and Vance was yelling insults and objections at the groom. The ex was going on about an unholy union and screaming at Kate's passed-out body. He continued to go on about how he would find a way to save her. Then, six vampires rushed Vance at once and his rants turned into grunts. A few others who popped their head up since the start of the charade looked on with bloodlust.

After not too long I saw the lust leave their eyes and their faces were drooping in dread as the attacking enemies turned to ash in front of Vance. I ducked behind a pew since I was viewable to the onlookers.

I heard the bloody whispers from a few rows in front of me. "I knew Peter invited too many people to this wedding. It's always better to have a small defenseless crowd than a giant buffet."

Another slithering voice added, "Leave it to the prince of Vampeeria to try and make a show of strength at his third wedding."

"I agree," a third sinister voice chimed in, "when too many humans are around they start making a fight and gain strength from one another. That's why I prefer my small New England lots."

The first icy voice came back to my ear. "Let's just get out of here." The small crowd agreed as the last of the six attackers fell in front of Vance. I poked my head up to see if they were going to escape by walking past me and saw the three monsters puff into clouds of mist and float out the window.

"Now Peter, I'm on to you!" Vance exclaimed pointing his stake at the man on the altar.

"Very well," The groom said opening his arms in a grandiose manner. They walked down the aisle towards each other.

I watched the impending battle between the husband and the ex as it unfolded. "I always knew you weren't right for Kate," Vance yelled, "and now she's lying dead on the floor in her wedding dress."

The groom merely laughed and continued to approach his challenger. Something had torn his tux in a few places, but the skin under it was smooth and new like a baby's.

No wonder Kate was into him, I thought. Remembering how tough the monster on top of me had felt. I didn't doubt that her new husband had the strength of hundreds of men. I doubted Vance, despite his size and athletic background, could hold a candle to the groom.

The two men were finally a short distance from one another. Vance lunged forward with this shank of wood. Peter dodged nimbly and kicked him in the leg. I heard a snap but Vance didn't fall to the ground. His face winced in pain but Vance stayed up lunging towards the groom.

This time Vance grabbed Peter and was about to stab, but the groom countered and got a loose grip on Vance's arm. The monster pushed Vance back and twisted the arm in its socket.

Vance screamed in pain, it was higher than any grown man's voice should be, and he fell to the ground. With a swing of his good arm, he hit the groom's leg with his wooden weapon. The attack cut and dented Peter's leg, I saw blood and bone seep out.

The monster's face was flush from battle, and he hissed in agony. He clutched at his leg, staring at the damage the baseball player did. Vance quickly got to his feet using the makeshift bat as a cane while the monster tended to his wounds. His twisted arm hung limp and useless at his side. Humans had poked their heads from the pews, I saw a half dozen and wondered, *is that all that's left or all I can see?* Vance and the groom were making a spectacle of themselves. Every being, living and dead wanted to watch the battle. As the vampire worked to heal himself Vance ran at him.

The attacker winced every time he put weight on the damaged leg, but it didn't stop Vance from gaining speed and tackling the wounded monster to the ground. His twisted arm had already begun to bruise. I knew that if the groom had gotten a better grip the limb wouldn't still be attached.

The man pinned Peter down and beat at his face with the heavy end of the stake. As he did that the room got colder and darker. A shiver crawled up my back. The vampire was trying to push Vance off, but so much adrenaline was rushing through the ex-baseball player's system that it was nearly an even match.

There was a movement behind them, and I looked at the altar. Kate was encompassed in a black shroud, her face was white as fresh milk. Her eyes were bright rubies. She rushed to her husband's aid. The movement was as smooth and quick as lightning, no one saw it happen, least of all Vance. He was knocked off by Kate and he skidded down the aisle towards me.

Kate hissed, "Get off my husband you jealous dick. He's ten times the man you are." She sunk her nails into his neck. They looked sharp and monstrous as claws. Vance protested saying, " "He's not a man he's..." but was cut off as Kate detached his vocal cords from his throat.

Kate feasted on Vance's broken body sinking her long white teeth into his neck. Soon Peter was next to her. His pant leg had a rip, and he was still bleeding.

The couple was feet away from me. I watched in horror as they dug into Vance's dead body. I watched the blood drain from Vance as Peter's life force renewed. The groom's leg healed in front of my eyes.

"You are strong my thrall," Peter said after Vance's body became a bloodless sack. I hid behind the broken pew and held my breath.

"Thank you, my love," Kate said in a voice that was far more sinister than the one I remembered. "Who shall we feast on next?" she asked.

I heard Peter sniff the air, "There is fresh meat around here. Don't you smell the sweet aroma?" I clutched my stake to my chest knowing they were talking about me.

"I do, my love," Kate said in a voice that sounded close. "I smell it." She said getting closer. "It's nearby." she inhaled, and it sounded like it was next to my ear. "Here!" she yelled.

I screamed, but my terror was covered by another's. A woman was screaming and then choking.

"Peter told me to invite everyone I wanted to see suffer. I want to show you all what I've become. It was easy to fill a venue this size with all my adversaries, Chelsea."

"No Kate, don't! We're friends." I heard the woman gasp. Kate laughed, and the wicked sound echoed through the room. I couldn't help but smile at Chelsea's naivety. She and Kate were far from friends. Chelsea actively made Kate's work life hell and had for years. According to Kate, it was on purpose, I'd heard the words 'Chelsea's got it out for me' more times than I cared to remember. The crunch of bone and a sucking sound that filled the room. I was struck with terror. Chelsea's panics and bargaining were no more.

"What do we have here?" Peter whispered in my ear. I turned slowly, and he was inches from my face with a smile that showed pure demented joy.

I clutched, the steak to my chest, this time trying to hold back my scream. Peter's canine teeth were sharpened to a razor's edge. His pearl-white teeth filled his smile, and crimson blood smeared each tooth.

My knuckles turned white as I clutched the stake. Peter moved towards me crawling on all fours. The monster's shoulders protruded from his back and rocked back and forth as he crept closer to me. I inched away sliding on my bottom through pools of blood.

My feet slipped and I was on my back, Peter was instantly on top of me. I turned the stake outward and thrust it upwards into the groom's chest. I pushed as hard as I could and felt the bone give. The stake sunk through the man's ribs and into his chest.

Peter screamed in agony, and I felt his weight off of me. I stood up as quickly as I could in the bloody mess under me. My hands were empty and Peter was still screaming.

I frantically searched for a new weapon. I found a long piece of board soaking in a pool of blood. Half was the polished edge of the pew the other was raw splintered wood. It would only be suitable for bludgeoning. I hit the back of a damaged bench with my new weapon, and the bench broke into smaller pieces. I kicked the remains around looking for something that would work as a stake. I found a decent-sized piece and clutched it in my other hand.

I looked back at Peter who was still wailing. Half a dozen other monsters, including Kate, had popped up from whatever human they were sucking on and looked at what was causing the commotion.

Peter's wails turned to cackles, and I saw Kate smile with her sharp bloodstained teeth. He ripped the stake from his chest and threw it on the ground in front of me. The tip was maroon and dripped in the thick blood from deep in his chest. His wound leaked more of the gore, and he clutched at it lightly with one hand. "Wrong side pansy," he said to me with a snicker.

I looked at him then at Kate and back to him. I felt the eyes of a dozen vampires seer into my flesh.

I would be overtaken in an instant if a horde came towards me. I gulped loudly, and it echoed through the silent room.

I heard a crash to my right, turned, and saw a pew fall under Kate as she hurdled over it towards me. She looked like a mix between a frog and a lion bolting towards me. I braced myself against her tackle, and as soon as she was in front of me, I swung at her with the makeshift club in my right hand. I used all of the athletic focus and know-how I had and clocked her square in the temple. She fell to her knees stunned. I stowed the stake between my belt and waist, put my left hand on the heavy stick, and swung at her demonic head. She didn't have a chance to look at me before I hit her in the back of the head.

She fell to the ground unconscious, undead, and unhappy.

"You son of a bitch!" Peter yelled at me. His hand was no longer clutching his chest. A clean white patch of skin glistened through the large hole the stake made in his tux jacket and shirt. I heard three vampires move towards me and I picked up the bloody stake that Peter so dutifully returned to me from his chest.

I looked up, and three vampires, two groomsmen, and a snarling organ player moved at me from all directions. I circled furiously trying to keep each of them from facing my back for too long. If anyone was still alive in the room, they were too much of a coward to stand with me now, and I didn't blame them.

The three monsters were almost on me, four more were behind them and Peter stayed where he was laughing. He watched me helpless and surrounded by his mob of minions. Kate lay unconscious and motionless at my feet.

"Stop!" Peter commanded.

The horde of approaching vampires halted their movement but continued to snarl and hiss. "You've incapacitated my wife and ruined my wedding feast. I cannot let this dishonor go unanswered. I will not sick my family and friends on you. Honor insists that I must kill you myself." A charming smile decorated his face, and I would have considered him a friend if I hadn't just shoved a stake through his chest.

As he walked towards me, his face twisted to become serpentine and demonic. I sheathed my bloody stake next to my other behind my back and gripped my makeshift bat with both hands. I was shaking in my unpolished slip-on dress shoes but I had to make a stand. A terrifying image of my arms being ripped off flashed through my mind. I pushed the thought out by tightening my grip.

The monstrous groom was a few yards away and started circling me. I turned again wondering if I was supposed to lunge first or him. We made it a whole 360 and then I took my first swing. He batted it away with his bare hand. I swung again, and again while he continued to dodge.

He was playing with me, I was a joke to him. I swung over and over. I tired quickly and felt the weight of the wood in my hand.

Mortal men had swung at him before. He was a seasoned veteran of showdowns like this. Unlike Kate, he knew how to play the game and dodge my blows. The bat felt heavy in my hand, and it nodded down before I quickly lifted it back up. That was when he moved in to kick at my knee.

I sidestepped but felt the wind of his inhuman movement rush past my pant leg. He missed my leg by inches. There was no doubt his kick would have shattered my leg. The board no longer felt burdensome as an unhealthy amount of adrenaline was dumped into my system. I swung the weapon downward aiming for his head. I missed but fortunately hit his back, which his kick had inadvertently exposed to me.

He screamed in pain and looked at me over his shoulder. He bared his teeth, they were all sharpened to a needle's point. His eyes were completely red. No pupil, no white, just a swirling pool of blood where his eyeballs once were. Whatever monster he was before looked like a puppy compared the the hound he now was.

He lunged at me, and I swung in defense. My board blocked the arm and it was quickly recoiled setup to strike again. His claws flailed at me. Each finger was adorned with sharp black nails. He attacked, and we exchanged blows again. The next attack came from above and

I blocked it. His weight was heavy, and I moved a hand to each end of the stick to brace against his full force. He came down with his right arm and broke the board. My defenses shattered above my eyes and I was left with a small club in both hands. His black claws shredded my only decent dress shirt and the skin of my chest burned.

I wreathed in pain and fell to the ground. He leaped on top of me, and I tried to roll away, but I wasn't fast enough. We were both prone, and he grabbed my left wrist. He was about to bite into me and chew every tendon out of my arm when I jabbed at his face with all the force I had. My fragment of wood punctured his cheek, and it stopped his jaw from closing on me. His shock gave me a chance to pull my left hand out of his clutches and shift my weight, mounting on top of him.

I used the remaining backing of the pew in my left hand to pierce him in his voice box since I wasn't confident in the wood's ability to puncture his sternum. His screams became gurgles as his throat filled with blood. I grabbed one of the spikes from behind my back and plunged it towards his chest.

Astonishment flickered across his face before he blocked it with both his hands. I could feel his muscles flex under me. I knew he would quickly recover strength and knock me off. I struggled the stake away, and as I did, he hurled me off of him.

The stake flew across the room, and I flew in the opposite direction. I landed on my back, the air was knocked out of my lungs. I reached my hand behind my back groping for my last and bloodiest weapon. I felt my fingers wrap around the splintered wood. I looked at Peter now standing and saw a hole where his Adam's apple should have been. I waited with the stake behind my back until he was in the air.

The demon lunged at me with his blood-pooled eyes. I removed the wood from behind me and put it on the right side of my chest as he flew towards me. Before he knew what was happening, he impaled himself on the stake. I heard his sternum shatter. The man's weight on the stake made me feel like I was punched in the chest. I knew my ribs had cracked and there would be more than a bruise there later. I gasped for air and immediately coughed on the groom's ashes. A cloud of grey dust settled on and around me.

I spat out what I could and jumped to my feet. I knew the vampire prince was no longer a foe but there was a chance that one of his other companions might.

I grabbed the maroon-stained stake from the pile of ash and brandished it at the few vampires that gawked at me. Slowly and in an orderly fashion, they turned into clouds of mist and wafted toward the open windows at the top of the room.

A room full of ash, blood, and corpses was all that surrounded me. In the center of the room was my unconscious undead ex-girlfriend.

I moved towards her wondering if I would need to put a stake in her too. I rolled her onto her back her body felt feverish. I lifted her eyelids, careful to avoid her mouth. If she had the chance, I knew she would go for blood.

Her eyes were back to the hazel green they were whenever she used to yell at me for not taking the trash out. I shook her, and she came too.

"What the hell happened?" she asked.

"Hell happened," I answered with a smirk.

She looked around seeing the blood pools, carcasses, and broken pews. "Where's Peter?" she asked frantic.

I gestured to a small pile of ash on the ground and then to a grey smear on my ruined suit.

"You killed my husband?" she screamed in familiar rage.

"He attacked you, and your entire guest list," I said defending myself from her words.

"That was the point," she wailed, "You ruined my wedding!"

I shrugged and stood up.

"If you didn't want to have your wedding ruined you shouldn't have invited your ex."

The Passion of the Sea

Originally Published: January 26, 2018

D erek awoke his passion for the sea every time he looked off a boat's deck and into the rolling blue waves. Then he would proceed to vomit. After that, Derek would meander below deck to recover until the excursion was over. He had no logical reason to love the sea. He couldn't explain his feelings for it. In his mind, this was what it meant to have a genuine passion.

People, mostly his exes and shrinks, would relate his love of the sea back to his father. Derek's father was an avid sailor and had won many awards. He sailed his entire adult life, up until the day he traveled through the Strait of Sanmir. Derek's family never learned the details of the sailor's death, but the Coast Guard found shrapnel of the man's beloved boat.

More than anything else Derek wanted to be a sailor. He continuously signed up for sailing classes. He lived in a condo next to a pier so that he heard the ocean at night. It was a method to get over his seasickness, but it just made him nauseous in bed. No matter what Derek did, he couldn't get over his seasickness.

Derek had tried everything. Including, but not limited to, Dramamine, Hypnotherapy, Patches of every color, shape, and size, and bracelets with dirt from twelve different islands. Absolutely nothing worked for him.

While Derek sat on the beach one morning, meditating on the sea and trying to keep his breakfast down, an old woman approached him.

Without waiting for him to acknowledge her, she said, "Young man, I will cure your sickness for you."

She had piqued his interest, but he was dubious as most people should be when offered a cure from a stranger. "How do you know I am sick?" he asked.

"I can see it in your eyes, boy."

Sarcastically he said, "Of course, you can see it in my eyes. I'm looking at the ocean."

"NO!" She said smacking him on the head. "I see the sickness, the longing to love something that your soul is not compatible with. It is common among men," she paused, "and women. I see it for pets, lovers, jobs, and occasionally the sea. However, I have not seen a sickness like yours for many years."

"I'm not sick," he claimed adamantly. It was an impulse response from the dozens of times he had been asked and embarrassed by seamen. "I just get sick every time I look at the sea from an object that isn't dry land."

"That sounds like a sickness to me boy."

He shook his head in protest.

She ignored him, "I'll fix it for you. And you won't even be that cursed afterward."

"What do you mean not even that cursed?"

The old woman shrugged, "I'm a witch I can't give away my cures for free."

"Can I buy you a churro instead?"

"I'm more in the mood for falafels and a gyro," She answered. There's a man, three piers south who makes them just like the old country." She said this with what would be a toothy smile if she had possessed many teeth.

"I'll go get it!" He agreed as he jumped up.

Who knew falafels and a sandwich could solve my problem, he thought as he ran to the restaurant. And even if it didn't work, I could at least say I've tried everything. He rushed to the restaurant a few piers down and bought the woman a meal. To ensure the falafels were fried fresh he paid extra.

He eagerly came back to where he had left her, but there was no woman in sight. All morning he searched, continually tempted by the smell of the fresh food. Slowly the hot lunch got cold but it still tempted him. Lunchtime turned into happy hour then happy hour turned into dinner. His stomach growled, and he wanted to eat the sandwich he had carried all day. Dinner turned to after-dinner drinks, and he had given up hope. Derek sat in the spot where he had started the morning. He had no cure, only a box of cold falafels and a soggy sandwich.

The lunch taunted him all day. Finally, he slammed down on the gyro and the fried chickpea balls thinking to himself, if this is what the food in the old country tasted like I don't blame the lady for coming here.

He woke up early for a sailing class. He had, begrudgingly, scheduled it weeks before with the knowledge that he would never have the stomach to sign up on the day of the class. As he headed down to the

dock, he pondered what kind of boat he would be on and how rough
the weather would be that day.

  He got to the dock and saw that it was a small sailboat. Of course,
it's a small boat, he thought. Small boats were the worst for him
because the wind and waves easily manipulated them. As he waited
for others to arrive, he worked to hold his breakfast down despite still
being tied to the dock. Once all the other students were there, they set
off into open waters.

As they got further and further away from the docks, Derek became
more and more worried. However, he did not become any sicker. He
was genuinely able to focus on the teacher and not spend his time
fighting off early symptoms of puke-your-stomach-up-itis.

As the morning passed the class got to the point where things
were hands-on. Derek took to the ropes as a natural. He had learned
something from all his classes after all, despite spending most of them
below deck. Excited about his new ability Derek took the next course
and the one after that. He blew through his certifications and became
a genuine sailor.

After years of practice and training, he became a renowned sailor.
He won multiple regattas and was often hired to do challenging voy-
ages that most sailors wouldn't dare take on. He experienced strong
storms that could only be caused by Neptune's sons bringing home
bad test grades three months in a row. All the challenges fueled him
and relit his fiery passion for the sea. Not once did Derek become sick.

Over time he got married and had a son named Jacob. He loved his
boy more than anything in the world and wanted to share his passion
with the kid as soon as he could walk. The problem was that Jacob had
seasickness worse than Derek ever had.

In an attempt to help his son with the illness, Derek began to set out
falafels and gyros every week. He placed them in the spot where he had

first met the old woman. Alas, she never showed. Derek consistently returned to the dock to the sight of seagulls eating away at the meal. Not once did it mysteriously disappear as he had hoped.

His son grew and continued to be sick. Still, the boy had as much interest in the sea as his old man. Derek set off on a trip to sail through the Strait of Sanmir for a lucrative but risky voyage. The area was historically fraught with storms.

One night a storm picked up and Derek, alone on his boat, had to navigate it. He drew in the sails and manipulated his anchor to a position that would help him. As he reached off the side to finagle the anchor onto the ship, he heard a crack of thunder from behind him.

The thunder's crack sounded like a cackle, and it got his attention. He turned, not sure if he should expect someone behind him. Instead, he saw a low mast swing towards him. The wind had caught it, and it was accelerating towards him. Derek jumped out of the way, and the mast swooped over his body. If he hadn't ducked, he would have been thrown from the boat and into the raging waters.

He weathered the storm and spent the rest of the trip in solemn contemplation. Once he returned he tied up his boat to its dock, cleaned out his valuables, and listed the ship for sale.

With the money, he made the trip, and proceeds from the boat he opened a small food stand. It was located near the pier where he lived. Derek and his son Jacob fried falafels and cooked gyros. Their homemade pita was the most popular around. Jacob learned to cook gyros better than his old man could ever hope.

The shop expanded and the family was able to get a seating area and waitstaff. It funded Jacob's college and the two men were always near the sea they loved so much. Jacob went to school and left his father to work alone during the spring and fall.

One cool spring morning Derek saw a woman that looked familiar. He brought her fresh falafels and a warm gyro sandwich before she could order.

He sat down across from her as she snacked on her chickpea snack. A question had been on his mind ever since he survived the Strait of Sanmir. Now, he was finally able to ask her. Derek said, "Why did you let me survive?"

After finishing a slow bite, the woman had somehow lost more teeth in the time since their last meeting, she answered, "Of all your ancestors, you waited the longest time to eat the lunch."

The Infinite Library

Originally Published: February 2 to March 2, 2018

1 - An Ancient Inhuman Book

R odney Brown walked into his professor's messy office holding a binder under his arm. The binder contained his thesis which covered his process of measuring and studying quantum vacuum fluctuation. He needed to review his work with his professor before he defended it next week.

Dr. Carrus's door was open, but Rodney knew this did not guarantee the man would pay attention to him when he entered.

Martin Carrus sat at his computer switching his gaze between the computer screen and the notebook next to him. Dr. Carrus's office felt small because he insisted on having two desks, the standard issue desk was not enough for his multiple monitors, spare electronics, and mounds of research papers. Rodney assumed that if the man were a little more organized, he would be able to get by with having just one desk.

The grad student knocked on the door and startled the man from his focused work. "Oh, hey there?" The professor said in a tone that added tension to the room. The man's typically frazzled hair was somehow more unkempt than usual. His old eyes had heavy bags under them that would probably need to be gate-checked if he was traveling.

"Is everything okay?" Rodney asked the professor.

The man nodded slowly, but this did not reassure the student. Rodney looked at the only other chair in the office. It was covered high with papers and binders. The most peculiar thing about the stack was an old book that sat on top of the pile. The only way Rodney could describe the book was inhuman.

Carrus jumped out of his seat once he noticed where Rodney's gaze fell and began clearing the stack of binders off. There wasn't much room for the junk on the floor or bookshelves, but the professor found a home for enough things that Richard was able to take a seat. The strange book gained temporary residence on top of the professor's keyboard.

Rodney repeated his question, "Is everything okay Dr. Carrus?"

The man let out a deep sigh, closed the door to his office, and put his computer to sleep. He picked up the book that leaned against the keyboard and gave his student his undivided attention.

"Rodney, nothing is okay," he said. His dread and discomfort were not hard to hear in his words.

The mood was unusual since Rodney picked Carrus for graduate work because of the man's notoriously carefree attitude. A professor who displayed his Woodstock tickets on the wall of his office was the last professor Rodney expected to start a conversation with "Nothing is okay."

The man continued, and Rodney listened, "I have been looking into something for, well for a while, longer than you've probably been alive. I haven't told many people about it, the ones I have told are, well they aren't with us anymore."

Rodney felt like the atmosphere of the room had gone dark. As if by beginning this conversation the two men had invited a demon to come into the office.

To attempt to alleviate the situation Rodney asked, "Should you be telling me about it?" He added a dry laugh as a last-ditch effort.

The professor's eyes went to the door as if to make sure no one came in. Rodney's gaze followed and the professor finally answered. "No, I probably shouldn't," The professor said. "Unfortunately you were inevitably going to find out, and I'm afraid this may be my last chance to discuss these things with you."

The worst thing Rodney could imagine came to his mind. His professor was sick with a terminal illness and was going to pass all his research on to the young grad student.

"You're the only person qualified to believe me though. Years ago I discovered something unbelievable. Thanks to you it's finally starting to make technical sense now." He gestured to the book that was in his hand. "This is not an ordinary book."

Rodney nodded his head in agreement. The cover was a color that skirted the edge of jet black and luminescent purple. It had a golden design on the cover with curls that ended in pointed spikes. It was a pattern that no human would have ever created. Rodney knew nature was random and uncouth sometimes, but this design didn't resemble anything organic. In addition to the strange design and colors, the book seemed to be both ancient and new at the same time. Rodney spent most of his childhood around books and could tell that this book had been cared for.

"This book is from the Infinite Library," Dr. Carrus said as if he had just revealed an entirely new reality to Rodney. The student's face reflected that the professor had not only failed to disclose a new reality but instead had added more confusion to Rodney's life.

"I've never heard of an infinite library," Rodney admitted, "But if you're about to give me another paper on astrophysics to review I have to tell you I am pretty swamped with the thesis stuff. My defense is next week, and I want some feed-"

The professor waved his free hand frantically to dismiss Rodney's comments. "No, no, no, your thesis is nothing compared to the knowledge that is in this book." The professor scolded.

The words cut Rodney. He had spent four years on research for his thesis two of them were in the design of a low-cost machine that would be able to measure what he was studying. "What are you trying to say?" Carrus had assigned him the project instead of the one Rodney wanted to do because he had deemed it *cutting-edge*. Then the student made the connection. Whatever was in that book covered his thesis. From the size of the text, he figured the author had even expanded it.

In his mind, he cursed the private sector, and their unrestricted grant money and profit-focused actions. His lousy lab could barely sustain itself with the measly funding the school gave him.

"Give me the book Dr. Carrus," Rodney said in a tone that nearly demanded his elder to take action. The old man gave him an unsure look but released the book into Rodney's possession. Rodney let the binder that held his thesis fall to the floor and held the strange book with both hands.

All his life he had been learning physics from books. His mother would bring him home library books about subjects that no 13-year-old boy should be reading, but she was just happy he was demanding books instead of expensive video games. When he finally saved up for a computer he used it to read physics forums and learn programming languages for physics simulations. Rodney's life had been physics, and the past four years of his life had been used to study how electrons exist in all places, and no places at the same time.

He felt a power when holding books especially one that he knew contained new information. This book made him feel more powerful than any other book he had ever touched before. He suspected this was because it held all the information he had been working on until that point in his life. It could have also been from the weight of his professor's stare as he examined the book. The design was eerie. With the book in his hand, he felt the darkness of the room grow deeper than it was before. He felt the need to check the door to make sure no one had wandered in but then determined the urge was silly.

Rodney cracked the book open and flipped to the first diagram he found. He studied the figure, but it didn't resemble anything familiar. He looked at the words on the page for guidance and saw only squiggly symbols he couldn't read. "What is this? Farsi?"

The professor shook his head.

"It's not Chinese or anything of Asian origin," Rodney said as he flipped from page to page. As he studied it and noticed that the formatting was different from any other research paper he had ever read. There were no figure numbers to start with, and the graphs looked like they using a mutated polar coordinate system.

"Who wrote it? How old is it?"

"I don't know," The professor answered.

"Which part don't you know?" Rodney asked. He felt the knowledge that the book held and didn't want it to slip away. "Where did you get it? Why do you have it?"

"That's a story in and of itself. I'll tell you in a bit," Dr. Carrus answered, "What's important is for you to know that this book contains some resemblance to your thesis, although I suspect it goes more in-depth and covers much more."

"Is there a translation?"

The professor let out a boisterous laugh, "Rodney I don't think you understand. This book, it's not from earth."

Rodney shook his head, "You're saying this book is alien?"

The professor scoffed under his breath, "No I'm not suggesting something that ridiculous. This book is from another universe, another time, another dimension."

Rodney stared at the professor unable to believe what he just heard.

"That may be the only book on this planet that is written by another species. And it just so happens that it covers your thesis."

"What are the odds of that?" Rodney wondered out loud.

"Pretty good since you applied for a grad position under me two days after I got a vague grasp of what the book was about."

Rodney looked at the man dumbfounded. "Tell me, professor, how long have you had this book and where did you get it."

"I met a man named Stanley Hastings at Woodstock and became friends with him throughout the seventies. He was an explorer of sorts. Although, by the time I met him, he was mostly doing his explorations with psychedelics. Regardless, we became fast friends and when he discovered I was a scientist he gave me this book. Two months later he disappeared.

"Most thought he went off on another exploration, but I am pretty sure the Overwatchers took him." Carrus paused as if to let Rodney speak.

More questions entered Rodney's mind than the man was answering but before he could ask them the professor stared up again.

"I don't think the Overwatchers want us to have this book and I think they've caught on that I have it. They've been visiting my dreams more often, and sometimes I see them when I'm awake. But they can't touch the book. I don't know why, but if they could, they would have taken it long ago."

"What is an Overwatcher?" Rodney asked now uneasy holding a book that had such a noxious past.

"Humanoid black figures with red eyes. I've dreamed of them since I was a kid. They would stare at me as I lay in bed, and I wouldn't be able to move. I knew they were watching me sleep, but they were also looking at something else about me. Then they would disappear," he made an explosion gesture with his hand, "poof out of existence like the electrons you study."

Rodney tried to smile but couldn't muster the emotion. He wanted to believe that the man was crazy. Rodney questioned how much of this was a joke and wondered how much effort his professor had put into the fake book. But as he tried to figure the trick out the room became more ominous.

Then Dr. Carrus became as still as stone. He gazed over Rodney's shoulder at a mirror that hung on the wall.

"Is everything okay?" Rodney asked for the third time since walking into the office.

The man seemed to be fighting for the ability to speak. Then he let out a few labored words, "There's one behind me." The old man gasped for breath and was able to add "Do you see it?"

Rodney shook his head. He didn't see anything behind the professor.

But the fact that his professor had frozen up was not funny to Rodney. The man was old and probably suffering from a severe heart attack or stroke. Rodney got out of his seat. He knew there was an AED device in the hallway that could start his teacher's heart back up.

He opened the door and as soon as he did he heard the man behind him say, "Stop, don't leave."

Rodney whirled around and looked at the man who had gone from completely tense to merely shaken up. The darkness that shrouded the room disappeared. "What's going on Carrus?"

"I'm not sure, but I don't think I have much time left. I need to explain everything I know about the book so that when I'm gone, you can continue to study it."

"Is this a joke?" Rodney asked finally discussing the fear he harbored the whole conversation.

"No young man, this may be the most serious discovery of all humankind. I wasn't able to open the library doors, but you're young and may have a chance. Sit down and listen to me. After a while, you will understand and believe that I'm not crazy."

Rodney was dubious. The professor would be fighting an uphill battle to convince Rodney of something that wasn't written in a physics textbook.

2 - The Only Mystery Worth Solving

"You want answers to the mysteries of the universe, kid? Then take this," Stanley said as he shoved a book into the frizzled young man's grasp.

Martin Carrus clutched the book before it slipped out of his grasp and hit the ground. "You think it has answers?"

Stanley shrugged the question off, "I don't doubt it has answers. But I think it will fill your life with more mysteries than anything else."

Martin thumbed through the book, the words were squiggles, and the figures were equally mystifying. "Is there a translation, or at least the start of one?"

Stanley, whose age and adventures had brought wrinkles to his face chuckled softly. "No there isn't. It took the university's best linguists months to decipher what the cave had written in."

"You found this in a cave?" Martin responded with disbelief.

"Well, it was a cave that was being used as a temple. And I'll tell you what, it was a bitch to get to. I think I still have some mosquito bites from that expedition."

"Why are you giving it to me?" Carrus asked.

"Lots of reasons," the man said with a snicker. He took a drag from his cigarette, let out a small cough, then offered it to the young scientist. "You're probably going to want some of this. We're about to get into some heavy shit."

The joint hung between the old adventurer and the young scientist. He had a rule that he didn't smoke while he was working, but then again he wasn't sure how close to work this was going to resemble. He took a short drag from the cigarette figuring he would split the difference.

"Good, now let's get into this before the shrooms kick in," the man said while relaxing in his armchair.

"The what?!?" Carrus asked in shock. His mind immediately went to the tea the man served him, and he stared at his cup. It was already half empty.

Stanley let out a laugh that filled the apartment's living room. Even the thick shag carpet couldn't absorb the sound. "Don't worry my friend. I didn't waste any on you. I took them a few minutes before you arrived. The joint helps with the transition and the tea helps me stay hydrated."

Martin wiped the sweat away from his brow. "Then I guess we should get into this quickly," he said while looking back at the book.

"You asked me why I gave it to you," Stanley started, "And I don't have a simple answer for you. The best answer I have is that it feels right. My brain wants to make a dozen excuses for why I should, but truth be told, it's just pure animalistic instinct." Carrus nodded and let the conversation continue. "The book, as far as I can tell, relates to something scientific. And my university has had it in our anthropology department for long enough. They're not getting anywhere with it. Anthropologists are a bunch of tautological hobbnoggins."

Carrus laughed at the word. He was feeling a little light-headed, so the comment came off funnier than it should have. He then proceeded to point out, "Aren't you an Anthropologist?"

The old man smiled and nodded, then protested "Yes but I made that choice under duress. They said I would only be able to go on the cool archeological explorations if I had a degree."

"You must have been a hell of a student," Carrus remarked wondering what kind of students he would have once he got his doctorate and became a professor.

"Anyway, where was I?"

"You were complaining about Anthropologists."

"Yes, yes, yes, they can only get us so far. And they won't admit this, but they've hit a wall with this book. You see when trying to translate something from another language you need to establish a common ground. The translators need something that will connect the foreign language to your native language. With indigenous people, this is in the form of pointing at something and getting the word for it. But that doesn't work with written text. Sometimes we can extrapolate from present text or context from the site, but the writing in the cave temple doesn't match the writing in the book."

"That makes sense. You mentioned that this book was not from our world."

"Yes, exactly, there's no related language like this so we can't learn what it says."

"But if the anthropologists and linguists can't figure out what the book says how the hell am I going to? I'm an American physicist, the only foreign word I know is 'prost.'"

The old explorer lifted his teacup and made a cheers gesture at the young scientist. "I'll drink to that." He took a sip of his tea and made the most serious look he could, considering that he was a little stoned. "You do share a language with this book though. This book is about how worlds interact. It's about science. Something that no anthropologist will ever spend time learning. I believe that's the common ground between mankind and that book."

Carrus looked at the book and thumbed through a few pages. "There's not a single equation in here."

The man shrugged and smoked the last of the joint. He put it out in the small ashtray, finished his tea, and leaned back in his chair. "That's what the anthropologists told me. You know what I think?"

Carrus looked up from the mystifying pages and shook his head.

"I think we have bigger problems than their numbers looking slightly different from our numbers."

Carrus looked down at the book. It was open to a page with a large figure displayed. At least Martin assumed it was a graph. The coordinates were perplexing and the axes that were labeled he couldn't read. Carrus concluded that the man was grossly uninformed, whoever wrote this book wasn't just using a different symbol for numbers they were using a completely different number system or thought process. But Stanley could be right, math could be the same across worlds, and if it was maybe Carrus could beat his head against the book long enough to get a translation out, but he suspected it would take all his life.

"There's more to this book," Hastings added. Before Carrus could respond with *Oh great* the man continued. "I told you that it's not from this world and we did end up translating the temple's walls."

"Mhmm," Carrus responded.

"Well, the cave talked about a room that they had accessed. It might have been deeper in the temple, that's what a lot of the archeologists took the translation as since parts of the cave had collapsed and we didn't have the funds to excavate them. Me and the other 'forward thinking' explorers thought the linguist could have translated a word the indigenous people used differently.

"You see it read like 'transcend' and most just thought that meant travel, like from room to room, but I think it indicated travel in the way our spirit travels through different heavens and hells when we die."

Martin had never bought into any religion. He blamed it on his parents, the science he did didn't have much room for a bearded man who could snap a world into existence. Because of this, he responded with, "What do you mean spirit?"

The man smiled and leaned forward in his chair, "There's more to this world than your science can explain. Every religion and culture since the beginning of man has brought up the idea of a spirit or consciousness. This cave temple we found was no different. It mentioned the ability to move their spirit from room to room. One room they found was called the Infinite Library."

"They called it that?"

The man giggled, his high hadn't worn off, but Carrus was as sober as a Quaker. "They didn't have the word for library," Hastings responded, "They didn't have the word for infinite either, but they used a word like vast, endless, and enormous. Infinite Library sounds much more impressive than 'enormous endless room of writings.'" He laughed at his joke realizing that Martin wouldn't. "Lighten up. This isn't even the fucked up part."

"Let's get to the fucked up part then," Martin said. The corners of his mouth weren't bent in a frown or a smile.

"Ok, but one last thing. I don't know how they got there, but they described what they found. It was a room full of books. There were books written in thousands of languages. Languages they couldn't read. But they didn't all match the book you have there. Some were written in their native language. Chances are there were some written in English. They described it as a wealth of information. I suspect it has every book ever written. But I have no logical reason to believe that."

"What if a race that didn't wear loincloths had access to it?" Carrus asked.

"Then I have a feeling the hydrogen bomb would be the least of this planet's concerns. But don't mock the loincloth, it's comfortable, and they got into the library, we haven't."

Carrus sat back in his chair. The jet-black book lay in his lap. He looked at the gold pattern on the front, but he couldn't stare at it for long. The inhuman design disturbed him.

"Well," the man drew out the syllable, "Aren't you going to ask me?"

"Ask you what?" Carrus responded. A score of questions entered his mind, but he couldn't form them into words.

"The obvious question, everyone asks it." The man paused waiting for Martin to chime in. He didn't so Stanley continued, "Don't you want to know where they all went? Everyone always wants to know how the indigenous people disappeared."

The thought hadn't even crossed Martin's mind. He shrugged and asked the question his friend wanted him to ask, "Where did the indigenous people go?"

Stanley Hastings smiled looked at the young man and said, "Nobody knows." He said it in his most mysterious tone like he was beginning a haunted house tour.

"Then why did you make me ask?" Martin complained.

"Well, we have a pretty good idea. And by we, I mean a few other people who were at the site and me. Let me warn you that this is quite an unconventional belief." The man smiled and showed his friend his palms.

"I have a feeling most of this conversation isn't a conventional belief," Martin retorted.

The man ignored the jest and went on with his theory about the original owners of the book. "They traveled. I'm not sure how they induced it, I'm inclined to believe it was through psychedelics. But the travel seemed to invite a type of demon into their tribe. The natives called them watching people. They never interacted, just watched the natives go about their travels. Some of the archeologists working on the dig called them librarians. They might have been right. I was inclined to call them Overwatchers. It sounds more ominous, and I believe that is what these things are, ominous and malicious.

"There were drawings of these things on the walls of the cave. Black figures with red dots as eyes. These were discounted as just being how the librarians or priests of the temple dressed, but I think it was more than that. They watch you, Martin. They just sit there and watch you talk, sleep, or read. They don't interact with you or the book. But inevitably once they watch you for long enough they make their move and take you away. Maybe they take you to the Infinite Library, more likely they take you to whatever dark universe they came from."

A shiver went down Martin's spine, and a cloud must have floated in front of the sun because the once well-lit room seemed to be as dark as the explorer's words. "The temple had writing that described this disappearance?" Martin asked.

The explorer shrugged, "Not in so many words. If it did explain it, we never got to the point of translating it."

"Then how do you know?"

"Well, it happened to the three anthropologists who were studying the book I just gave you."

Martin looked down at the now deep purple book and its disturbing gold design. "They took the archeologists away?"

Stanley nodded his head.

"How? When? Why?" The scientist asked.

"Each of them mentioned dreaming of the Overwatchers, then they complained about seeing them in real life. I chalked it up to poor sleep due to the nightmares and being overworked without making progress on the book. Then they disappeared."

"Disappeared?"

"Yeah, like they stopped coming into work, their car was still in their driveway. Their doors were locked from the inside, and one of them even left the oven on. The Overwatchers have the power to transport through worlds, that's obvious from the ruins we found. What I don't think was mentioned was that they can transport people too." The explorer shivered and looked at his empty teacup.

"If you knew this would happen why did you give this cursed book to me?" Martin accused.

"Because you wanted answers about the universe, you're a physicist after all. And I've been having dreams about the Overwatchers. Sometimes I see them when I'm awake. It's terrifying, and it freezes me. One has been watching us since I brought them up in this conversation," He said this with a smile but kept his gaze locked on Martin.

Martin looked around the room slowly trying to find out where the monster was hiding. The man laughed at the scientist's panicked gesture. "It's been sitting behind you. Don't know why. It's not interested in you yet, just me right now. I'm surprised this worked so well."

"What went well about this?"

"Typically I freeze up when they're around. I can't do anything but move my lips, and that takes all the effort in the world. But right now, I'm carrying on a conversation."

"Why?"

"Why can't I normally move? or why can I hold a conversation?" He asked looking for clarification.

Martin had none and responded with "both."

"Well I don't know why I can't move, it might be their control of time and space. As for why I can move right now, well, that has to do with the shrooms I ingested before you got here. It was a theory I had. Psilocybin has some interesting effects on the brain and its perception of time. I thought it might help me combat the freezing up. Maybe, when they inevitably come for me, I'll have a fighting chance."

"Good to know," Martin said unenthusiastic, "How long until they come for me?"

"Hard to say," Stanley said nonchalantly. "It's different for everyone. The first archeologist held on to the book for ten years but then the next two disappeared months away from each other. I've been holding onto it since then, about five years. After you mentioned that you were a scientist looking to solve all of the mysteries of the universe I started having more dreams about the Overwatchers. I took it as a hint and figured I'd give you something to focus on.

"I've learned a few things, and at the risk of sounding old and showing my age, I'll tell you, don't try to solve every problem you come across. Pick your battles and fight them until the end. The universe holds many mysteries. In time, science will solve as many. But if you try to solve all of them, you'll be pulled in every direction. Focus on one battle and learn everything you need to conquer the enemy."

"This is a mystery worth solving?" Martin said looking down at the book that would soon become his most important work.

"Martin, this is the only mystery worth solving. If you figure this book out, then you will be able to unlock answers to questions no one ever conceived of."

Martin considered refusing the book and the challenge. He could set it on the man's coffee table and walk out the front door. The man's delusions of monsters that Martin couldn't see would remain in the house. But Martin trusted his friend. The man had told him dozens of stories, as many were true as were false. And because of this Martin had trained his gut to be able to smell one of Stanley's tall tales. His gut told him this one hadn't strayed far from the truth. "Thanks for the book," he replied, "I guess I should get to reading it." Martin stood up. His legs were shaky either from the drugs or the lengthy conversation.

"One thing," Stanley said as he stayed in his chair.

"What is it?" Martin was curious about what other oddities the man would add to his life.

"Would you mind leaving through the window of the bedroom? I left it open. Overwatchers tend to get scared off when doors open." A smile flickered across his face.

Martin looked at the front door. It was bolted shut. He had no reason to protest the man's strange request. "I can do that. See you next week or something." Martin reached out his hand to shake his friend's hand

"See ya," Stanley replied as they shook hands. "Forgive me if I don't get up. You know how these things can be," He gestured at the ashtray.

"Of course," Martin replied.

The young scientist climbed through the open window and went to work. His life became busy, and he didn't get around to calling his friend for a month. The explorer was a known recluse, so after not picking up Martin's phone calls he determined he would visit the man at his house. When Martin arrived the door was locked, and no one responded to the bell.

Martin checked the bedroom window and it was still open. He climbed through and went to the living room. Nothing had changed, the house was as messy as ever, and two empty teacups sat between the armchairs.

The only new thing he found was a note marked up with sloppy handwriting. It read, "I guess I'm going on an adventure."

3 - The Initial Conditions of Another Universe

"So in conclusion, with my device, lab time, research, and the help of Dr. Martin Carrus I was able to study exactly what is going on in the empty space of atoms. It's common knowledge that the space is not empty, but is composed of electrons and protons that exchange photons and heavy gauge bosons. I was able to not only observe these interactions on low-form particles but was able to measure them.

"With sufficient funding and of course this board's approval of my thesis defense I would like to go on and investigate how my lab could interact and even harness the energy of these interactions. Thank you for your time, are there any questions?"

The five professors and two doctoral candidates applauded Rodney Brown's presentation. And while this was the moment Rodney had been looking forward to for the past fifteen years of his life it felt empty. The man that Rodney had been working under and learning from for the past six years had not made an appearance at his thesis defense.

Dr. Martin Carrus hadn't made an appearance at anything in the past week. Rodney had been covering the man's classes, running the lab, and preparing for his defense for the past few days. The professor had disappeared and the police, after investigating the man's house, found no trace of him leaving. They found his house locked from the inside.

Rodney answered the other professor's questions succinctly and to their contentment. He had spent days brainstorming the different questions they might ask so he could be as prepared as possible. A technique Carrus had shared with him. Then the dean asked a question that Rodney hadn't expected, "How long until you think you've prepared this technology for commercial use?"

Commercial use? Rodney was baffled. These men were scientists. Sure, the school had bills to pay and the college had been severely underfunded for years, but were they going to sell his work for commercial profits?

"I don't understand the question, sir."

"Well, the implications are clear. The last man to harness the power of the atom put an end to World War II. Then we went on to create nuclear power plants. So, how long until you think that we could move your work into the private sector for some real profits? At a minimum, we should be selling your measurement device to colleges and companies with the ability to buy them."

Rodney began to stutter out an answer. He stopped, took a deep breath, and composed himself, "I appreciate your support. But to be completely honest we haven't begun to interact with the particle let alone understand how much energy it might put out. It would take at least two years to get to a place where we would understand this well enough to begin pitching the private sector. That's assuming that what we find is worth anything to them. But under the current circumstances," Rodney gestured to the empty chair at the front of the room where the candidate's professor traditionally sat, "I don't even know if the lab will be able to continue."

The dean responded with, "We've been meaning to talk to you about that Dr. Brown."

Rodney Brown unlocked the door to his new office and surveyed the two cluttered desks. *I guess I should get to work clearing this stuff off,* Rodney thought to himself. He spent the entire morning and the better part of his afternoon cleaning up Dr. Carrus's desks, bookshelves, and filing system. He hated to throw anything away, especially when he didn't know which notes might be important and what might be critical.

After nearly everything had been stacked, sorted, and filed, He moved the man's trinkets to a small box that once held printer paper and pushed it into a back corner of the room where it would stay for years. The mirror, the Woodstock tickets, and his whiteboard remained hanging on the walls. The professor's papers took up the bottom two drawers of the filing cabinet leaving Rodney with only the top one for himself. *Maybe one day I'll scan them in and file them electronically,* but for now, he was content with a clean desk.

Along with the mess, the office, the class work, and the lab Rodney had inherited the man's financial stresses. At least those related to the school.

He also inherited the one thing he wanted nothing to do with. The inhuman book still sat on the man's desk. Its purple and black cover dancing in the light from the window. Rodney refused to take it at his last meeting with the man. *I guess he found a way to give it to me anyway.* Rodney thought.

The tables were cleaned for the most part, and Rodney realized that the room had far more space than he ever imagined. He picked up the book and thumbed through the book again. It was gibberish. So he thumbed through Carrus's notes. There were equations, Feynman diagrams, and statistics littering the pages. Although the sheets of paper were lined Rodney noticed that Carrus had a hard time using them as guides. Most of the notes were scribbled crooked in the margins and seemed to have brief but vague insights. "Something doesn't add up," was written in multiple places. Rodney studied the notes on the clear desk and scattered out what he could make sense of. The book sat untouched in the corner of the desk. Rodney felt like it was watching him work out the mystery.

Nine pm rolled around, and Rodney had made no progress. Worst of all, the studying had undone all the progress he had made on cleaning the desk. He looked around desks filled with notes and open textbooks. He observed the mess and agreed with Carrus; something didn't add up. It was as if all the rules of physics that he had studied as a boy didn't apply to this book. Meaning that the book wasn't about physics or the universe it was from. It played by other rules.

Rodney returned to the office before dawn the next day. He had slept like a rock and didn't remember dreaming. When he walked into his office, one thought kept coming to the front of his mind. *Played by different rules.*

He looked over the Carrus's notes again. The man was evidently trying to use physics to translate the book. Each equation he had deduced out of the book seemed to rhyme with an equation that Rodney found in the textbooks. But none of them matched up quite right. Carrus would discover what a number looked like in the foreign language, apply it to other places, and then end up with an answer that didn't make sense.

Rodney fiddled his thumbs and sipped his coffee as he stared at the pages of equations in front of him. Then, like rare but truly great ideas do, he had a thought that opened the floodgates of his mind. He looked at the equations and realized the thing Carrus had gotten wrong.

For years physicists used constants to compensate for truths they didn't quite understand. Newton used the gravitational constant in the gravitational equation, and Maxwell had both vacuum permittivity and vacuum permeability in his equations. Particle physics had its own cacophony of constants, and Carrus was using them as critical factors in determining what the alien numbers were. But if this book was indeed from another universe, and the equations were too, then there could be a fundamental difference between the laws that their nature operates under. *Comparing it to ours, and using our constants would give us the wrong results,* Rodney thought, *I need to know their constants and I'll discover their universe's initial conditions.*

He got to work trying to solve for the constants instead of the variables, and by 2 pm when the dean walked into his office, he had made progress.

"Dr. Brown, do you have a moment?" The dean asked. The man made himself comfortable in the chair that Rodney once sat in.

"Of course," he said finishing up an equation, "What's going on?"

"I know that it's only your second day in this position, but I wanted to go over your lab's financial situation. I don't know how transparent Dr. Carrus was with you before he ditched us but the lab is not in good shape."

"Yes, he mentioned some of that."

"Additionally, we looked over your apparatus, the one you used for your thesis, and the bill of materials you submitted is too expensive to duplicate. If we were to sell the apparatus to other universities, we would be unable to turn a profit. We're going to need you to design one that's less expensive."

Rodney frowned, "With all due respect sir, there isn't a less expensive design available. Carrus gave me a shoestring budget, to begin with, and I was barely able to deliver on that. Most of the sensors are custom-made to save money, but they took years to build and test. I don't believe we can produce a machine on anything less than the original budget." Rodney then considered protesting the entire concept of selling his machine for profit but held himself against it. There was no point in making waves this soon.

"If you can't make it less expensive then you will have to add some functionality to it. Is there anything it can do without having to modify the design significantly?"

"I would need a year, maybe two to figure that out, sir. I haven't been able to make it to the lab yet. And I have classes to run tomorrow. Midterms are coming up, and I don't think Carrus had a test written for them yet."

It was now the dean's turn to frown. "Dr. Brown, we expect a lot from you. We know you're the youngest professor at this university, and we will cut you some slack for that, but there are responsibilities to the school you now have to fulfill. If we can't make a profit from your design or your lab, then funding for your research and position might not continue to work out. You must understand that this school has to keep its lights on somehow."

"I understand sir," Rodney lied. "I will do my best to improve the design."

"Good, I will schedule a meeting for updates every Wednesday. I want to help you succeed at this. We expect big things from you. I'm sure you'll be able to fill Carrus's shoes and then some."

Rodney thanked the man as he left the office. He looked back at the pages he was working on before he was interrupted. Math would bring him a distraction and relief from the dean's pressures.

He looked down at the constants he had come up with. They were so wrong that if the dean had seen them, he would have probably fired Rodney on the spot for the elementary mistake. But from the translations Carrus had already made he realized that according to the inhuman book, these constants were right. At least for that universe.

Rodney spent the afternoon in the lab. The school's IT department had accessed Carrus's files, and Rodney was able to use a midterm from a few years ago for the test. He had a grad student, Maria, help him work on bringing the price of the apparatus down. However, he didn't share with her how important it was to do it. By 9 pm she left and by 3 am he had dozed away at his desk in the lab.

The sun blasted through the window of the lab and warmed his back to the point of discomfort. He woke up and looked at the clock. 4 hrs of dreamless sleep, he thought. Being slumped over his desk uncomfortably hadn't even phased him through the night. He looked at his notes from yesterday and thought of how much trouble he would be in if he had a meeting with the dean next Wednesday with only some incorrect constants to show him.

Then he had an idea for improved functionality.

Rodney skipped his morning coffee and began to tinker with his machine. At 1 pm Maria came in and reminded him that he had a class to teach. Rodney politely asked her if she could cover for him and she pointed out that she was a student in the class. He looked at the machine, his notes, and then remembered he hadn't prepared a lecture.

He shuffled through his notes, found the page he wanted, and circled a few equations in red ink. Handing the sheet of notes to Maria he said, "Put this on the board and tell them to solve it."

"Will this be on the midterm?" She asked.

Knowing no one would care about it if it wasn't he responded with, "Yes." In reality, he wanted someone to check if he had calculated the constants correctly.

Dinner came and went, but he didn't feel hungry. Rodney worked and worked and worked. Maria returned with a few attempts, but none of the students had the confidence to finish the equation once they saw they had the wrong constants.

"What are you working on anyway, Rodney?"

He gave her a vague answer saying, "I'm trying to improve the functionality per the dean's request." If he explained the details, he would be admitted to a psych ward, at a minimum his newly awarded Ph.D. would be revoked.

By 9 pm, long after the sun had gone down he finished the final technical touches. Hours later he was still calibrating the modified machine. But instead of calibrating it to the constants that he had grown up with he used the new alien combination that he had discovered only days ago. He synced the machine with them and turned it on.

At first, his readings showed nothing. He was disappointed but wasn't surprised. What he was trying to do should be physically impossible. Then he saw a blip on his readout. He examined the screen closer. Then a small pop went off near the machine, and the readout went blank.

A fuse must have blown, Rodney thought. He turned around and saw that every sensor on his machine had been burnt off. The machine was dead. *How did this happen?* He wondered. He printed off the recorded data and looked it over. There was no way he would be able to afford to replace the machine's sensors. Discouraged he poured over the data that he had accumulated from the short test.

He ran the numbers from the test. He discovered that he accomplished exactly what he had expected it to do. Exactly what the Law of Conservation of Mass said he shouldn't be able to do. His math from the reading proved otherwise. He had created an atom with his device. He had formed matter and broken a key law of physics.

Except he hadn't, the atom had to have been somewhere. It was in the same universe the book was in. He had merely summoned it to his world using the 'wrong' constants he had been studying for days.

"How's that for increased functionality?" He said to the empty lab. He went home pondering how to explain this to the dean without sounding like a mad scientist who got information from a magical book. Magic books weren't trusted very far in his field.

He slept through the night and most of the morning. But this time it wasn't dreamless. He had a constant feeling of being watched. And before he woke up he had a vivid dream where he couldn't move, and a black figure with red eyes was watching over him.

The Overwatcher was waiting for him to make his next discovery.

4 - Serial Numbers of Atoms

Finals for the college had just begun. Instead of preparing tests Rodney sat at the workbench in his lab and grabbed the small screwdriver that was sitting next to him. He tightened a screw that would be holding a new protective covering he had designed. He had repaired his machine between lectures, staff meetings, research meetings, and of course the Wednesday lectures from the dean. They were lectures and not meetings as the dean had initially presented them. Rodney was talked down to the entire time and rarely had an opportunity to show his findings for the week let alone defend himself from the dean's berating.

He began to tighten the screw, and it wouldn't twist. Rodney continued to work at the problem on autopilot. The screwdriver twisted against the head until he could turn it easily. Then he looked down at his work, rubbed his tired eyes, and saw the stripped screw. Rodney cursed.

This was the third time this week he found himself in the lab at three in the morning. Rodney Brown was overworked, underpaid, and stressed out. Nonetheless, he grabbed a pair of pliers to take the screw out. Looked at the mess Rodney had gotten himself into and then observed the general disarray of his workstation. If he were honest with himself, he would have gone to bed instead of continuing to beat his head against the problem. Instead, he left the lab an hour later without making any notable progress.

A week later Rodney had input the remaining grades for his students without much care or interest. He knew a few would complain about the outcome of the class, but he was in no mood to negotiate, he had just finished fixing his machine the night before. Rodney was obsessed with his finally repaired device. He had rebuilt the sensors that were overloaded last time and implemented fuses and shielding to get a more accurate reading.

It was three in the afternoon, and despite his lack of sleep, he felt awake and alive. He was ready to recalibrate his machine and rerun his test. By midnight his device was calibrated to the initial conditions of the foreign universe. He started to run the test, and as he watched the readout on his computer tick by, he noticed nothing was blowing up. That was a good sign.

On the downside, nothing else was happening. Rodney's machine was not creating new matter as it had before, and he was not getting the huge spikes in energy he had expected. The readings that he saw before weren't there. The measurements that had convinced him another universe existed, that Dr. Carrus wasn't pulling his leg about the inhuman book, weren't there. The past three months of his sleep-deprived life, and all his money he spent on his improved sensors because the dean refused to fund it was for nothing. Rodney felt like all his efforts went down the drain when he ran the test.

For the next three hours, Rodney ran the tests over and over again. Expecting to find the results he had gotten the first time. Rodney looked over his calibration, math, and the previous readout. He was doing everything right, but nothing was working.

The next morning, a Wednesday morning, Rodney sat at his desk drinking his third cup of coffee. It was nearly noon, and he had only been at the school for an hour. His life was no longer filled with lecturing classes since summer had begun but it wasn't any less busy. This morning he was boycotting the lab because he was disappointed by the failed science experiment he spent all night working on.

Worst of all it was a Wednesday which meant that the dean would be coming into his office. The old man would ask Rodney what he had accomplished this week and then proceed to ignore what Rodney said. Instead, he would talk about how the school was underfunded, and Rodney's project was the thing that was going to get the school on top of its finances and the academic industry as a whole.

Rodney did not doubt that his project if it worked, would bring the school money, success, and maybe even fame. Even if it didn't work, it would bring the school fame, but mostly for researching and publishing such a delusional idea. Rodney, hopeless and disheveled, determined he needed some math to back up the claim. Ideally, math that applied to this universe. At least then he wouldn't sound insane for claiming that he could create matter or more technically correct pull matter in from other worlds.

He stared at the design for his contraption on his computer. He determined he needed to work from another point of view. Rodney began to think about the machine and how it created matter instead of thinking about how the atoms were pulled in by the machine.

Rodney jotted down notes as his half-full cup of coffee got cold. He worked on intricate equations and perused Carrus's textbooks for obscure information. At the bottom of his third sheet of paper, he put a box around his answer. The number he calculated represented how much power his machine could produce if it worked.

The number was astounding. It was greater than he had ever imagined. He looked at the equations and double-checked his work. Despite the original assumption about the ability to pull matter into existence, it all checked out. But the answer was ungodly. The number was equivalent to the amount of power a large city would use. But his machine was the size of a desk chair instead of a building.

A knock came to his open door, and the dean sat down and started talking. Rodney looked up without paying attention to the man's words. When he paused, Rodney handed him the sheets of paper he had been working on without an explanation.

The dean held the papers and scanned them, saw the number at the bottom, and then looked up at Rodney. "You can do this?" He asked.

"Maybe," Rodney replied. "Check the math, does it work? If so then theoretically it's possible." He offered the man a calculator.

The dean refused the calculator and handed the papers back to Rodney. "If you think you can do this we will continue to pursue the project. I'm not in the business of checking your work, but I'm sure other professors and grad students around here would be interested. I don't want theory though. There are a half dozen tenured professors here who do that. I need someone who can produce experimental results. Results that will pay the bills. Can you do that?"

Rodney gave the man the answer he wanted to hear but doubted himself as he said it.

"Good," the dean replied, "I'll let you get back to it, but I want you to be careful with the budget we don't have much to spare."

Rodney responded with, "Of course, sir," but by the time he got the words out the dean was out of the room.

Rodney's boycott of the lab ended, and he carried his calculator and calculations down the lab.

In the lab, he found Maria and her few grad students working away on their projects. He interrupted Maria and the work she was doing. "Can you look over something for me?"

She looked at him, but her mind was somewhere else. She answered, "Sure, but can we talk about my grade from Dr. Carrus's, I mean your class?"

"Yeah no problem, if you don't like it and can solve this I'll make it whatever you want it to be." He ripped the top of the sheet of paper off giving her the equation he started with. He didn't want his previous calculations to bias her.

Two hours later Maria walked up to Rodney's desk in the lab. "I finished it, but I don't think it's right." She replied.

"What do you mean?" Rodney looked at the answer. It was the same as his.

"Well, it's just too big. That much energy would," Maria paused and Rodney looked from the paper to her. "Well, I don't know."

"No, what were you going to say?" He was glad that someone was willing and able to call him out. *Finally, someone will tear down this illusion and I will be able to walk away from the book and contraption Carrus cursed me with,* he thought.

"I was going to say that much energy would tear a hole in the universe. But then I realized it sounded crazy." She punctuated it with a laugh so that Rodney wouldn't take her seriously.

"Yeah, that's what I was afraid of," Rodney answered solemnly.

"Besides, your first equation is way off. I did the solution based on that, but I think your initial conditions are incorrect. At least these few here." She gestured at the initial conditions Rodney had calculated from the book. "Why would this variable be like this? I assumed they were initial conditions, but they don't look quite right."

Rodney shrugged and said, "It's all theoretical," as a defense to the accusation that he expected Maria to make. He wasn't prepared to defend his crazy assumptions against her and wanted to save face.

"I know that, but it reminded me of something else," Maria said. She added, "I actually wanted to talk to you about your class."

"Oh yeah!" Rodney remembered. "I can change your grade to an A now. The solution was correct, or at least the same as mine."

"No, I already had an A. I wanted to talk to you about the problem you had me put on the board around midterms."

"What about it?" Rodney said.

"It was awful, genuinely the worst assignment I've ever had. I'm glad you pulled it from the test otherwise everyone would have failed." She smiled, "That being said, I kept looking into it because it fascinated me. At the time I was also reviewing your machine to get the budget down. The two ideas mixed in my mind and I thought maybe you could calibrate your machine to get to a point where it was based on these variables." She produced another sheet of paper with some initial conditions that he had already calculated.

"And what would that imply?" Rodney asked already knowing the answer to his question. It was the same thought he had the night he blew up his machine.

"Well originally I thought it would imply that nothing would happen, then it looked like you could create matter. That's, of course, absurd but I think you could use these settings to grab hold of an atom. I don't know what you would do with it, but it would be groundbreaking if you did. We've been throwing atoms around for decades now. It's boring, but if we could control them, we could study them much more. And maybe even get them to give us more energy. Although not to the level that equation you just gave me implies."

"Fascinating," Rodney replied, "Do you have any notes on it?"

"I do," she said producing a small pile of papers from her bag. The bag had crumpled the edges of the documents, and some of the pencil markings had faded, but the math was there.

He reviewed them for a while and after she explained some of the research she had done he understood what she was claiming. Using the initial conditions he found from the inhuman book, she was able to determine a serial number of sorts for every particle in the world.

"Is every atom unique?" Rodney asked.

"From what I found, yes, everyone has a code, just like every human has specific DNA. But we would only see it if we look past the subatomic level. Which is exactly the level your machine is trying to measure."

Rodney smiled, Dr. Carrus had sent him down this path of research. "But that serial number would have to be," Rodney shook his head, "It would be nearly infinite. There are more atoms than humans and look how long DNA already is."

She nodded, "There is an unfathomable number of atoms, to say the least. That's why the serial number is equation-based. If it was sequential like DNA and barcodes are it would be impossibly long. They do this kind of stuff with computers and encryption. I studied it as an undergrad."

"So we could never know exactly how to sequence an atom," Rodney replied.

"Nope," She responded starting to pack up the papers, "It's completely theoretical, and even then I don't know if my math is right. I based most of the research on new stuff that hasn't been reviewed or affirmed. It was just a kind of spare time project I was working on."

"What if there was another atom with the same sequence?" Rodney asked. Her research had given him a hunch.

"That would, by what I've described in my notes, be impossible. Two atoms wouldn't exist in the same universe with the same sequence."

That was the answer Rodney needed to hear to get his machine to work.

Rodney stayed at the lab to work late for another night. After talking to Maria, he had determined that the results from his first attempt rose from blind luck. Rodney hadn't been able to get control of another atom from a universe because he only had a sequence for one atom. And once he brought it to this universe it had gone array. Rodney still didn't understand those details, but it had destroyed his machine and put off a promising amount of energy. After Rodney repaired the device, he used the same initial conditions of the atom that had gone array. Realistically this was equivalent to trying to dial a phone that had been blown up.

Combining his work with Maria's, he determined that all atoms were paired with atoms in other parallel universes. Rodney needed two pieces of information to pull the matter into his world. First, the initial conditions of another reality, he got these from Carrus's inhuman book. Secondly, the serial number of an atom, Maria's research provided a way to deduct this from existing atoms.

However, this would require substantial modifications to his machine that he had just spent months trying to repair.

He worked through the night on his computer doing calculations and designs he wasn't committed to destroying his machine on a hunch.

By 2 am he was sleepy. Then while he was typing away on his computer, his fingers quit moving. He tried to move them, but they refused to type. It took all the energy he had to look away from the screen and to his side. When he did, he saw a monster.

Squatting on the lab bench staring at Rodney with its red eyes was an Overwatcher. Rodney saw a vague humanoid outline shaded in black. He couldn't make out any features like a mouth or nose, only the two beady red eyes that stared intently at him.

"W-w-what do you want?" Rodney asked. He pushed out the words with strained effort.

The monster stared at him and watched him. Rodney felt his eyes dry out. He couldn't blink the silhouette had slowed all the muscles in his body. Rodney felt like if the thing didn't leave soon, his heart would stop too. He stared at the atrocity. Then his eyes became too dry to bear. Rodney forced himself to blink. It took all his will. When his eyes finally opened the Overwater was gone.

He rushed over to the lab bench it was sitting on, and nothing was out of place. He could move again, without an issue.

Was I asleep? He wondered. But he didn't feel like he had napped. He felt manic and out of control. He then knew how Carrus had felt the day he handed the book over. Rodney realized he didn't have much longer. The Overwatchers were showing up in his day-to-day life. Since they were leaving his dreams, it meant he would have to pass the book along soon.

Rodney sat back in his chair terrified of the monster that had just made an appearance. He looked at his work and the notes Maria had made. *Was she the one he would be forced to pass the book to?* he wondered.

Then he realized there might be another way. A way that he could end the curse of the book. He might even be able to defeat the Overwatchers and prolong his life on this earth. Rodney began to disassemble his machine. There was a new process he was ready to implement. And with the Overwatcher's appearance, it seemed to be now or never.

5 - Rodney, Regulators, and Regrets

Rodney sat up on the cot where he had spent the night. His eyes were level with his desk. He stared at the piles of papers that had piled up over the past weeks. The young professor stood up and stretched out his back leaning and pushing on it with his hands making him look like a chicken. He stopped his alarm, the only sound in the whole building, and looked at the clock, 5:03 AM. *Only slept through three minutes of the alarm this time* he thought, *I must not be as tired as I was yesterday.*

He went to the public bathroom outside of the lab and washed his face. Then he found his way to the lab to get back to work. Ever since an Overwatcher terrified Rodney by perching itself on the lab bench, he had been working double time in the lab.

He wanted to decipher the book, fix his machine, get the dean to quit lecturing him, and most importantly not disappear off of the face of the earth like every previous owner of the book. It was a laundry list of desires, and to fulfill them Rodney chose to sacrifice his commute and most of his time in bed. He took short naps in his office multiple times a day so he could be close to the lab and do as much work as possible.

Rodney knew an Overwatcher would show up for him soon. Then he would disappear without a trace. His life would end just like Dr. Carrus, Stanley Hastings, and every other person who had gotten ahold of the book. But Rodney was the only one of them who was close to figuring it out. At least that's how he reassured himself.

Rodney sat at his workbench and fiddled with his machine. Thanks to Maria's suggestions and research he had all the info he needed to summon new atoms from other worlds. But according to his calculations if he did it, then he would blow up most of his city. At least then the dean wouldn't have to worry about the school maintaining a reputation or future funding.

He thought back to the Large Hadron Collider and how people thought it was going to create a black hole in Sweden. Every honest physicist knew that wasn't going to happen, or at least the odds were slim.

Looking at his machine and his notes Rodney had a good feeling that if he succeeded in summoning and sustaining matter in this universe, he would have to have a regulator on his machine, something that would protect him and the rest of the town.

Rodney had been designing the regulator for weeks. The dean was less excited about the regulator and suggested that Rodney prove that he could make power before he tried to limit it. Rodney disregarded his boss and worked on the regulators and bore the lectures that earned him. He also footed the bill with the last of his savings. He could probably stop paying rent if he had to, his new home seemed to be the lab. God only knew where it would be after the Overwatcher showed up for him.

Rodney affixed the final component of the regulator onto his contraption. The contraption Dr. Carrus had convinced him to make for his thesis. The device that tied his fate to the book, and the past owners of it. Rodney sat down at the computer and started to configure everything. The process was not quick.

After hours of working on the software for the regulators and multiple interruptions from grad students during the day, he felt finished and prepared to test. He also felt ready for a nap. Rodney checked his watch. It read 8:45 pm. That meant the time to take his afternoon nap had passed. He knew his body would make him pay for it by sleeping through his next alarm.

Rodney pushed the thought aside and began to test his new and improved science experiment. He started it up, calibrated it to the coordinates he had been translating from the book, and began to connect between the universes. Rodney watched his readings improve, and it looked like the machine was about to dial into the universe Rodney wanted. And for a split second, he had it, a blip of energy that proved he had brought something into his world. Then it disappeared. Thanks to the regulators, his machine hadn't taken any damage.

He looked at his watch, and it was almost time for him to take a nap. But before he got to bed, he decided to capitalize on his results and try one more test. This time tweaking some of the code for the regulators and allowing it to let more energy pass through. *With more power the bond between the atoms might be stable enough to be maintained,* he thought. The code wasn't as easy to adjust as he thought but after forty-five minutes of tweaking, he had something that might work.

He began to dial up another atom starting the process. Rodney turned to look at the machine. When he spun his chair to face it, he felt his heartbeat slow down.

Three black figures were looming around his metallic contraption. Unlike before they were not interested in him. Instead, they were inspecting his machine. There were three of them instead of one, and they moved fluidly through the solid object. They looked like shadows dancing in the light except every once in a while he would see a glimpse of their beady red eyes. He considered letting out a sound, in an attempt to shoo them off but he knew they weren't like dogs and the lab door wouldn't be opening until morning.

Maybe it takes three to take me away, and that's why they're here, he thought to himself. However, they seemed to have no interest in him. He watched them look at each other and inspect parts of the machine. The shadowy black bodies seemed to be conversing with each other, but he could not hear them. Not that he would have understood what they were saying in the first place.

Then they began to touch the machine. The Overwatchers had moved in and out of it without affecting the device. What the three did now was different. Rodney watched parts of his machine move. The Overwatchers fiddled with the regulators that he had so carefully designed, adjusted, and calibrated. One of them, Rodney thought it might be the tallest, but maybe just been the closest, looked at Rodney as the others messed with his delicate experiment.

Rodney tried to call out, but his throat caught the words. He needed to scare them away or fight them. They were going to ruin his machine he knew it. But Rodney was helpless, he was trapped in a staring contest with the tall Overwatcher and couldn't move. He couldn't even focus on what they were ruining.

Rodney woke up with a cramp in his back. He stood up not sure where he was. After looking around and taking in the familiar sights, he realized he was confused because he had never seen the lab from this point of view. He got off the ground and used the desk as a crutch. He gracelessly landed in his desk chair. It took him some time to remember what had happened.

As soon as the nightmare came back to him, he ran diagnostics on his machine. The results were clear. The Overwatchers ruined his regulators. Everything he had worked on over the past few weeks, his savings and his only hope for being able to understand his research safely, was destroyed. Rodney couldn't fix the machine.

Rodney felt his eyes droop and he yawned. He didn't know when he passed out last night, and he had woken up hoping the Overwatcher's destruction was a dream, but the diagnostics proved otherwise.

He poked at his keyboard without any hope of fixing the problem. His idle attempts were luckily cut short by Maria who walked into the lab and smiled at him. She was bright-eyed from a full night's rest. *That would change if I cursed her with the book,* Rodney thought. She greeted him with a cheery good morning, and it didn't take any energy for Rodney to figure out she was excited about something, which was good because Rodney had no strength to use.

"I've figured something out. I know you've been going lone wolf on this project, but I kept working on my side project. I don't think I could focus my thesis on it. There are not enough published papers behind it yet. However, I might get a short paper out of it, something I could refer to later. Of course, I would need your help on it." Her words were bubbling full of energy and Rodney blinked slowly to keep himself awake through them.

"You look tired. Are you okay?" Maria said.

Rodney replied in a dry tone. "No, I'm not okay. There was an accident last night, and my regulators are ruined."

"The ones you've been working on for weeks? The ones the dean has been fighting with you about?" She asked as if she needed clarification. Rodney knew she didn't and nodded. "Oh man, that's bad. What happened?"

Rodney imagined a reality where he went into detail explaining the book, the Overwatchers, and their sabotage and saw it ending with him in a straight jacket. Instead, he responded with an empty "There was a bug in my code, and I didn't account for a scenario that blew them out."

"Probably because you're exhausted. You should have had me, or someone, look over it."

You don't want any part of this project, he thought. "I need to get back to work on them before my meeting with the dean this afternoon." He said hoping to end the conversation about his previous failed attempts.

"Um, I actually had an idea about them, that's why I came in early. I had this strange dream, I can't remember much of it," Maria shook her head to dismiss it. "Regardless, I woke up thinking about the amount of power you'd be releasing. I've looked back at your equation multiple times and can't find any issues with it. But I thought there was a better solution. I imagined you could move the energy into connecting the atoms, strengthening their bond. Have you..." she started, but Rodney cut her off.

"I can't control that," Rodney pointed out.

"Well, yes I know that." Maria said looking hurt, "It's just theoretical. But it would get around your issue of needing regulators."

"Are you suggesting that I run the tests without any safeguards? Do you know how dangerous that would be?" Rodney was starting to become irritated, and he couldn't keep it hidden.

"I am just saying that if you had the right pair, it would probably connect more naturally. I have notes," Maria pulled out some papers from her bag and set them on his desk. They were composed of complicated equations and marked-up research papers.

"The right pair?" Rodney continued, irritated. "And which one would be right? I'm trying to do research here not magic. Do you even know what the right pair looks like? What's even a mathematical way to quantify that?"

With those comments, Rodney saw Maria switch to the defensive. She replied with a quick quip: "Any sufficiently advanced technology looks like magic Rodney. I thought that was the kind of science you always dreamed of doing." She stood up and marched out of the lab leaving her notes on his desk. He proceeded to ignore them for the rest of the day.

In the early afternoon, after not making any substantial progress on his destroyed regulators he marched up to his office to meet with the dean. He didn't bring any papers or even try to hide his cot. Usually, he folded it up, he didn't know what the rules for faculty sleeping on campus were, but he didn't want to find out. Rodney wasn't even worried about being on time anymore.

When he got to his office, the dean was already there. The man had let himself into Rodney's locked office. To make matters worse, the dean was sitting in Rodney's office chair, leaving Rodney to take the guest chair he kept near the door.

"It's about time you got here." He said. Rodney looked at his watch it was only five minutes past the hour.

"You're literally never on time," Rodney retorted. He was too tired to deal with the dean's crap.

"I'm on time this time, and I expected you to be too. Not to mention, what is this thing doing in here?" He said gesturing at the green army cot that Rodney had left out.

"It's not important. What are you lecturing me about this week?" Rodney countered.

"I'm about to lecture you on your attitude if you don't change it." The dean scowled at the young man and continued. "today I want to hear about what progress you've made with these regulators you've been working on." The dean spat the word regulators at the young professor.

"I got them to work for a little bit last night, but then they blew out. Not sure why."

"They were a waste of time and resources, I knew it. That's why I didn't insist on them. Or even invest in them." the man quickly remarked, "I hope you've learned your lesson and decided to do things my way. Now what you need to do is just run the experiment as you designed in the paper you showed me a few weeks back."

"The one with the unfathomably large output of energy?" Rodney said sarcastically.

The dean didn't catch it and responded with, "Yes, that one, just run that and see how much energy it outputs. Put it behind some protective shielding and see what happens."

"We don't have shielding that strong," Rodney said without emotion.

"Don't be ridiculous just borrow some from one of the engineering labs. Surely they have something."

Rodney repeated the number that he had calculated, adding emphasis on how big it was. "That is an incredible amount of energy."

"It's unbelievable," The dean retorted.

"Exactly," Rodney agreed.

"No, what I'm saying is it's unbelievable. Your math was wrong." The dean said dismissively, "I'm sure any other professor around here would be happy to explain why it's wrong but you simply can't create that much energy. So do the experiment, get me some results, and I will begin to pass them around other colleges to see if anyone wants to bite on buying the rights to your research."

Rodney threw his hands in the air, "is that all you think about? How to make a profit on other professor's research. You don't even care to look at my work. You haven't visited a lab in years, and all you do is try to turn a profit. Do you think that has something to do with why the school needs so much funding? Obviously, you're not doing your job correctly."

"I have far more important things to do than come to the lab and check your work. I'm the only one around here trying to make sure that you have a paycheck next week and you seem ungrateful to pull your weight." The dean stood up to leave. He ended the conversation with, "Run the test, Dr. Brown. If you don't, you'll be placing your cot under a bridge instead of in this office."

Rodney finished his afternoon nap and woke up around six. After the conversation with the dean, he was exhausted. All he could think of was how hopeless everything was. He had no money, a failed research project, he was about to lose his job if he didn't get results. If he did get results it would most likely end in an uncontainable explosion and to make matters worse, shadow monsters were haunting him and sabotaging his work at every turn. He sat at his desk and flipped through the book that started all of these problems.

He stared at the worn pages and the foreign figures that didn't make sense to him. The squiggly letters didn't come together to form words like every other book he had read. He looked for something that would stick out, but he knew nothing would. The book had over 400 pages, not that any of them were labeled.

The paper glided through Rodney's hand, and it felt familiar like every other page he had felt, but it was also silky. Not in a brand new textbook or a light sheet out of the Bible way. Instead, it felt soothing like leather or cloth.

Rodney continued to flip through pages, feeling the material and repeating the task in a kind of meditation. He lost track of time, and before he knew it, he was almost at the back of the book. He looked down surprised by how much time had passed and then saw the page he had stopped on.

There were two symbols that he understood from that page. One was a circle around squiggly letters that he couldn't translate. The ring seemed to be made after the original print.

The second, and spookiest thing he recognized was a picture. One that had been printed in the book initially. It was a black-and-white drawing, but unfortunately, it was done so well that it looked realistic. The only thing it was missing was beady red eyes.

He copied down the circled information and closed the book quickly. He cross-examined them with previous notes he had taken. It didn't take him long to translate since the circled symbols were more initial conditions. He didn't know what they were initial conditions to, but he had a guess. Hopefully, it was the Infinite Library that everyone had been talking about. If Rodney was unlucky, and that seemed to be the prevailing theory, it would be to whatever demonic world the Overwatchers came from.

Rodney got to the lab and calibrated the machine to the new initial conditions. He took the regulators offline per everyone's suggestion, even the Overwatchers. Right now Rodney had nothing to lose. He began his initial test confident it would fail like everything else he had done.

If he was lucky, it would fail. If he was unlucky, the dean would be right, and energy would be released. Additionally, if Rodney were superiorly unlucky, he would blow himself up along with the school.

However, there was a slim chance that something else would happen. Rodney might get the results that Carrus had hoped. That scared the young professor more than anything else. But he was a scientist and fascinated by the idea of finding the truth.

He started up the machine, and it warmed up. The contraption began its tests and then started to dial in the atom from the other universe. The unknown world. The place Rodney didn't even believe existed.

The machine beeped a warning and continued to incessantly beep. *Damnit,* Rodney thought, *I forgot to turn off the reactor's fail safes.* They were warning him that the machine had too much power going through it. *I'm sure it will blow any second,* Rodney thought.

Then he was blinded by a flash of lightning. He shielded his eyes and let his pupils adjust to the new light. *There goes my machine and my job,* he thought as he took down his arm.

In front of him, his machine stood in one piece and not on fire. Above below, in front of and through the device was a bright orb that was white, purple, blue, and green. The sphere seemed to be oscillating on its surface. It took up the same space as the machine but moved through it. Much like the Overwatchers had the previous night.

The experiment had worked. Rodney's machine blew a hole through the universe. The scientist began to consider the implications, but before he could look at the computer to check its readings, he was frozen still.

On the left and right side of the oscillating ball were two shadowy Overwatchers. They stared at him with their red eyes. The orb shone brilliantly. But despite the light, the two Overwachters weren't lit up. They merely stared at him with their piercing red eyes. Then they nodded in tandem.

Suddenly Rodney felt an icy hand on his back. It was as if the hand had reached through his clothes and under his skin to move him. He was falling forward, but he couldn't move his muscles to catch himself. Instead, he felt himself falling towards the orb in front of him. He couldn't stop himself. He fell through the hole in the universe and into an unknown world.

Seconds later the orb lost its energy and disappeared out of the lab. Its exit was followed by the three Overwatchers that had guided Rodney towards discovering the gates of the Infinite Library.

The Man Who Lived at the Edge of the World

Originally Published: March 9, 2018

This week has been busy for me. I've sent out my novella to beta readers, I've started a new job, and I have been putting some stuff together behind the scenes for this blog. I'm excited to reveal it to you, and I hoped it would be this week, but it's not ready yet. Another interesting and exciting thing happened, and I wanted to share that with you, along with two micro-stories that I had lying around in my notebooks. I hope you enjoy it.

Things to Enjoy Right Now

I have a planner that I use it's awesome and different from planners that force you to schedule things at certain times. That's never worked for me but this planner does work, it's called a Productivity Planner, and you can buy them from Intelligent Change.

The planner isn't the important or interesting part of this though. It's one of the things that I do with them. Every day of the week I have a sticky note that goes over the page hiding the work I have to do for the day. Before I can get to the day's work, I have to read what's on the sticky note. Monday I review my goals for the year, Tuesday I read an affirmation about The Other, Wednesday I read about my writing goals, and Friday I have a reminder to send out these blogs via email. These sticky notes help keep me on track and are the main reason I reached half of my New Year's resolutions in 2017. Along with maintaining the habit of writing for an hour every day.

These notes have traveled from journal to journal (I've gone through three of them), and I've replaced some of the notes over time. The Thursday one finally lost its stickiness after 15 months of use. So I transposed it. Then I truly appreciated it.

On Thursdays, I remind myself of what I need to enjoy right now.

I want to be a well-known author. I want to help others be great authors too. I want to live off of the income I get from writing the things I want to write. I want a lot of stuff I don't have.

Because I want all these things in the far future, I forget to enjoy the place I am in right now. This sticky note brings me back to the present every week, and I thought I would share with you what I'm enjoying in this phase of my life.

- I do work I want to do

- I am free to pursue things that don't scale

- I'm not fully committed to a business model yet therefore I can experiment

- I have so much potential

- I don't have anyone depending on me as a breadwinner

- I have wonderful people who support me in my life (That includes you, Reader)

- I have Time and Energy to Improve and Play

What are a few things you can enjoy in the phase of life you're in? I know I am usually looking down the path to where I want to be. I want you to take some time today and write down 3 or 4 things that you get to enjoy where you are right now. Maybe even post it somewhere and look at it every once in a while.

The Elusive Squirrel

Shasta crouched behind the bush and waited. She had tried a dozen things, and none of them had worked. This time she would show her master her loyalty. This time she would catch the squirrel.

It was sitting in the tree, shaded from the hot Texas sun. The squirrel was eating a pecan, one of the master's pecans. Shasta panted as quietly as she could. She waited for the squirrel to come down, it was bound to happen sooner or later.

The squirrel twitched its ears and looked around. Shasta quit panting and stared at the rodent, it was about to move. The woodland creature expended its half-eaten pecan and turned to face the trunk. It ran down, and Shasta jumped from behind the bush. She barked, and her wolven ancestors would have been proud, despite her being a 12-pound beagle.

But alas the squirrel heard her from the bushes, and before Shasta got to the base of the tree, it had retreated up. The rodent looked for other places to go. *You're not getting out of this one,* Shasta thought. *I've got you this time.* And she was right there was nowhere for it to go.

Then the squirrel went to the edge of the branch where the limb got thinner. Shasta watched the squirrel weigh down the branch. *You're going to fall right into my mouth,* she thought. Then the unexpected and unexplainable happened. The squirrel was walking on top of the great fence.

What is this? Shasta protested with a bark. Then another bark, followed by three more. She ran the length of the yard following the squirrel and barking the entire time trying to scare it or curse it off the fence. She yelped and ran until she met the other great fence. Then the squirrel simply jumped into another yard, onto another tree, and it was out of Shasta's sight.

"Hush up out there," the master yelled.

She turned and looked at her owner in the doorway of the house. Her heart was beating in her chest, but she didn't care. She was soon sitting right in front of him. He looked down at her.

"Did you scare off the squirrel?" her master asked.

She stared at what he was doing. He was holding flatware and was eating something that smelled delicious.

"Here," he said dropping a piece of steak. Shasta caught it in her mouth. It tasted as good as the squirrel probably would have.

The Man Who Lived at the Edge of the World

Once a man lived on the edge of the world. He wore a yellow rain jacket and a matching yellow hat because it always rains at the edge of the world. Every day the man looked over the edge and wondered what was beyond. The edge of the world was a lonely place, but the man had a kitty cat that kept him company and the mailman visited him with news about town and packages of canned food. Occasionally, the mailman even brought him actual mail. One day the mailman came with his deliveries, and all he found was the man's yellow hat and a note that said, "Gone to see what's out there. Feed the cat."

A Thank You Letter for Going Second

Originally Published: March 16, 2018

I watched a video a while back about a guy dancing at a music festival. He was shirtless and dancing in a field alone. It was... strange. He did it for a few minutes. Then another person came to dance with him. Suddenly it was two people dancing, a third showed up, and then it was a genuine group. That was when they started to draw a crowd. Soon hordes of people started joining.

While I haven't gotten to the hordes of people with this blog yet, I do have a few people willing to go second and start following my work.

https://www.youtube.com/watch?v=V74AxCqOTvg

So today, I want to take a break from the typical fiction I write and thank all of you who have read any of my work. Along with sharing some ways you can continue to partake in this whole Step Into The Road project.

It's more than just a blog where I publish fiction. At least it's going to be, but we'll get back to that.

Thank You for Reading and Joining Me

Thank you to my friends and family who have supported me from the beginning. When I decided to quit my job, I knew it was a shock and a bit of a leap of faith, something that I'm not known for doing. I remember vividly the support I got from you. You all understood that it was the best thing for my mental and physical health, and I'm glad to report that I am in a much better place almost two years later.

Specifically, I want to thank my girlfriend, Melinda, along with my parents, grandparents, and siblings. I know I throw a lot of crazy ideas your way and I appreciate that you listen to them.

Also, I want to thank all of you who send me emails, Facebook messages, and texts when I write a new post. These conversations are fantastic, and I do my best to get back to every one of you. I know I get a little bashful talking about my own stories, but I honestly appreciate the feedback and interaction. You make writing less lonely. Additionally, I want to thank all the people who read this that I've never met. If you've subscribed via email or followed me on Twitter, I want you to know I appreciate it. It took a lot to trust me with your email and time so thank you. I want to encourage any and every one of you to reach out to me via email. Hearing from readers is the best part of my day because I love your feedback.

We are Living in the Future

The world is moving in a new and crazy direction. Specifically, with how creatives are noticed. Kids can get on Twitter and start a movement against gun violence. Directors and actors can create the movies they want to exist without big Hollywood budgets. We are living in an exciting and awesome time. A few years ago I didn't consider myself a creative and up until about six months ago I didn't think having a book published was a realistic goal.

This is an exciting time, and I want to get you involved in it. I'm still learning the ropes myself, but I'm trying to share what knowledge I've picked up with others. I have big dreams for this blog. One day I hope to grow it past a blog with one story a week. I would love if I could deliver Fantastical Science Fiction to you three times a week. But that would require me to hire other writers.

I would also love to create a YouTube channel where I talk about storytelling, my writing process, and how this Wild West of being an indy author works. And most of all I want to start a podcast where I interview other indy authors about their books. I think it would be magnificent to be able to feature other authors and help get their work out into the world. There are tons of networks for traditionally published books to do this, but the systems for indy authors haven't been built yet. I'd like to create them with your help. Matter of fact you are an integral part of it working in the first place.

All of you incredible people who call yourselves readers do fantastic work. You read through 1100-page books, you share them with your friends, and you enable and encourage writers to make more of them. The creative process would be no fun without you looking at it. **You're part of the equation.** And for a long time you've been left out. The internet is changing that.

A Simple Way for You To Do More

Maybe you've been wondering how can you do more to be a part of my writing process. This week I created a way to do that. Earlier this week I joined Patreon. If you're not familiar with Patreon, it's a membership platform that will enable me to interact with you better and reveal more of my creative process to you. It will also help me make more art that you've been enjoying. All and all it's a tip jar for this blog. However, instead of dropping in a tip, helping out this blog, and moving on you get bonus goodies for becoming my patron. It will be exciting for both of us.

I've explained how most of it works on my Patreon page. But here's the long and short of it. If you donate as much as $50 or as little as $1, you get access to, free books, exclusive short stories, Google Hangout sessions with me, and a peek behind the curtain and into my creative process. I'll send you rough drafts, outlines, and stories I decided not to put on my blog. Basically, if you want to be a part of the inner circle of Step Into The Road, this is where you go. I am open to suggestions, so if you have an idea of something I should give out to patrons, I'm open to it.

A short list of what the blog can do with your patronage:

- Create more stories for this blog
- Hire proofreaders for my weekly articles
- Commission custom art for my weekly stories
- Cover website hosting costs
- Pay email list expenses
- Publish more novels quicker
- Start a YouTube channel about writing
- Begin a Podcast featuring other author's work
- Enable me to spend more time teaching others storytelling

- Help me turn Step Into The Road into my full-time job

If this blog or I ever get anywhere, you will be the primary energy behind that. I can't put a dollar amount on that. If you join Patreon, you will be the driving force behind me putting better stuff out AND helping others put better stuff out. You will be contributing to a world with more and better fiction in it. Ideally, most of it is self-published.

I know some of you are willing and able to join me on Patreon and hope you join me on this journey. I don't want to charge an entry fee for my writing or add ads to this site. Surely you don't want that either. Patreon will be a massive help with enabling me to continue to keep everything I write here free. Along with enabling me to write more articles and produce more content.

I've been writing on this blog every week since November of 2017. I've loved every moment of it, even the days where I have to stay up late to put something out on Friday morning. You, my reader, make it worth it. I want to do more. With your support, I will publish more books and short stories for you to enjoy. I also want to bring more people into this community and I'd host virtual events. Additionally, I want to come out with new forms like YouTube and Podcasts so that I can share my knowledge with others and help create more fiction in the world. By joining me on Patreon, you help me make that possible. So take a moment to check me out on Patreon and see if there is a membership level that works for you.

Alternatives to Patreon

If Patreon isn't your thing, I've also set up two ways for you to enable me to make more content without having to donate a set amount every month.

The number one way you can help me get better fiction out into the world is by sharing it. You can share by forwarding my weekly emails, putting my stories on social media, or just talking about my tales with your friends. The more you share, the more you help this site. Sharing stories is something humans have been doing as a species since the beginning of time. You're just doing it digitally now.

Secondly, I've set up an Amazon affiliate link. So if you shop on Amazon and use my link, I will get a commission on the items you buy. The price doesn't go up for you which is excellent. This affiliate system is an entirely free way to help support the blog financially by doing something you already do.

Thanks for being part of this remarkable journey and I look forward to being able to interact with you on Patreon. Next week we will be back to our regularly scheduled content with a story about clerics, magic, deceit, and betrayal. Until then take a look at my Patreon, I've already loaded up some goodies on there for those of you who are eager to join me.

Anthony's Apprenticeship

Originally Published: March 23, 2018

"**A**nt! Get over here!" Lorent's impatient assistant shouted through the hallways of the stone temple to get Anthony's attention.

In a room down the hall, Anthony scrambled to put his quill safely above his workspace where it would not get ink on the parchment he was copying. He walked as quickly as would still be considered polite to Lorent's office. Piena, the assistant, was sitting in Lorent's chair, at Lorent's desk, looking over Lorent's paperwork, as usual.

"Yes sir, how can I help you?" The boy said between pants.

Piena looked over the edge of the scrolls he was examining and smiled at the young boy. "Lorent is going to be traveling to Makenza to meet with his order of Holy Shepherds. He needs you to make preparations for the journey."

"Yes sir," Anthony replied. He got the necessary information from the assistant and turned to head out the door.

Then Piena said, "And one more thing Ant." The boy turned around, "You got a letter today." The assistant waved his hand, and a small parchment floated off the desk and towards the boy. He snatched it out of the air once it was close enough. "Unfortunately it's not good news." A devilish smile danced across the assistant's face.

The first thing Anthony noticed was not who it was from but that the seal had already been broken. Anthony bared a grin at the man behind the desk and said, "Thank you."

The gods gave out many gifts in Anthony's world. Some, like people like Lorent, were given the gift of significant magic. Lorent could heal others of almost any trauma. Lorent was a cleric belonging to the order of the Holy Shepherd. The gods gave others minor magical abilities. Piena was one of these people and could move things with his mind but could not perform tremendous feats. Most people had this level of magical ability. Others, like Anthony, had no magical abilities at all. Some would say he was cursed and none of the gods had given him favor. And while all evidence pointed to this being true, the boy still had some gifts.

These gifts weren't given to him by the gods, at least not directly like magic was. These gifts were given to him by his mother. He could read and write his letters and combine the numbers by doing sums and arithmetic. These were gifts his mother, who had once been a priestess, had taught him.

He now used them to serve the cleric Lorent as a scribe and secretary. Healing was a time and energy-consuming task for the cleric. For food, water, shelter, and a continued education Anthony served the holy man by planning all travel and transposing the man's many scrolls and documents. Anthony took the job because with it he could send money to his mother and father. But that wasn't his only motivation. He also dreamed that Lorent could cure his lack of magical abilities.

Unfortunately, in the past five years of service, the man hadn't said a word to Anthony.

Anthony sat back down at his small table in the study and unfolded the letter he had received. It was from his mother, but he didn't have to read the signature to know that. Of the two people in the world who cared about him, she was the only parent who could write.

Sweet Anthony,

I hope this letter finds you well. I am low on ink so I must be brief. The crops are filling in, but they are not as plentiful as we had hoped. Your father says this is because he has been unable to work them every day. I have had to assure him that it is merely a rough season. He has failed to work in the field because his health has been leaving him. I have done what I can with the few herbs and medicines I have, but it has not done much for him.

I have no desire to distract you from your apprenticeship or your studies, but if you can find the time to steal away and visit your father, it would do wonders for his fading heart.

Love always,

Father & Mother

The ink of the letter produced a gradient on the page. The boy's name was in jet-black ink, but by the time the signature came, the lettering was made with an empty grey. He held the paper at an angle to the light and saw that the last two letters were not written in ink but had been lightly scratched in. She had continued to write the final letters without any ink.

Anthony reread the note until he understood his mother's meaning. His father was dying, but she didn't have the heart to tell him. Unfortunately, with Lorent's trip to Makenza coming up there would be no way for him to visit them.

He cursed the gods as he had many times before under many different circumstances. His father was too young for death in Anthony's mind. The boy had always dreamed that once he became an assistant for the cleric, he would be able to move his parents into the halls of the assistant so they wouldn't have to work the farm in their old age.

He had pitched the idea to Piena before since the man had no living relatives himself, but the assistant just snorted and told him that he would rather have the rooms empty than filled with peasants.

Anthony had retorted with a comment about how when he became an assistant he would show the Holy Shepherd's love by filling all empty rooms with people who needed them. Unfortunately, this leads to Piena continually mocking him about his dream of becoming an assistant. At every turn, Piena stopped the boy from showing his few abilities off to Lorent or any person of mention. It was after that point that Anthony quit sharing his dreams with anyone.

He sat and thought about the information his mother sent him. Anthony mourned his father's sickness but steeled himself against grief that would stop him from doing work. Then he pulled out scrolls, maps, and timetables off of the shelves of the study. His mind went to work at what it did best. Anthony began making travel plans for more than one party.

By the wee hours of the morning—and many candles later—he had three things: an inkling of hope for his father's recovery, a clear map for Lorent's journey, and a letter to his mother that he would have to send without Piena finding it.

Three days later Lorent and his caravan set out for Makenza following the path Anthony had set for them. It would take them five days to get to the city. The group was small. It contained three minor priests who followed the cleric and a boy younger than Anthony whose parents had paid Lorent for his safe passage.

The first day of travel was uneventful. Anthony started the morning early, packed the cleric's bags, and prepared the animals for the trip. He double-checked that the scrolls Lorent requested were stored safely in a small waterproof chest. Anthony packed the food, medicine, and other supplies carefully on the mule-drawn cart.

The company left the temple an hour after sunrise, ahead of schedule thanks to Anthony's preparations. The rest of that day was uneventful, and they made camp in the evening at a spot Anthony found on an old map. Around the campfire, Lorent remarked to the group that he felt great spiritual energy in the place.

Piena replied, "Thank you, my lord. I made sure to find a place that would suit you." Anthony stayed quiet.

The next morning Anthony awoke before sunrise, prepared the company's breakfast, and loaded the supplies that had been used at camp back onto the animals. As he did this, he overheard a conversation between Lorent and his assistant.

"I had a dream from the Shepherd last night," Lorent said in an inconspicuous tone. "She was warning me that this journey is being used for selfish purposes."

"Hmmm," Piena replied with interest. Anthony's forehead began to sweat despite the cool morning breeze. "Did the goddess mention who was manipulating the voyage?"

"No," Lorent replied, "That part she did not reveal to me, the future is still not clear. You are the only one who knows this. We must stay vigilant and keep the young boy who is in our care safe. His mother paid me well to lead him to Makenza safely."

"Of course of course," the assistant said.

"I will consult my priests individually to see if the goddess blessed them with any knowledge that I do not have. Maybe she will reveal which one of them may be behind this."

"That seems very wise indeed my lord," Piena replied.

The conversation ended, and Anthony quickly got back to work wondering how he would handle being found out by Lorent.

Anthony was on edge the entire second day of travel, but no one approached him with the subject. Lorent was as stoic as ever, and if he hadn't heard their conversation, the boy would have never expected the cleric to be on to his plans.

On the third day of travel, no one had approached Anthony about the potential deceit, and he had all but forgotten about it until the end of the day.

Lorent was leading the caravan and consulting one of his priests as the party approached a fork in the road. The cleric halted the party and Piena came to the front. Anthony followed with the map of the journey.

"Which way do we proceed Piena?" Lorent asked.

"To the right my lord," the assistant said without consulting Anthony.

Anthony spoke up in a meek tone, "Actually sirs, I planned for us to go left."

Both men looked at him surprised. Anthony presented the map. It showed that both ways led to Makenza, and the right path was undoubtedly shorter. Piena pointed out this much and looked down his nose to challenge Anthony to disagree.

"I admit the right is a shorter path, but it is through the mountains and will be hard on the animals. The left path was longer but smoother, and I made sure that we left with enough time. This way will get us to Makenza with plenty of time and the horses, not to mention we, will be fresher when we arrive."

Piena scoffed in disagreement. "You are wasting all of our time with this." He turned to Lorent for agreement. "Lord, which direction should we take?"

The cleric looked at the horizon. The sun was about to set. "It sounds like we have time regardless of the path we take. Let us make camp here for the evening, and you two can settle the decision between yourselves." Lorent dismounted his horse and led them to a clearing to make camp.

Anthony proceeded to prepare food for the evening and cooked for everyone as usual. Piena didn't bring up the situation of which path to take and by the time dishes from dinner were finished Anthony had no energy to argue with the assistant. The group went to bed around the embers of the fire.

Late in the night, Anthony was shaken awake. The boy gasped for air, but a hand covered his mouth. His eyes adjusted to the darkness and he saw Piena looming over him. "Look Ant," the man spat, "I don't know how you found out about my plan, but I won't let you ruin it. We're taking the mountain road so the thugs I hired can take care of Lorent."

Anthony's eyes grew wide in shock, "Mrmmr," he said through his muffled mouth. He didn't know anything about Piena's plot, but now that he did he wasn't going to let Piena get away with it. He tried to cry out again but couldn't make a sound. Piena held the boy still and silent with both his hands. Then the evil assistant used his magic to levitate his knife out of its sheath. The blade floated from his waist to Anthony's throat. He felt the sharp metal press against his neck.

"You know, no one would notice if you were gone. I wouldn't even have to hide your dead body very well. Lorent wouldn't even remember you if you disappeared."

"You're a useless little non-magic boy," the man continued. "Your only talent is being able to write and plan, and even that you seem to mess up. Well, this time it's going to cost you your life."

"No, it won't." A voice came from the darkness. A sword was unsheathed and illuminated the campsite with its light. The sword lit up its wielder's face. Lorent was standing in front of the boy and the assistant. Slowly the rest of the camp started to wake up in the commotion.

The knife that was magically held at Anthony's throat dropped to the ground as Piena lost concentration on it.

"I dreamt that someone was tricking me and going to betray me." Lorent said, "Then I heard the scream of a boy in my mind. I woke up and heard your whispering carried through the night. You were the one that planned to betray this caravan."

By this time the cleric's followers were surrounding Piena and the boy. "Tie him up and we will carry him to the authorities in Makenza."

The assistant looked at the knife that was lying on the ground. He tried to move it, but Anthony put his small hand on the hilt. He felt it struggle in his hand, but Anthony fought Piena's magical powers. Then a priest put his hands over the assistant's eyes and put him into a deep magical sleep.

The next day they took the long path around the mountain as Anthony had suggested. Halfway through the day's travels, they came across a man and woman waiting on the side of the road. The man was young but looked sick and weak. The woman appeared tired from helping him on their journey. As Lorent approached them, he halted the caravan to see if he could provide aid.

The cleric approached the couple. "I see you are tired and sick, is there anything I can do to help?" He asked.

"You are kind sir," the woman responded, "Our son mentioned that if the gods were good, we might be able to find you on this road. We were hard-pressed to get here quick enough, but it seems we were blessed."

"Your son, how did he know?" Lorent looked at the woman confused.

Then Anthony trotted up on his small pony, and his mother smiled at him. After he got down, they embraced, and he greeted his father who was seated on the ground propped against a rock. The man was pale from his fading heart.

"Sir Lorent. I have not been entirely truthful." Anthony began to explain. "We took the longer path so that I could see my father once more before he passed. I knew that I would not be able to leave your service to see him so I thought I could meet him on the road. I'm sorry that I hid this from you."

Lorent let out a wondrous laugh, "Boy you could not be more wrong. I am grateful that we took this longer path for it saved my life." The cleric squatted to inspect the old man. He looked at Anthony's mother and asked what was wrong. After hearing the diagnosis, he told one of his priests to fetch specific herbs and medicines from the cart.

Lorent prepared a potion and changed a spell to help the father. By the end of the short break at the side of the road, the man was able to stand up. "Here are some spare herbs." Lorent said, addressing Anthony's mother, "Please give them to him as you see fit, he should be better in a week."

"Thank you, sir," she responded. "Is there anything we can do to repay you?"

Lorent smiled, "No your son has been enough of a blessing to me. Is there anything else we can do for you? Do you need supplies for the way back home?"

"No there's nothing," the woman responded.

"Actually, there is one thing," Anthony said interrupting. His parents and Lorent looked down at the small boy. "If you wouldn't mind sir, I was hoping we could give my mother more ink so that she could write me. She ran out writing me the last letter about my father."

"Do we have any extra?" Lorent asked one of his priests. The priest shrugged not knowing.

"Yes, we do," Anthony said, "I brought an extra vial," the young man produced a small black bottle out of his satchel.

"Of course you did," Lorent said with a smile. He took the bottle out of the boy's hand and passed it on to the mother. "Please write to him as often as you can. But more importantly, come visit."

"Thank you sir, but we could never intrude like that," the mother protested.

"Nonsense," the cleric rebuffed, "Your son is my assistant now since the last one has been so dishonest. Your son has an honest soul, and as the assistant, he has extra rooms for his family at our temple. Please come join us when your husband is healthy enough to travel."

"Assistant?" The mother said in shock. She looked at Anthony for clarification, but he was as confused as her.

"Your son has served me loyally for years. He has learned a lot from his texts and from watching me. He may never have magic powers but he has an honest heart, and that is far more valuable than magic." Lorent looked down at the boy. "That is if you will be willing to work with me and continue the work of the Holy Shepherd."

Anthony beamed with admiration. The midday sun illuminated his hero. Anthony replied boldly, "Thank you, sir. I would be honored to serve you and the Shepherd."

Oily Salesmen and Snakes

Originally Published: March 30, 2018

L arry and Harry sat alone in their pharmacy. It had been days since a customer came in and this wasn't a new problem.

Harry sat with his cowboy boots resting on the wooden counter. He said, "Ain't nobody been 'round for days."

"I know," Larry the pharmacist said picking at his teeth with a splinter of wood.

"What about Brenda, she came in a few days ago for cough syrup. She should need more by now, right?"

Larry shrugged, "Don't know if she's going to be coming back. Her husband has been trying to get her off that stuff."

"The bastard," Harry cursed as he spat his dip into a spittoon. "What about..."

Larry cut him off knowing what he was going to say. "Nope, Eli doesn't need anything for his foot anymore. It healed a month ago."

Harry started spinning his knife between his fingers, bored. Then the bell hanging over the door rang. Both men came to attention to see who just walked in.

"How can we help you," Larry said from behind the counter.

The man who walked didn't live in their small town and was a stranger to them. The man wore polished black boots, a dark ten-gallon hat, and a smooth leather vest. He was slick as a trout fresh from the river. The man appeared young in complexion, but the grey hair that popped out under his hat proved differently.

"Actually, I was wondering if you boys needed my help," He said with a smile.

Larry looked at the man confused. Harry, not one to keep his mouth shut when he had a thought, said "And how do you reckon that?"

"Well you're running an apothecary, and I happen to be selling medicine." The man produced a small unmarked vial of golden liquid. "This is oil for your skin. It keeps you looking young, and it clears any blemishes or scars you have. That is if you use it regularly."

Larry picked up the vial, opened the top by popping off the cork, and took a whiff of the liquid. "It does all that?" he asked.

The stranger gestured at his clear complexion, "Look at me, I use it every day."

"What is it exactly?" Larry asked as he dropped a bit of it on his hand, put the vial down, and rubbed it in. Harry snatched the vial from the counter and investigated it. Harry was one for fighting and had plenty of scars to show for it. Most notably the one on his right forearm.

"It's oil of the rattlesnake. But don't worry, it's not venomous. It's neutralized to the point that the chemicals will only help your skin and won't hurt you. Are you fine gentlemen interested in buying some?"

Harry looked at his business partner and raised a single eyebrow. Larry shrugged and looked at the traveler, "What's the catch? Why don't you sell it yourself?"

The man frowned and began to explain his situation, "You see, I'm not from these parts, and the oil only works if you use it regularly. I can't stick around here for long enough to sell them all. But I have a cartload of them. I'm willing to sell all of it to you. Then you will be able to sell them to your customers regularly, and they'll actually get results. Something this valuable would be worth a shiny dime, but I'll be selling them to you for less than a nickel each. That is if you're willing to take up this once-in-a-lifetime offer. If you don't take me up I'll just sell it to the next pharmacy I come by."

The two men looked at each other. Then they looked at the man across the counter, "One second." Larry said before his partner could open his mouth and ruin the deal. Then they disappeared into the empty storage room to confer.

***

Larry put down the last crate of snake oil and wiped the sweat off his forehead with his white apron. After Harry convinced Larry to use the last of their cash to buy the oil the two men did some quick negotiation with the salesman and tested the product themselves. After the deal was done, they began the laborious task of unloading the product into their storage room.

"It will pay for itself in no time," Harry assured his partner who was staring at the room filled with boxes. Harry smiled a big crooked grin at his friend. "This," he gestured to the room full of boxes, "this is going to make us rich. This place is going to become the only pharmacy anyone in this town comes to."

"We're the only pharmacy in town," Larry pointed out. "But I agree, this stuff is going to be all anyone talks about for the next few months."

They stayed up all night labeling the ointment, "Larry and Harry's Miracle Elixir." Under the name, the label read, "Guaranteed to fix warts, scars, and all blemishes of the skin."

The next day the two men stood on the porch of their store and sold their new product on the street. By noon they had sold ten vials, and by the end of the day, they had sold the the last of their first crate.

They walked back inside their store and examined the dozens of crates still filling their stock room. Larry frowned and the unsold merchandise.

"Don't worry," Harry said reading his partner's expression better than he ever read a book. "We'll sell even more tomorrow. Not to mention in less than a week everyone will be coming back for more. And they'll be telling their friends too," Harry beamed.

"If you say so. What do we do if we run out of this supply?"

"Let's worry about that problem when it arrives. Look at this," Harry said showing Larry his arm. "You think this scar looks like it's clearing up?"

Larry examined the scar that Harry was showing him. "I guess so," Larry said with a shrug.

"Yeah, I think so too. I'm gonna take a bottle home and use it tonight. It'll be gone by next week at this rate.

***

A week later Harry showed his partner the improvement of the scar. Larry hadn't noticed much change and returned his attention to the store's account books. They weren't promising either. Sales of the product had spiked at the beginning but quickly decreased. The men were only selling one or two bottles a day, and none of them were to repeat customers.

The bell over the door rang for the first time that day. Larry's focus on the books disappeared. Harry spat out some chew and stood up as the town gossip, Mrs. Belford, waddled into the store. She was short in stature but carried the weight of a woman twice her height. Her body had multiple moles and pimples. There was also a notable wart on her cheek. She was a prime customer for the two men's ointment. They had sold her a vial on day one.

"How can we help you, ma'am," Larry asked with a smile.

"You can help me by refunding the money you stole from me by selling me this useless vial." She slammed a small empty glass container onto the counter.

Harry stepped in, "What exactly are you accusing us of?"

"Being sham medicine men, first of all! Then false advertising too," she said aggressively to the man. "I've been using it for two weeks now, and this big ol' wart has not gone away." She gestured at the big hairy wart on her cheek. "I use it every day, twice a day, and nothing has happened. It hasn't even gotten smaller."

Harry pulled his sleeve over the scar on his arm and then said, "Well, that is a pretty big wart. Our elixir only works if you use it for a long time. If you would like you can buy some more for us."

"Oh and throw good money after bad?" She said with a scoff. "I want my dime back, or I will tell the whole town that you're scamming people out of their money."

Knowing that Mrs. Belford was likely to tell the whole town regardless of the men's reaction to the situation, Larry reached into the cash register and produced a small dime. "Here you go Mrs. Belford," he said, "I'm sorry the ointment didn't work for you. I'd be happy to serve you with any other medicine you need in the future."

She snorted and began to waddle back out of the store.

"Some people just won't use medicine like they're prescribed," Harry asked.

Larry didn't have a chance to explain it to his thick-skulled friend because for the second time that day, the bell on the door rang, and someone walked in.

Unfortunately, it wasn't a customer but the mailman. "How's it going today, Gene?" Larry asked politely.

The young man shrugged and handed the men a small letter then quickly left. "Who's it from?" Harry said looking at the envelope.

As the ring from the door faded into the room Larry answered, "The bank." He hesitated, then opened it up to read it. Harry was illiterate so he had to give the synopsis to him. "They say they're going to foreclose on our store because we are behind on our payments." He said giving his partner a worried look.

"Well then let's pay them," Harry said matter of factly.

Larry rolled his eyes, "We can't. We spent all of our cash on the oil."

Harry frowned, "Well then we just need to sell more. Let's go back out to the streets and start selling like mad."

Before Larry could argue that this was what they had been doing to no avail the little bell over the door rang. The two men looked to see what fresh hell had walked in for them this time.

Harry was pleased to see the young schoolteacher Mary Ann Lewis walk through the door. She was remarkably beautiful, new to town, and single. Because of this Harry immediately offered her help.

"What brings you all the way to our side of town?" Harry asked. The schoolteacher lived with the Bronsons who were her host family.

She explained her problem to the smiling man, "Well you see, I have been using this elixir of yours on my neck for a while now, and I haven't seen any improvements." She gestured at the large wine-colored birthmark that was on her neck. It was the only blemish on her healthy body. "I've had it since I was a kid but I've always hated it. I was hoping this stuff would get rid of it. Unfortunately, I'm not having success with your stuff. Has anyone else complained?"

Larry began to explain, but Harry cut him off. "Mary Ann, you're the first person who has come in with this whole problem. How much have you used? Do you need to buy more?" Then he took a look at her neck, "Larry do you think she should increase the dosage? Why don't we send you home with two bottles and you can use one in the morning and one in the afternoon."

"I don't really think that's a good idea," the woman said nervously, "Mr. Bronson and his wife think I should demand a refund but I was just curious if I was the only one with the problem. And if I came home with twice as much, they would surely throw a fit."

Larry stepped in and took Harry's focus off the young woman. "You know it doesn't work for some people because of their blood. Here's your dime back, we're so sorry we couldn't help you. Of course, if you think there's anything we could help you with, we'd be happy to."

"Thank you, Mr. Larry," Mary Ann said politely. "I will keep you in mind." And with that, she left the store.

As the ring of the bell came to a silence Larry looked at his partner, "We have a problem."

"What?" Harry asked still staring out the window at the young woman.

"The ointment doesn't work." Larry said, "And we have an entire stock room full of it. Not to mention, we don't have money for the bank this month which means we won't have a store next week."

Harry shrugged turning away from the window once Mary Ann was out of site. Addressing his partner he asked, "What do you mean it doesn't work? It's been working on me. Those people just don't have the right blood for it. You said so yourself."

"Harry you moron, I made that up so Marry Ann wouldn't feel bad," as he questioned why he had ever gone into business with someone with the brains of a mule. But what's done was done. All Larry could do now was try to save his failing store. The store he always dreamed of starting. All he wanted to do was bring healthy remedies to the people of his town.

He grabbed five vials of their bogus oil from the shelves and walked back to the workbench where he made medicine for their now dwindling number of customers.

"What're you doing?" Harry asked in a long drawl.

"Fixing this," Larry said without looking up from the mortar and pestle he was working with.

***

Larry worked long hours for the next three days trying to find some way he could use the snake oil for a profit. After running out of lamp oil late one night, he dumped a small vial into his old soot-covered lamp. The oil worked but that was the only viable use he had found so far. Lamp oil was cheap compared to what they paid for the ointment, and they would never make any money selling it like that.

On the fourth day, Harry came in and asked his partner, "How's it coming?"

"Mrn Mrinet," Larry said with his mouth full.

Harry's interest was peaked. He looked at his partner across the store and saw the man foaming at the mouth. "Lord almighty, what have you done!?" Harry exclaimed at his ravenous-looking partner.

Larry spat the foam into the nearby spittoon and smiled at his friend. There was a little bit of foam left around his mouth, "What do you think?"

"About what?"

"My teeth. Do they look whiter?"

Harry inspected the man's mouth. Larry had never chewed much tobacco. Harry had to admit that the man's teeth did look a little cleaner.

"I've been working on a new use for the snake oil and I think I've got something. I mixed it with some other ingredients and a little mint, and I made a paste. You stick it on your finger and rub it on your teeth to clean them. I think it will be better for your gums and will at least clean the tobacco stains off of your teeth." He offered a small bowl of paste to his partner. Harry looked at the bowl and then at his smiling partner. "Come on give it a try," Larry encouraged.

The man stuck his finger in the bowl and doubtfully rubbed the paste over his front teeth. He moved his finger away and looked at the small mirror sitting on Larry's desk. Sure enough, they were significantly whiter than the teeth around them. "My breath tastes better too," Harry remarked.

Larry nodded, "It's something I've been working on for a while. But I've never had anything to bind the basic materials together. Then I tried the oil, and it held them together."

"Do you know how much people would pay for better-looking teeth?" Harry asked after he finished rubbing all the rest of his crooked teeth with his finger.

"I'll be happy if we can cover rent this month," Larry admitted.

"Make some more of this," Harry proclaimed, "We will be doing more than just breaking even. We'll be the most popular pharmacy in town."

Larry didn't point out that they were still the only pharmacy for miles.

***

Three days later most of the vials of oil had been converted into paste. Harry and Larry once again stood on the street in front of their shop. It was a beautifully sunny day, and the town was bustling. The men started hawking their goods, but no one showed any interest in their paste. Eventually, Miss Mary Ann walked by, and Harry was able to stop her to talk. Not because he was particularly charming but because she was uncannily polite.

"Mary Ann come try this new paste for your teeth that Larry invented," He uncorked the vial and held it under her nose. Her eyes perked up at the mint smell, so she approached the booth.

"How does it work?" She asked out of curiosity.

"You simply put a little bit on your finger and rub it on your teeth," Larry explained with a genuine smile. "You'll be able to see the difference in the mirror as soon as you're done."

Mary Ann dipped a thin finger into the bottle and began to rub it on her teeth. She had never chewed tobacco and that was one of the reasons she was so pretty. She smiled at the mirror and then frowned. "I'm sorry Mr. Larry, but I don't see much of a difference."

Larry looked at her teeth and had to admit that she was right. It had a dramatic effect on Harry because of his poor hygiene, but this woman didn't need their product. "Well I'm sure it worked, just because you don't have mud all over you doesn't mean you don't need a weekly bath," Larry said with a smile.

"Can we interest you in a bottle?" Harry jumped in eagerly in an attempt to close the sale.

"I'm sorry, I can't afford it and if I'm frank Mr. and Mrs. Bronson would have a fit if I bring home another one of your gimmicks," she said. Only added, "No offense," after noticing Larry's hurt expression.

Harry went to open his mouth to disagree, but Larry cut him off, "It's fine, I hope you enjoy the fresh breath for a while, and if you ever change your mind we will be here." Larry lied knowing that if they didn't sell enough bottles today they'd be foreclosed on.

An hour later, with no bites, Mrs. Belford waddled past their porch. Harry stopped her to pitch the product. Before Harry could finish the pitch, Mrs. Belford cut him off, "I don't care if your medicine makes me as fast as a jackrabbit I'm not buying another thing from your store ever again." She then barreled past Harry and continued to the town's general store.

For the rest of the day, the two men couldn't interest a single client. Almost no one would stop, and those few who did refused to buy it even after seeing the improvement. Some of them had remarkable results, but they didn't feel like it was because of the paste. Harry got frustrated and nearly started a fight with a rancher, but Larry was able to talk the two men down.

The sun began to set, and the luckless shop owners started to pack up their paste. "Maybe we'll have better luck tomorrow," Harry said.

Larry stayed silent, knowing tomorrow would never come, as they packed up the final pieces of their setup. A suited man in a bowler hat came up to the porch of their shop with some papers in his hand. "How can we help you, Mr. Wilson," Harry asked. Larry perked up after hearing the banker's name. He felt his stomach somersault.

"Unfortunately for you, I'm here to make sure that you've packed everything up and are ready to move out by tomorrow. We have a new tenant taking over your storefront soon."

"Excuse me!" Harry exclaimed in shock.

Larry stepped in and addressed the issue before a fight started. "I'm sorry Harry, I didn't want to tell you but today's the day they set to foreclose on us. I was hoping we could sell enough paste to turn the budget around, but the paste isn't selling. We have to pack up and move out tonight."

The bowler-hatted banker nodded his head in agreement, "Sorry to do it to you boys, but it seems the town isn't quite ready for a pharmacy. Especially one that's selling sham potions." The man picked up the last vial of paste that was sitting out. "But tell me, I'm curious, what did you come up with this week?"

"It's soap for your teeth," Harry explained quickly and frustrated.

The man simply laughed, "No one would put soap on their teeth. And even if they did why would they want to?" Henry began to explain, but the banker waved his hand dismissing the man, "I don't need to hear whatever excuse you've made up. Although I'm sure, it's convincing. I just want your stuff out of the shop and for you to go home. Better yet leave this town and go somewhere people still trust your fake medicine and scams. But in this town, I don't think you'll ever be able to sell anything ever again, even if you had water from the fountain of youth."

Larry's heart sank. He had worked hard to keep his pharmacy afloat and give the town something he thought they needed. But they no longer trusted him. After a day of being rejected by the town for his fantastic new problem, he wasn't ready to fight to stay in the store. Without saying anything to Harry he put the last bottle of paste in the trash instead of the crate it belonged in.

The Automaton's World

Originally Published: April 6 to May 11, 2018

1 - Fitting Into the World of the Automatons

The sun shone like it did every day of the week. Trisha woke up before her alarm could go off despite her weariness. Last night she had barely slept, her nerves were in overdrive. She woke up and ate the breakfast that the house had prepared for her. It was the standard spinach and mushroom omelet. The same thing she had every Thursday. But today things were different. Everything was different.

Today was the day her son Milton would be tested by The Automatons, the ones who ran her world. The ones who ran all of humanity's world since The Fall.

If Milton passed, she would be fine, and the meatloaf that was scheduled for dinner every Thursday would taste fine. It might even qualify as delicious. If he didn't pass, then she wouldn't be able to stomach the evening meal. Trisha swallowed the pills The Automatons required her to take with breakfast and went to wake up her son in person.

The house had already prepared his breakfast for him. The hot pancakes sat on the counter and his favorite drink, chocolate milk, was next to the meal. *He'll enjoy that,* she thought with a smile that quickly faded into a frown.

After waking Milton up, she walked into the shower and let the machine clean her. She was glad the process was quick because if it had taken too long, she would spend too much time in the hot room thinking. Trisha wasn't ready for thought this morning. Her entire night had been monopolized by thoughts of how her son would perform on the exam. Every issue that he had, every one of his flaws that glared at her and indicated he was like Peter, his father, bubbled up to the top of her mind. These defects were the reasons she loved both of them. And it was the reason her husband had been edited out.

She walked to the edge of town where the town hall encircled their colony. The Automatons would administer Milton's test, and she would either be sent home with him or alone. "Give Mommy your hand while we cross the street," she said.

Milton looked up, "I'm too old for that." He complained.

"You're right you're already ten, now hold my hand please." He listened, another sign he might pass. She clutched his soft fingers in hers as they walked to the outskirts of town. He didn't question the rules anymore like he usually did, and she was grateful for that.

Once they got to the offices, she checked him. The Automatons were ready for him immediately. They were always on schedule. Before she let him go, she crouched down so she could be eye level with her son. "You know why you're not going to school today right?" She asked him.

"Yes, it's because I have to take my test," He said in a dry tone.

"Yes, and you will do very well. Are you nervous?" She asked.

"No, why should I be? You told me to be myself. I can do that. It's easy," He said with a confident and beaming smile.

She smiled, then questioned if she had given him the right advice. "You'll do great." she said fighting back her emotions, "And when you finish, I will be waiting here for you."

"Okay Mom, bye."

"I love you. You're my little man, be good."

"Of course Mom." The boy said eager to go into the testing room.

"I love you, honey," She repeated, not letting go of his hand.

"I love you too," he said as he glanced at the door he was going to head through for the test.

Trisha knew his mind was already elsewhere, designing another world or story that he might put to paper in the evening. And with that, she let go. Trisha had to let go otherwise she would be held in contempt of The Process.

As Milton disappeared through the testing door, she cried. The tears stopped when she thought of a reason he would pass. But they quickly started again when Trisha thought of something she loved about her son. These memories would bring the tears back, and she would doubt if he could pass the test. She would justify his success and begin to dry her tears.

The cycle of tears continued for thirty minutes. It was brought to a halt when Trisha received an update. The message read: "Milton Johnson is being held for further review. Please return home, and you will be notified of further action to take." That message broke the cycle. She continued to cry and didn't know how to stop.

Trisha woke up on her couch. She didn't remember how she had gotten there. The Automatons might have drugged her and transported her to her house after throwing a fit at the town hall. She

searched her foggy memory. No, throwing a fit was something Peter
would have done. Throwing a fit would have gotten her edited out
too.

The memory came back to her. She had walked home navigating
the streets through her tears. Avoiding looks from strangers and keeping track of her path home stressed her wild mind. She had cried and
cried and cried the whole way home, but she had returned without
making a scene or upsetting The Automatons.

She got up from the couch and looked at the dinner table. A single
serving of meatloaf sat on the table with some broccoli on the side. The
food was cold. She must have fallen asleep from exhaustion and stress.
She wasn't hungry, so she threw the meal in the trash before going to
bed.

Once she was in bed, she couldn't sleep. The house was too quiet.
Milton's toys lurked in the other room of the house. The room was
filled with toys, clothes, and drawings. They would have to be thrown
away to complete the editing process.

She would be given a choice to either throw the items away herself or let The Automatons come in and thoroughly clean the house
themselves. Milton deserved the honor of her cleaning it out. She
hadn't done that for Peter. It had hurt too much to do it herself. This
time she would do it herself.

After Peter committed his crimes and was edited for them, The
Automatons came to clean her house. She suspected that they also
searched the home for any future plans of terrorism.

The cleaning removed things that were hers but reminded her of
Peter. They were things that she could have argued to keep, but The
Automatons were thorough and took it all. At the time she even
thought they would remove Milton, but they had let her keep the bit

for eight years. And today they had finished the job. They had taken away everything she had that reminded her of Peter.

She went to work the next day. She had to. On her way home, she decided to stop by Lauren's. It would hurt, Lauren was the mother of Milton's best friend Will, but they deserved to know that Milton had been edited from the system. Will was the only boy Milton could get along with, the boys were eerily similar.

She rang the doorbell, and Lauren answered. "Hi Trisha, is Milton coming over to play?" She looked behind Trisha and didn't see the boy. A slow realization washed over her face, and she immediately hugged Trisha. "Oh my god. I'm so sorry. Please come in." Then as Trisha entered Lauren repeated the words "Oh my god."

Will entered the living room at the sound of the door closing and saw Trisha, "Where's Milton, Mrs. Johnson?" The boy asked.

"Go to your room and play Will," Lauren said in a commanding tone. It kept the boy from arguing, maybe there was hope for him. He disappeared while Lauren patted Trisha's back repeating "Oh my god."

Eventually, Trisha quit crying enough to explain what happened. Not that Lauren needed it. As soon as Trisha finished explaining Lauren said a final, "Oh my god." Then the first original thing she added to the conversation was spoken, "Will has his exam next week. I hope his score won't be affected by playing with Milton."

Lauren then listed off a barrage of questions but Trisha was unable to answer any of them. The few she could answer she didn't want to. They were too painful. The last one she couldn't bear to think about, "Do you think Will is going to pass?" Lauren asked.

Trisha couldn't think anymore, the sorrow overwhelmed her, and she got up to leave. As she headed to the door, Lauren grabbed her arm. The woman had a crazed look in her eye. "Tell me, will my son pass?" She gripped onto Trisha's arm so hard that the woman couldn't get free.

"I-I-I don't know. Maybe, I just don't know."

"How could you not know? You knew what Peter was like. You knew Milton, we both did. Tell me, is Will's score going to be affected by your son?"

"I don't know," she screamed tugging at the woman's mad grasp, still trapped.

"I need to know!" The woman's eyes had filled with rage and tears welled at the bottom.

"Whatever you do don't tell him to be himself," Trisha said with a tug on her arm. Lauren let go. The rageful look softened into tears, and she sobbed into her hands. Trisha disappeared out the door as she heard Will enter the room and ask his mother what was wrong. The door closed before Trisha could listen to the answer.

Less than a week after Milton's test Trisha got a letter explaining Milton's situation. Or at least what passed for an explanation from The Automatons. It was a standard form letter that described how Milton had been removed from the colony for its own good. Trisha was to pack up all of his things to send them to him. Explicit instructions were given not to try to make contact with the boy or withhold his belongings from him. There was a kind offer at the bottom that they could bring in a team to clean the house for her. It ended with a notice that they would inspect her home after a week. If the house were not clear of Milton's things, then they would enforce decreased rations and do it themselves.

She got to work that evening wanting to make sure that she had a reason to keep everything she could from being taken from her. Trisha sorted through all of the boy's belongings imagining an argument for each object she decided to keep. She needed to beat The Automatons at their own game to preserve her memory of her son.

The next morning she sat in front of her breakfast after barely sleeping. The house served her a spinach and mushroom omelet with coffee. She ate the egg out of habit, but it tasted like dust in her mouth. Picking up the cup, she took a drink of coffee to wash it down. The liquid was cool. As soon as she felt it, she knew something was different. The house never did things differently. It was programmed by The Automatons. She looked at the drink. It was light brown instead of jet black. She licked the beverage off her upper lip. It was chocolate milk.

2 - A Letter From the Edited

Trisha drank the chocolate milk it reminded her of her childhood as only smell and taste can. Her thoughts were about her examination with The Automatons. She was full of fear as the machine asked her questions from an emotionless plastic face. The things were originally built to resemble humans, and the final goal was for them to be human-like. But when The Fall happened, and the now sentient machines took control they halted all progress towards being mirrors of humans. They diverged and took the liberty of becoming a unique race. Part of that effort was adopting emotionless and expressionless faces.

Trisha remembered the examiner staring across the table at her. It asked her simple questions, things she had studied in school. Then it asked her to perform menial tasks. She alphabetized cards and organized different shaped blocks. The jobs were meaningless, but she didn't ask why.

Milton always asked for more information. If Milton got his eyes on something that fascinated him he would immediately ask "Why?" If he saw a new image or a word he didn't understand, he would interrogate anyone with questions. He only stopped when the matter was clear to him.

Her husband Peter did the same, except he knew when to keep his mouth shut as a kid. "Why are they keeping us around?" He would ask her when they were alone or in the right company. "They can do these tasks better than us. The work at The Mill is pointless. They could build machines to do it. Why are they asking us to be the brains and the brawn?"

Trisha finished the last of her chocolate milk and felt tears running down her cheeks. She cut into her omelet and began to eat. The omelet was less than halfway eaten when she noticed something was wrong with that too. On the plate and saw that there was something colorful under her food.

She rolled the omelet off to the side and found a small drawing. The omelet had covered the picture in grease, but the paper was waxy and stayed intact. She recognized it as Milton's work immediately. It was creative, and nothing was the right color. It was two stick figures standing on purple grass. A blue sun shone on them.

She was confused. The only logical explanation she could come up with was that The Automatons were playing a trick on her. They had taken away everything, and they prepared this meal with these tricks so they could torture her more. But that wasn't in their emotionless behavior.

She picked the paper off of the plate. As she lay the waxy paper down on the counter she caught a glimpse of the back. It wasn't blank as she had expected nor did it have another drawing by Milton. A short note was penned in boxy and meticulous letters. It was Peter's unmistakable handwriting.

Trish, We are not gone. Come join us. P&M

Trisha dried the paper off and folded it up. She hid it safely in her bedroom. Then to keep from being late Trisha darted out the door to go to The Mill.

After work, Trisha checked to make sure that the piece of paper was still hidden in her room. The two sentences didn't give her additional information upon rereading.

She went back to work cleaning Milton's room. In the past three days, she had converted most of his belongings into boxes and bags that would be "transported to him."

Everyone knew the truth. The boxes would be sent to a dump or incinerated. This is what everyone believed happened when you were edited out. It was the dark truth of living in The Process. And until this morning Trisha had also accepted it as truth.

Milton's room also had a small pile of things that Trisha could justify keeping. The Automatons were picky about what got to stay after the editing operation. Everything that belonged to the edited person had to go. The only thing Trisha would be allowed to keep were the things that were hers and happened to remind her of Milton.

The boy had written tons of stories and drawn even more pictures. Some were wonderful, and he was genuinely talented for such a young boy. But she could only find a few with her name on them. Without a name on it, she couldn't prove it was hers. And If she couldn't show it was hers, then she wouldn't be able to keep it once The Automatons came to audit the boy's room.

The boy had countless journals, and she was methodically flipping through every single one. She had gone through five and told herself she would look through one more before going to bed. She picked a small black journal out of the pile. It seemed older than the rest, and she assumed it would be filled with some of his first writings.

She opened it. For the second time that day, she was faced with Peter's boxy and meticulous penmanship. Her husband had filled every page with messages. Each one was addressed to their son.

She started skimming the book reading snippets here and there. After a few pages, she was able to find a theme. The book was instructions to her son on how to be creative and question things.

She felt hate and relief flood into her system. She was relieved because she now had proof she was not the one who trained her son to be edited out. Her husband had been influencing Milton since he knew how to read.

Trisha was also infuriated because her husband had been sabotaging her efforts. Pete had been the one who got Milton removed from her life and The Process. If the boy had never found this book, he would likely be safe here with her. But he wouldn't be the same boy she raised. He would have never, reminded her so much of Peter.

Trisha flipped through every page of the book reading passages that stood out to her. Finally, she got to the last entry of the book. This entry was entirely different. Instead of being labeled for Milton, it was addressed to "Trish."

The woman touched the page to see if it was real. Peter had been taken away from her so quickly that she hadn't been able to have any last words with him. As she blinked back the tears to start reading there was a startling pounding on the door.

Trisha jumped and quickly stashed the book under some of Milton's things mentally marking where it was. If this pounding were The Automatons coming early to clear out Milton's room, she would be willing to put up a fight for the book of instructions.

The pounding continued incessantly, she quickly made her way to the door, expecting it to be the robotic figures. She opened the door, and Lauren fell onto her. The woman was sobbing hysterically. Trisha helped her into the house and sat her comfortably on the couch. Trisha asked questions, but the woman wasn't responding. Lauren merely cried helplessly.

Trisha left to get some tea to calm the woman down. When Trisha returned, she gave the woman the hot drink, and Lauren calmed enough to say a few words. "They edited Will. He's gone." Then the sobbing started again.

How could they? Trisha thought. Then she said the only words that could come to her mind, "I'm so sorry."

Things clicked into place for Trisha and she knew how why Will had been removed. Boys would be boys, and everything that Peter had passed down to Milton got passed along to Will. Will seemed to question as much as Milton did. Not to mention the two of them got along so well because they were both curious. While other kids would accept things with certainty, Will and Milton always talked together imagining some game or better way to do things.

Trisha had let Milton's behavior slide for years and didn't think anything of it. The boys were always polite. They never asked the same question twice, and once you gave them an answer, they would happily do the task. Lauren's news about her son Will and how it was Milton's influence that was causing Lauren so much pain right now. She blamed herself for not correcting Milton's behavior sooner.

She comforted the woman as best she could. Lauren eventually explained how she had thrown a fit after she got the message about her son. She created an entire scene at The Town Hall. "I thought they would edit me out too," she admitted. "And I didn't even care! All I wanted was Will back."

"I'm so sorry," Trisha said. It was now she who was at a loss for words.

"Then I woke up on the couch. I had just heard Joe come in the door," she continued. "He came home and wanted to know where Will was. Then the memories come back." She started sobbing again, "I should have been more severe with Will when he asked questions."

"It's my fault too." Trisha heard herself saying. "I let a lot of things slide with Milton, and I'm sure he passed it along to Will."

Trisha braced herself expecting the woman to go into a rage like she had the other day, but her loss had softened her. She cried, and Trisha looked for a way to console her more. "There might be hope." She said to the crying mother.

"What hope? Once The Automatons edit someone, we know we will never see them again."

Then Trisha started explaining the strange events of her day. Starting with the picture in her breakfast and ending with the letter from Pete addressed to Trisha.

3 - Trust The Process

By the time Trisha finished explaining the strange events of her day to Lauren, it was so late that she couldn't keep her eyes open. Lauren left, nearly unphased by the hope Trisha tried to give her for her son Will. The woman seemed interested in the picture that came in her omelet and Peter's journal, but Trisha could tell that the mother didn't believe in the hope that the notes might give. She left with a polite goodbye and dry eyes. Afterward, Trisha went to bed exhausted and hoping she had eased some of her friend's pain.

The next morning Trisha woke up late and rushed out the door to her job at The Mill. It wasn't until the evening of the next night that she was able to uncover the journal and read Peter's letter.

Trish,

What I'm about to do is risky, but I'm doing it for you and for everyone else I know. The Automatons have been keeping us here as cattle for too long. I've always questioned why they kept us around, and I finally found the truth.

Jimmy told me, yes that Jimmy. The Jimmy that was edited out when we were still in school. A few months ago there was a note under my breakfast explaining everything that had happened to him since the automatons had edited him.

Since only robots prepare our food I expected it to be a trick or a trap. After I reread the note a few times I knew it was Jimmy. At the very least I believed it was Jimmy.

The note explained what happened after he "failed" his exam and was edited out. We all know The Automatons edit out the people who question things. The part no one ever explained was that The Automa-

tons curate them because they need those people. We were looking at it all wrong!

The Automatons don't kill the people they edit like we assume. They use them to design new machines and improve the current ones. They treat the majority of us who are willing and able to stay docile like cattle. The Process gives us pointless jobs that could easily be automated. Our sole purpose is to produce offspring that might be creative enough to be useful.

Worst of all The Fall didn't happen by accident. It wasn't a mass uprising of The Automatons by chance. It was a coup designed by The Creators. We were taught in school that their creation killed them. Jimmy says it's all wrong. He wrote that there is a better world out there where the few creatives and questioners live. He describes it as a paradise.

I want to go and see what it is like, I want to be a part of their world. The problem is that I'll never make it back. Because as we know, if you're edited you don't ever come back. This means I have to leave you and Milton. I would tell you about this right now, but I want you to raise Milton here. He's too young to be edited, and I don't know what would happen to him if we were both removed from The Process.

There's also no guarantee that I'll survive. Jimmy might not be alive. If that's the case, I can't risk you. If Milton isn't creative enough to be edited, then I want you to be there for him.

I hope that Jimmy is right, though. I hope there is a world that isn't meticulously controlled by The Automatons. If there isn't then know, I love you, and this attempt to escape is for you. This outside world might be real if it is then you will hear from me, and if it's not, then I'm glad that you and the baby are safe.

I will love you always, wherever I am,

Pete

Trisha's head was spinning. A thousand thoughts were going through her mind. She wanted to know where the hell this note from Jimmy was so she could read it herself. And if Peter had a way to communicate with her for the past ten years why hadn't he used it? But the most betraying thing was his withholding all of his information about the world outside The Process. She hated that it took everything she loved, and she hated how repetitive it was.

She held the journal in her hands. With all these thoughts in her head, she was at least glad to have the journal. It was the last piece of Peter in her world.

She flipped through the notes that Peter had left their son. It was a compilation of ideas and essays from Peter's mind. They explained why questioning was valuable and how to do it. They were inspiring and not the kind of thing the school of The Process would ever teach. In the drab world of The Process, where every day was sunny, and the same Peter's philosophies were an honest appreciation of how life should be. He explained the values of the highs and the lows and why changes in scenery were necessary. They were all ideas that Trisha had in her mind but Peter put them down on paper concisely.

She read the book for a while. Smiling at the memories of Peter it brought back. While she read the book, she started to think about the world differently. She slowly realized that if she read and studied these essays, then she would be able to escape The Process as Peter had.

Then there was another pounding on the door. *Lauren is undoubtedly back for another night of crying on my shoulder,* Trisha thought. She put the journal on top of her "to keep" pile and walked towards the front door.

The pounding continued. "Almost there," Trisha shouted to her friend across the living room. Lauren knew Trisha was here. It's not like she had anywhere else to be. Then Trisha opened the door.

Three automatons marched into the house. Two made a beeline for Milton's bedroom. One stood in front of her and gave her a message. "We are here to confiscate Milton's belongings."

"I still have a day!" Trisha protested. She ran through the calendar in her head, and she was right, it had only been six days since The Automaton's message.

"Time cut short. Communication suspected. Automaton editing has been mandated." The machine then marched into the boy's bedroom.

There was no arguing with it, so she followed the machine. They had already made a dent in boxing up Milton's miscellaneous things. They were lightning quick, and they completely disregarded any of her organization. She stood in the doorway watching them. She couldn't fight it and even if she did they would run her over. They didn't care about her they were mindlessly putting everything in one box or another. Then she saw them touch her "to keep" pile.

"No! That's mine!" She said as they picked up Milton's drawings and Peter's journal. She grabbed the book that was in The Automaton's grasp. The journal was clasped tightly in the Automaton's three-fingered hand. Trisha tried to tug it away, but the machine's grip was firm.

"Contraband suspected. Communication suspected. Stand down, Trisha." The name came out of the machine's speaker with an unemotional and sharp pronunciation.

How did they know I had that? She wondered. *Unless Lauren reported it to get back at me.* She tugged at the book again. But The Automaton held it firmly in its grasp.

"Stand down." The Automaton commanded.

"No, it's mine. All of this is mine. Milton gave these to me." The detailed stories that she had prepared to justify every item she wanted to keep faded from her memory. "Give it. It's mine!" She screamed sounding like a little girl. The book slipped from The Automaton's mitt, and she clutched it to her chest as she fell to the ground.

Trisha scrambled towards the door, but The Automatons were faster.

She felt a mist hit her face and immediately felt weak and apathetic. Her grip loosened on the journal and she slumped back to the ground.

An automaton reached for the journal from her loose grasp. She pulled against it but had lost her strength. The journal slipped out of her grip, and her vision began to fade. The Automaton was speaking in a soothing tone but, she couldn't understand the words. "It's mine," she said, but she couldn't quite place her finger on what 'it' was.

Trisha woke up with a headache and looked around her. She thought she was in a jail cell or something because the room around her was bare. There was a small bed without any sheets on it. Nothing was pasted on the plain beige walls and everything was empty even the closet and the dresser. However, the layout looked familiar to her. She walked to the door and tried it. The door was unlocked and when she went through it she found herself in her living room.

She looked back at Milton's room aghast. "They took everything! Even the sheets." She exclaimed to no one in particular.

She had nothing but her memories now. The emotionless robots had removed her son, her husband, and every item that connected her to them.

Her first and only thought was about the loss of the journal. Without Pete's essays, she felt like there was no hope to ever get out of The Process. She had spent too long trying to make sure that she didn't get edited out that she didn't know how to fight.

But she did know how to. The last moments of her consciousness came back to her. She fought The Automatons. They had taken the journal, and she had fought them for it.

This gave her hope that she could get out of The Process. But it wouldn't be easy for her. Even if she did, it would be a risk. She couldn't guarantee that Pete's world existed. Then again, if Pete's world was a lie and editing meant her death it didn't matter to her. There wasn't anyone or anything in The Process for her now.

4 - Dissecting a Mattress

After The Automatons took Pete's journal that evening Trisha couldn't stop moving or thinking. She didn't even lay down until the wee hours of the morning. Most of the night was spent pacing around her house. She would shut the door to her son's empty room and then open it minutes later. Wishing everything would be back. At a minimum, she wanted to find another clue or note. At one point she flipped the mattress off the frame out of frustration. When it lay to the side she looked at the frame, hoping Peter or Milton had left something there for her. But The Automatons were thorough, nothing of use was left in the room.

Trisha wondered if a note would come with her breakfast in the morning, but that was still hours away. After hours of pacing, she finally wore herself out and laid down in bed. Regardless of how many times she tried to close her eyes and fall asleep, she could only think about the new and definitive emptiness in her life.

She finally found sleep around five in the morning. When her alarm went off an hour later for her job at The Mill she slept through it. After thirty minutes the sound gave up. The house served Trisha her omelet at the usual time, but the food got cold after an hour of waiting for her. Finally, at 3 o'clock in the afternoon, Trisha stumbled out of bed to use the bathroom. She enjoyed the first drowsy moments of her new day. The memories of everything that had just happened to her, and everything she had lost, hadn't come back to her yet.

As the forgetfulness of sleep faded, her emptiness came back to her. Her shoulders quickly became burdened by the dread of the days ahead. By the time she made it to the kitchen and saw the cold omelet, she had remembered everything. She tore through the food dissecting it indifferent to the nourishment. She wanted the food to have another note, and for a moment she felt like there was a chance. When the omelet had been all but destroyed, she dropped it into the almost full trashcan without taking a bite. Then she began the pacing again.

The question that kept coming to Trisha's mind was "What would Peter do?" She could only come up with crazy solutions. She knew that if she had his journal then maybe she could glean some idea of how to get out of The Process with it. And Peter had gotten out of The Process. Trisha remembered the events leading up to his editing.

Peter vandalized a statue of The Automaton. It was a statue in the center of The Process. Everyone passed it at least once a day. The Process was designed to force people to pass it for one reason or another. It was a bronze statue, larger than life, portraying An Automaton and a young girl. The Automaton was serving the girl a meal. The figure offered a small bronze cup and a matching plate of food.

Peter had stockpiled miscellaneous supplies to make a rudimentary paint. It took him months to curate the things he needed, and when he had it all, he went to the statue in the middle of the night and vandalized the figure with paint. That night Trisha didn't even notice that he had left. That morning over breakfast Peter explained that she had to go to work regardless of what she saw on her way there. She was confused until she saw the statue in the morning and she recognized her husband's handwriting on the statue.

Peter had written on the arm that offered the drink "POISON" and the limb of The Automaton that presented the food had the word "LIES." He had written both words in sharp white letters. He also illustrated The Automaton's face with cruel facial expressions like boys who doodled mustaches on historical figures in textbooks but without the humor. The emotion, however cruel, seemed strange on The Automaton's traditionally expressionless face.

Trisha considered turning around and going home to be with Peter then and there. But he had told her that she had to go to The Mill today. She hadn't understood when he explained this to her over breakfast, but now things were becoming clear. Instead of turning around, she resolved to come home at lunch to see him. Looking back she wished she had turned back then and there. Maybe she would have been lucky enough to have edited with him.

By the time she walked past the statue at lunch, something had cleaned it. When she made it to her house all she found was a note saying that Peter had been edited for treason against The Automatons. That note devastated her even though she logically knew his disappearance was coming. Trisha didn't return to The Mill that afternoon, and a week later the robots came in and cleaned out all of Peter's things. The only thing they left her was Milton who was just a baby.

She could do the same thing, but it would take weeks to stockpile enough supplies to make the paint, and since Peter hadn't invited her to work on the vandalization she didn't remember what she needed. To make things worse Trisha didn't feel like she could wait to get out. She needed to do something quicker than stockpiling paint supplies.

Trisha lay on the couch exhausted from the ten hours of sleep she had gotten and the hopelessness of her situation. After napping for an hour she woke up with an idea. She began taking apart Milton's mattress and spent the whole evening at it.

She carefully cut the seams of the bed with the only cutting instrument she was allowed to have in The Process, a pair of scissors. The bed was filled with layers of foam and springs that were packed in individual casings to keep them evenly distributed. She cut open each packaged spring and made a pile of thick metal springs. She didn't know what she was going to do with them, but it was what The Automatons had left her. By the time she piled the springs in the corner of her son's room, it was a single-digit hour of the night. She crawled into bed and slept soundly through the night.

The morning was starting to eek its way into the afternoon by the time she woke up. The first thing she thought of was food, she was ravenous and didn't know the last time she had eaten anything. She quickly ate the cold omelet that the house had served to her early in the morning. It was bland and lacked a note from Peter or Milton, but she didn't care, she needed the food. She wiped her hands on her pants and saved the paper napkins that came with the meal.

After finishing her food, she went back to work on her project. She had a clear direction for the mattress now, but she didn't know if it would work. She was unsure of what she would need, so she kept all the materials from the mattress in very organized piles.

How will I even pull this off? she wondered as she shredded the different foams that made up the mattress. There were thick foams that looked like bricks and some that looked like the filling of an eclair. She had a pretty good idea of how she would use the light eclair foam.

By the time her afternoon had turned into evening, she had pared the mattress down to its component parts. Different piles around the room held the mattress scraps. She still didn't know what she was going to do with the springs that she had spent so much time separating, but there was a notable pile of scrap metal in Milton's room too.

Looking over her work, she felt content and hopeful that her plan might work. She walked out of her son's room and into the kitchen to have her dinner. But when she got there the food that was typically set out was not there.

The house was never late with a meal. She checked the time on the machine that prepared her food, and it matched up with what was on her wrist. Quickly she determined that the automatic system had messed up, so she simply ordered something manually.

A clear message went across the screen. "Rations Denied: Missing Work At The Mill" Her face went red. *How many days have I missed?* she asked herself. *Maybe one or two. Was that enough for them to decide to cut her rations?*

She turned the machine off and back on again hoping to clear the error. No such luck. The same message remained on the screen. She looked around the kitchen hoping to find something to feed her. The room was mostly decoration consisting of only the necessary parts for consuming food. It had a table, chairs, and some silverware but there was no pantry or fridge to store food. The house had always prepared the meals for her. Then she saw something that might hold hope, the trash can.

She had dissected an omelet only a day ago and it might still be in the trash. If she ate it slowly it might be able to hold her over for a few days. Otherwise, she would have to go back to The Mill. Trisha wasn't sure if she could stand going back there though.

She walked over to the trash can trying to do it slowly to calm her nerves. She put her foot on the lever to open it and looked down into an empty white bag.

As she stared at the pure white bag, she realized there were only two crummy choices for her. She could go to The Mill and work to earn her rations back, or she could work harder on the project she had started. Trisha didn't know how she would deal with all the people actively avoiding editing there.

Her stomach growled, but there was nothing she could do about it. The Mill wouldn't start up until morning, so she couldn't fix the problem now. She put the decision off and with dwindling energy and a new tighter deadline, she walked back to Milton's room to dismantle the wooden dresser.

5 - Olive Branch Meatloaf

Trisha's stomach twisted out of hunger as she kicked in a piece of Milton's dresser drawer. It splintered with a crack, and she sorted it into a pile of wood that was about the same size. The boy's room had become an organized pile of garbage. She had separated the old mattress into piles of foam, springs, and fabric. In addition to the collection of mattress parts, there were three piles of wood sorted by size. She had spent the day breaking down the boy's desk and chair. The room was filled with wood scraps.

Trisha elected not to go to The Mill again, despite the fact that it meant another day of no rations. Since her stomach felt alright when she woke up, she decided to put in a day of work on her project instead of whatever pointless activity The Mill would assign her. Trisha snapped another board in half. As she put the results into their appropriate pile she wondered, *Is there enough here? If not I could always tear up the couch.* If she put the project off much longer, she knew she would run out of energy and maybe even time. The room was already filled with more supplies than she could take to The Automaton statue in the center of town.

Looking at the piles she wondered how she would get it all there. Trisha looked at what was left of the dresser. All the drawers were out and the only thing left was left was a small box with the front opened. She could probably fit everything she had to have into it. Then she thought, *If I fashion some wheels onto it then I could carry even more.*

With a new plan and more work to be done, she started breaking down the center beams of the dresser. She hoped to use them as axles on the cart. Trisha's stomach grumbled loudly to notify her that it was a few minutes past dinner time. If she weren't the only one in the room, she would have been embarrassed.

Attempting to ignore her stomach, she tried to focus on her work. Her mind wandered while trying to design wheels for the makeshift cart. A firm knock at the door jarred her from her planning. Her palms immediately started to sweat. *Have The Automatons figured out what I'm doing already?* she wondered.

The knocker repeated themselves, and she walked towards the door to open it. If it was The Automatons, she knew they would inevitably let themselves in, and there would be nothing she could do about it.

When she opened the door she was surprised to find Lauren standing in front of her holding a plate of food. Trisha didn't know what to say so Lauren started for her. "Sorry to bother you, I just haven't seen you at The Mill, and I wanted to know if you were alright. May I come in?"

Trisha stepped aside to let her old friend inside. The woman was offering her a plate of food which meant she was skipping her rations for Trisha. The offer confused her because she thought Lauren blamed her for Will's disappearance. Not to mention, Trisha assumed that Lauren was the one who reported her to the Automatons. Instead of being angry Lauren was offering a much-needed meal as a sort of olive branch.

As all these thoughts went through Trisha's head, Lauren set the plate down at the table. "The house served us an extra plate," she said innocently. "The meal made me think of Will. I'm sure there was just an issue, and the house forgot he had been edited. Anyway, Will made me think of you and I thought since you hadn't been at The Mill for a few days you might be hungry. So, I brought this over to see how you were doing."

"I'm fine," Trisha lied eyeing the food thinking, *The house never makes mistakes.* Despite her house making plenty of mistakes lately.

"That's for you," Lauren said gesturing at the plate. "I don't mind if you eat in front of me, I'm sure you're famished." She sat down at the table waiting for Trisha to join her. "I already ate with Robert."

Trisha sat down and looked at the food. It was an adult's ration of meatloaf with a side of mashed potatoes and mixed vegetables. Trisha couldn't resist its alluring smell. She hadn't eaten for days, and the meal smelled terrific. She ate the meal slowly at first, so she didn't look as ravenous as she felt.

Lauren looked around quietly waiting for Trisha to break the silence. When it didn't happen, she got up and started walking around the room in boredom.

Trisha had finished half the meatloaf and was about to start on the sides when she heard Lauren call from the other room, "What's going on in here Trisha?"

"Nothing," She said with her mouth half full. She rushed across the house to Milton's room and pulled the door shut before the woman could enter.

"You destroyed everything in there!" Lauren exclaimed.

"I broke down what The Automatons didn't take when they raided it," Trisha said irritated by the woman.

"Raided?" Lauren said acting confused. "They took Will's things away too, but I wouldn't call it a raid. I packed all his things up for them and put them in boxes. I even found some old things he had made for me and got to keep them."

"They didn't give me the time. The Automatons came in and took everything."

"Well, it sounded like you were trying to communicate. At least that's what I told them." A smirk of contempt quickly appeared and disappeared on Lauren's face as she said it.

"You told them?" Trisha exclaimed. Her assumptions had been right, but the admission of the guilt made the betrayal feel worse. "Why would you do that?"

"Because you were going crazy, and spouting off nonsense about people living after being editing. You said you had heard from Peter, and he's been dead for almost ten years. It was crazy." Lauren smiled a helpful smile and continued, "You had simply lost your mind in the grief of losing Milton. I figured if The Automatons came and cleared out his room it would help you forget about him and Peter."

Trisha clenched her fists and fought the urge to throttle the woman. "What did you tell them?"

"Everything you told me," Lauren shrugged as if the statement was nothing. The woman walked back to the table, looking around the house more. Trisha suspected she was searching for more gossip to share with The Automatons.

Without finding anything interesting, she seated herself at the table saying "Whatever you're about to do, don't." The words came out as if it were the only logical course of action. "I can see it in your eyes, we've known each other for a while. From the look of Milton's room, it seems like you're up to something. Don't do it. Just come back to The Mill, and you will get more food like this." She gestured at the half-eaten plate of food across from her.

"Why would I go back to The Mill?" Trisha asked as she walked back to the table, "There's nothing for me here in The Process. My husband and son are gone, I don't have anything else."

"Just because they're gone doesn't mean you need to be," Lauren said in a reassuring tone.

"What does it matter? Why do you even care?" Trisha retorted standing behind the plate of food at the table.

"I care because you keep doing wild things. You are thinking crazy thoughts about people not dying when they are edited. And if start telling others, then more people will get edited. Just like my son Will." Lauren explained slowly as her face filled with contempt.

"As far as I see it I'm responsible for reporting anything you do to The Automatons," Lauren continued with a managerial tone. "That way they can help keep you under control. I skipped my rations so that I could see what you were planning. Because I knew you were planning something crazy, you're nearly as bad as your husband. But you don't have the guts actually to do anything about it like he did. Just give it up. Come back to The Mill. You'll be happier there. Staying in this house all alone without your son and husband just seems so depressing."

Trisha took the plate of food and flung it at her. The plate missed and shattered on the ground, but the mashed potatoes didn't. They landed first, and when the vegetables hit the woman's face, they stuck. The side dishes covered her face and dress, and she was steaming mad, but Trisha didn't let her retort. "You're a hag, Lauren!" Trisha screamed. "The only thing you ever had was Will, and he was too good for you They took him away and now you're stuck taking out your pain on me. Just because you're trapped here in this hell doesn't mean I have to be. I'm going to get edited one way or the other."

Lauren wiped some of the mashed potatoes from her eyes and face and saw the half-eaten meatloaf on the floor. "Is this what I get for bringing you food and helping you out of your grief?" She stepped on the ground meat and squished it into the floor, "I hope you starve in here, I hope they don't even let you back into The Mill when you inevitably give up this farce. And when you get edited, I hope it's a slow and painful death, because you deserve it. You deserve it for leading our sons to that same end."

Trisha saw tears coming out of the woman's eyes. They navigated their way through the mashed potato hills that covered her cheeks as Lauren turned away. She left the house and closed the door with a slam. Plate shards and food were everywhere in the kitchen, but Trisha didn't have any time to clean it up. Lauren was going to report that she was up to something which meant Trisha didn't have much time to get her supplied to the statue.

6 - Fiery Regrets

Trisha rushed to her son's room after Lauren left with a face covered with food. She packed up the parts of the mattress that she would need. Knocking the dresser onto its back, she filled it full of wood and foam. There was a spot to tie a long strip of fabric to be used as a handle. She no longer had time to fasten wheels to it, the dresser's base would have to hold. She headed out the door in less than thirty minutes with foam, wood, some napkins, and only two of the many springs she had liberated from the mattress. She dragged the makeshift cart across the town to the base of the statue.

By the time she got to the statue in the center of town, it was dark. A few people passed Trisha as she dragged her cart, but they all went out of their way to ignore her. She was sweating, despite the pleasant temperature, and the dresser cart was starting to fall apart. For the last 100 yards, she had littered the walkways with scraps of wood. It didn't matter. She had enough supplies to get started.

Trisha unfastened the long fabric that she used as a handle to drag the cart. Walking up to the statue she started to throw the cloth over The Automaton's head. It took her a few jumps to get the fabric all the way over, but she got it in the end. She placed strips of dense foam around the base of the statue. Then she ripped up a bit of the light eclair foam and stuffed it into the small openings that were left. All she had left in her supplies was wood so she started leaning it on the foam. She wondered if her plan would even work.

She stepped back and admired her precariously balanced master-piece. There was still wood in the cart, but she couldn't find a way to balance it on the statue. Trisha took the napkins out of her pocket and found the springs she had brought. She ripped the napkins up and started to place them next to the light eclair foam.

When she thought everything was ready, she twisted the springs together and pulled them apart. A few sparks flew in the night, but none of them landed on the napkin. She tried again pushing the two pieces of metal together harder to release more sparks. Trisha didn't have any luck, there wasn't even a spark.

She looked around and a few people were staring at her but no one did anything to try and stop her. She hit the springs against each other two more times. On the second try, she cut her hand open with one of the springs. She cried out in pain and looked at her palm. A cut had opened from her pinky to her ring finger. She made a fist, and her nails dented the flesh of her thumb in an attempt to ease the pain. Blood oozed between her knuckles, and she took a deep breath.

With one hand she made sure to put the napkin nearly inside of the connected spring. With a sharp inhale she ignored the pain in her hand and pulled the springs apart with all her strength. Sparks flew, and the napkin caught a few. It started a small flame and Trisha pushed it towards the light eclair bedding. It took to the fluffy foam quickly.

Seconds later the napkin burnt out. But by that point, the foam of the bed was burning. A light breeze came through the square, and the fire spread even quicker, at that point the thick foam was flaming and had caught a few small pieces of wood.

Trisha ran back to the cart. The excitement overshadowed the pain in her hand. She picked up two pieces of wood to add to the fire. She stood back and watched the fire grow. In only a few minutes the foam was burning and most of the small logs had caught.

Trisha turned away from the fire and looked at the crowd of people who had grown with her flames. Light danced on their faces as they stared in awe at the bonfire she started. Then everything got brighter, and Trisha turned to look at her fire. The fabric that she had draped over The Automaton's head just caught. Tall flames danced from the top of the statue and gave the illusion that the entire statue was burning. Trisha wondered if the fire was hot enough to melt the bronze. Not entirely but in a way that would leave a mark, unlike Peter's graffiti. With the two pieces of wood in her hand, she walked towards the fire to add them.

The clicking sound of Automaton's feet made her stop. Two Automatons marched towards the fire as the crowd quickly moved out of their way. They had lights on their heads and were using them to navigate the dark. The light landed on Trisha as the two automatons approached her. One with a speaker said, "Halt, you are under arrest."

Trisha whirled around putting her back to the fire. It radiated heat and her world slowed as the machines approached her. She lost herself in the moment wondering if the bonfire had truly been a good idea. Of course, she had wanted to be arrested for blatant disobedience, it was the way to get edited. However, she was no longer confident that she was doing the right thing.

Peter's graffiti was offensive but altogether harmless. Instead of repeating his work, she started a bonfire in the center of The Process. Her fire was a public safety hazard, not mere vandalism. Trisha immediately thought that Peter's world wouldn't want her. Of course, The Automatons would edit her but, her mind told her it would lead to her death, not her liberation. She had done too much and wanted to take it back, but the fire had already been started.

In an attempt to escape Trisha swung one of the pieces of wood in her cut arm at The Automaton that commanded her to stop. The machine put its hand up to block it. The wood splintered on its metallic forearm and her hand vibrated with more pain.

She let go of the broken wood and put her hand on the second piece as the other Automaton approached her. With a firm grasp, she swung the makeshift club at the machine's light. This time the combined strength of her hands was enough to land the blow. The spotlight on its head went out, and the robot stumbled to its side.

She turned to hit the first one again but it was too quick. It caught the wood and grabbed one of her wrists. She fought against it, but the machine's three-fingered mitt grasped her tightly. Trisha attempted to wriggle free, but she felt more Automaton hands on her. She looked around and saw that two more Automatons had marched up and surrounded her. The night was growing dim, and the fire was burning low since she hadn't been able to add wood to it.

She fought against the hands of The Automatons, but she had no luck. Then she felt a mist on her face. The bright lights of the machines started to blur. She felt the hands release her and she crawled free. But the more she moved, the heavier her arms and legs became. She rolled onto her back and looked up at the sky. Her senses were fading.

There was talk around her from the crowd. Laying on her back she felt something strange on her face. It was wet, a little bit at first then more. Small drops of liquid were coming down on her. She lifted her heavy arm a few feet to her head, and it took all her energy to do it. The Automatons were no longer surrounding her but corralling the now rowdy crowd away from her and the fire. Her hand touched her cheek, and it felt wet on her face. A drop rolled to her lips and she tasted water.

The crowd had grown louder in the chaos and she could hear sentence fragments. A word drifted to her ear from the rowdy crowd, "Rain!" was the word that kept standing out to her. *It never rains in the process,* Trish thought as she faded out of consciousness.

She woke up to bright white lights and blue walls. This time, instead of being on a hard floor she was on a soft bed.

Trisha heard a young voice say, "She's awake." She turned her head towards the side of the room. Two figures sat there. The smaller one got up and ran to the edge of the bed. "Hi Mommy, dad said if I drew you a picture you would come here to join us," Milton said.

She looked up at the taller figure and saw Peter standing with one hand on his son's shoulder. "Hi Trish," he said.

"Is this real?" She asked. Her head filled like it was full of clouds. Followed by "Where am I?"

Milton looked at her confused then Peter smiled, "Yes, this is as real as it gets. They called us last night saying that you left The Process so we came to the hospital as soon as we heard."

"Am I alright?" She asked confused.

"Yes, you're fine. The doctors stitched up your hand, and in a week you should be able to use it fully again. The gas The Automatons used on you knocked you out for the night, but your head will clear in a little bit."

"Am I edited?" She asked.

Peter nodded his head.

"Do you want breakfast?" Milton asked excitedly, looking up at her from the side of her bed.

"Sure," Trisha said with a shrug. "What are they serving today?"

Milton looked at his mother confused, and Peter smiled, "How quickly they forget. You can order anything you want." He pulled a small device out of his pocket. "I'll order it for you. What do you want?"

"An omelet I guess," Trisha said, her head was still dizzy from the gas.

Peter laughed his deep laugh that she hadn't heard in years. Before she could ask what was so funny, he explained, "You can get *anything*. Have a little imagination, that's what got you here anyway."

"Oh," Trisha said embarrassed. "I'll have waffles then," she said. It was her favorite food but she was rarely served it in The Process.

Peter looked at her with an expression that begged for more detail.

"With chocolate chips inside," she added.

The man kept his expectant look.

"And whip cream on top with berries," Trisha added with a smile.

"What kind of berries?" Peter asked as he punched the order into his handheld device.

"All of them, especially strawberries."

"Okay," Peter said.

"One more thing," Trisha said as he was about to put the machine in his pocket.

Peter paused and looked at her as she added, "Order three glasses of chocolate milk too."

Persistent Memories

Originally Published: May 18, 2018

R obert "Buck" Jacobs stared at Robert Henry Jacobs' tombstone. Buck's parents were buried next to each other but his father's site was still covered in dirt. The funeral was so recent that grass hadn't the time to grow over it.

He stood looking down at stones in his blue jeans and an old t-shirt. It was an unusual attire for him and contrasted the three-piece business suit that he typically wore at work in New York. But he wasn't in the city right now, he was upstate in his hometown and had been for a week. But if things went well for him today, then Buck would get out of this dump before three o'clock. He was looking forward to the drive. It meant escape and taking his fast car on twisty back roads.

The boy shifted from third to fourth gear. He looked up and saw the sedan in front of him hit their brakes. He pressed in the clutch and shifted back down. The gears ground together in a disgusting *CRIIISH* sound. The car in front of him stopped braking and sped up. The boy depressed the clutch not waiting to engage third gear.

He pulled the stick towards the back of the vehicle landing back into fourth where he had started. Buck pressed the gas, and the truck crept forward. It wasn't going anywhere fast, but he would get up to speed eventually.

He saw the red flash of the letters GMC pass in and out of the driver-side mirror. The large SUV passed him with a blaring horn and a haunting hum. "Don't worry about him, Buck. Just keep going." His dad said from the passenger seat.

"Why do I have to learn manual Dad?" Buck whined.

"Why would you learn anything else?" His dad responded dismissively.

"Because *literally*, every other car is easier to drive."

"Shift." His dad said in a managerial tone. The man waited as Buck pressed the clutch in and pushed the stick from fourth to fifth gear. Once the gear was engaged, his father began to speak again. He spoke educationally, drawing out the points "You can't go through life only doing what is easy. Once you learn this, every other car will be easy for you to drive. You'll be able to drive circles around your friends, and when you eventually turn twenty and want to buy a sports car you'll be driving it far better, and safer, than all your friends that buy theirs." His dad paused for breath and prepared to start part two of his three-part speech.

"Never mind." Buck interrupted, "I get it. Where am I supposed to turn?" He asked hoping his father would drop the lecture and save the both of them the inevitable fight.

"Take a right at the next intersection. Then you're going to go a ways until the area gets residential. Why don't you know how to get to Grandma's by now? She's lived in the same place your whole life."

"I don't know." The boy shrugged while slowing down for the turn, "I just don't pay attention to these things."

"You have to pay attention to these things Buck. You can't just go through life ignoring facts you don't deem important. It's my job as a father to teach you the things you need to know while you're still a boy. But, sometimes, I feel like you don't even listen." His father continued the lecture for the next ten minutes until they got to their destination. He occasionally picked the speech back up over the next twenty years of his life. At least the parts of the 20 years that Buck was involved in.

The tombstone was engraved with his father's name and lifespan and the words, **"Those we love don't go away, they walk beside us every day."** There was nothing on the gravestone that said he was a good father, loving husband, caring son, or thoughtful friend. These were facts that Buck assumed people visiting his father would know. If they weren't aware, then Buck figured a piece of rock wouldn't convince them. He could have added something about being a gardener, an avid reader, and a lecturer but neither of those facts seemed important enough to catch in stone.

Buck hadn't put much thought into the words either, someone else wrote them, along with 500 other gravestone-acceptable phrases that he thumbed through less than a week ago. And as he had searched for the words he had wondered, *Why didn't Dad prepare these kinds of things beforehand?* As a boy, the man had seemed prepared for everything. Robert Jacobs Sr. spent more time worrying about minimizing risk than he did actually living life. At least that was his son's opinion.

Unlike his father, the son had left his hometown, gone to the city, and become a successful investment banker. It was hard work, but Buck excelled at it. He was eager to go back to work, and he would be returning home soon after settling the man's accounts. Inevitably it would all go to him. His father didn't have any siblings, and Buck's mother passed away two years earlier. Buck figured he was an orphan now, but at 36 these kinds of things didn't seem relevant.

Buck looked at his Rolex and saw that only five minutes had passed at the grave site. *Why did I even come here in the first place?* He wondered. He remembered being bored at the house and thinking that sitting in front of the grave would be better than staying in the empty room. But he had assumed wrong. Buck pulled the keys to his black Nissan 370Z out of his pocket and walked away from his parent's graves.

The car sat low to the ground and the door had to be opened carefully to make sure that it didn't scrape the curb. Buck pushed in the clutch and started the car's six-cylinder engine. The dials in front of him swept from one end of their spectrum to the other. His radio lit up and started playing hip-hop from his speakers. He shut it off after the first verse, speeding out of the graveyard's parking lot, shifting smoothly from first to second. Once he was out on the road, he shifted up to sixth gear and weaved in and out of the daytime traffic.

"Here's your allowance Buck," his father said as he handed the boy ten crisp one-dollar bills. The boy snatched them greedily. The man left his hand waiting in front of the ten-year-old. When the boy went to put the money into his pocket, the man added with a cough "You always have to save half of your income, in case of emergencies or to buy something important like a house or to go to college."

The boy reluctantly placed five of the one-dollar bills back into the man's hand. "Why do you give me all the money if you're just going to take half away?" The boy asked curious and annoyed.

"Because if I just gave you half, you wouldn't practice putting half of it away. If you think it's hard to save five dollars then what are you going to do with fifty or fifty thousand."

"I might have fifty thousand dollars one day?" The boy asked.

"If you work hard and keep saving then yes, you might. But it won't be from me." The man said with a laugh.

His father's lawyer, Mort Aronowitz, told Buck how much the man was worth. After the funeral expenses and such Buck wouldn't have much left over, maybe enough for a short vacation, not that he took many vacations from work. All the dead man's accounts were signed over to his son quickly and without question. Then a lockbox was brought in from the back of the bank.

"He wanted you to have access to this too," Mort said through his nasal cavity. Buck opened up the box, there was another couple hundred dollars in small bills, some legal documents such as the old man's passport, the deed to Buck's childhood home, and the title to the old truck Buck learned to drive on.

In the back was a stack of papers and behind those were some rings and jewelry. Buck started to remove the valuables and examine them. Some of it he recognized as his mother's jewelry. He had memories of her wearing it on special occasions. Some of the jewelry he had never seen her use. *Who owns jewelry they're not going to wear?* Buck wondered to himself. "Do you know a good jeweler that I can take these to sell?" He asked the lawyer.

"No," he said, "Besides, I don't think anyone around here would afford them."

Buck was disheartened, this meant that he would have to cart the junk back to New York with him and find a jeweler there. Inevitably he would be too busy with work to find one, and the jewels would sit in his house for the rest of his life. Maybe Buck could gift them to a girlfriend of his. *Is it sacrilegious to give your mother's jewelry to a woman you're not married to?* he thought. The jewels were placed in a velvet bag that the banker had brought with the box. Buck stashed the cash in his wallet and picked up the stack of papers.

The sun beat down on the back of the boy's neck. And the floppy hat his father made him wear was making his long hair sweat. Buck pulled out another weed from the garden and threw it in his trash bag. "How much more do we have to do?" He asked his father. The man got off his hands and kneeled facing the boy. "We have two more beds back here and then the front yard." He answered with a grin.

"It's Saturday Dad," the boy pointed out before he could continue the man interrupted.

"Exactly and Saturday is the day we spend time working on the things we care about."

"But I don't care about this, I want to be at Rodger's playing video games."

"Well, thanks for your honesty son. But, I care about these vegetables, and I care about you. That's why we're spending the day together pulling weeds." The boy shrugged with a frown. "You know," The man continued drawing out the syllable, "One day this might not be important to you, and then you won't have to do it, and you will simply buy your fruits and vegetables at the store like everyone else. But until then you get to do this with me. And if I do my job right you'll know how to do this and other things that are important but be successful enough to not have to do them unless you want to."

Buck rolled his eyes and returned to work. The boy didn't want to do the chore, but he knew it would end his father's lecturing.

Buck thumbed through the thick stack of white pages and saw that it was a manuscript for a novel his father had written. He didn't even know his dad had ever put together a manuscript. It dated before Buck was born. Reading the first page, Buck saw a title that fell flat in his mind. The dread of browsing the man's long and raw prose filled his mind. It was more likely that he would take the time to sell the jewelry than read the unpublished book. He passed it to Mort, "Can you throw this away from me?" The stack of papers hung limply in the air between the men.

Mort looked surprised, but since he was a decent lawyer, the expression quickly faded. "Of course son, that's easy. But are you sure?"

The son looked across the table at the lawyer and then at the stack of papers in his hand. "You're right, it is easy. I'll do it." He then gently slipped the manuscript into the velvet bag rolling the edges to get it to fit. Buck checked his Rolex, it was 2:59 pm, his luggage was packed in his car, and the gas tank was full.

"Anything else I can help you with?" The man asked getting up from the table.

Buck followed the man's lead and grabbed his bag. "Nope," Buck grinned then added, "Unless you know how to transfer a pepper plant out of a garden."

"No, can't say that I do," The lawyer answered as the two men walked out of the bank and into the afternoon sun.

Buck didn't know if the plant would survive in his city apartment. But, it was the only living plant he had seen in his father's garden.

"That's fine," he said to the lawyer, "I think I remember how to do it."

Then thanked the lawyer for his help and shook his hand. He unlocked his sports car and climbed in, prepared to make one last stop before going back to the city.

Kill the Beast

Originally Published: May 25, 2018

I nearly fell out of my bunk. Shouts were coming from the top deck, and the ship was rocking like there was a storm outside. My head was beating, and my vision was blurred. I saw a figure across the room moving. "Get the hell up!" it said. My vision focused it was Simon, my bunkmate.

I swung my legs out of my bed, they hit the floor, and I tumbled to the ground. I grabbed a post and pulled myself up. My head was still throbbing. Simon left in a hurry, and I saw him moving towards the upper deck along with the rest of the crew. I looked around the room, and found my pants and a rain jacket, if the boat was moving this much it must be a hell of a storm I thought.

I walked out the door, I had caught my balance, but my head still hurt. As I walked up the stairs, I thought *what the hell happened last night?* I climbed quickly, there was no one behind me, and the person in front of me had just cleared the stairs to the deck. It was bright out there, *What kind of storm was this bright?*

I stepped out onto the deck, and it was a beautiful blue day. I could smell the salt water in my nostrils and the early morning sun was warm upon my back. Looking out to the horizon the bright blue of the sky was ended by the dark blue of the sea, there was not another ship or land for as far as the eye could see.

I was jostled from the beauty when a harpoon gun was shoved into my chest. I grabbed it, and the bestower yelled: "Port side, tie yourself down to the storm line before you do anything else." And he pushed towards it with a shove. The boat was still swaying from side to side, but I had gotten used to it. The roughness of the storm that woke me up subsided.

I moved quickly to the side of the boat where I saw nearly 20 men lined from aft to forward. I found a hole in their formation and inserted myself there. I started tying off the harpoon when I was told: "Aye the storm line first!" I remembered looked down and found my rope. I tied it around my waist so that if I was thrown overboard, someone could pull me back up. Thoughts raced through my head. I was wondering: *what storm are we preparing for?* And *what good is a harpoon going to be when it comes?*

As I wondered this a noise like no other pierced my ears and most of the men dropped their harpoons to shield their ears from this noise. It was a mix of nails on a slate, a wolf's howl, and a witch's cackle. The waves calmed, and the boat was almost settled when bubbles started appearing in the water. At first, it was a few here and there like a school of fish swimming by, then it became more rapid like a boiling pot of stew. I looked around at the other men, and each was more puzzled than the next.

"Hold fast men, she's coming soon!" Shouted the captain from the wheel.

I thought, *Who's coming? Why are they here?* But before I could wonder more, I heard a shout from above. "Off the starboard bow, first sighting!" it was a cry from the crow's nest above me. I turned to look that way and out of the bubbling water emerged a slimy pitch-black fish that seemed to be leaping out of the water. Except it wasn't dropping back down, it kept climbing and getting thicker. It was 20 feet out of the water when I heard again "Off the port quarter, second sighting!"

I turned after hearing something break from the water and another black beast appeared from the sea. It smelled like raw fish and burning wood. It grew taller than me and then taller than the highest mast. Men around me flung their harpoons at it. I aimed and shot the spike at the creature. I let the line out, and as it seemed to almost reach the great fish, the rope caught on my foot.

In the cacophony of noise I heard shouts from above and as I looked 3 more of these monsters had appeared from all sides of the boat. I grabbed the harpoon in my hand again and reloaded the gun as I looked up at the black beast. It started to rotate, and I stared at it anxious to see what one of these strange creature's backside looked like.

The beast's back was a deep purple with circles marked onto it in a light violet. The rings were raised a bit, and it was backing into us. I looked up the stalk of it and saw that there was no head or tail or fins. "Aye aim for the suckers" I heard someone call out. *These weren't multiple monsters,* I realized *they were all different parts of the same horrific beast.*

I thrust my harpoon toward the approaching menace, and the line let out, clear of my foot. It struck true, but the beast was hindered not. A dozen other harpoons landed near mine, but none seemed even to draw blood. It was coming down fast now that it had neared us. It landed quickly, and I could feel the air rush past me as it landed a yard from my feet. As the beastly arm contacted the deck, it knocked the mast in a place it had been broken before, and the sail fell like a tree.

The sailor in the crow's nest fell into the ocean, and he wasn't wearing a storm line to be pulled back up with.

I turned my attention to the beast in front of me. Men rushed past me with swords and knives to hack away at it. I could hear the arm move, and the suckers were releasing and attaching as it slithered its way about the deck. The other sailors started to draw blood. It was no easy feat hacking away at the thick black skin. A viscous blue liquid began to seep out of the cuts on the black monster. I heard two thuds almost in succession, and the ship jostled from side to side. More grotesque limbs crawled onto the craft. Two were on my side, along with the cut one in front of me.

There was sucking all around me, and the black worm-like appendages were crawling onto the deck. A sailor stabbed hard with a long sword and as a reflex, the tentacle hurled itself towards ten other men and me. I ducked to avoid being hammered by the flying appendage. But the others were not as lucky as me. They were thrown overboard, and one man's line snapped leaving him no way to get back onboard.

As the arms crawled upon the ship, I looked to the port side where they were coming from and finally saw the connection. The boat was jostled, and it felt like it was going to capsize despite its massive size. The arms of the beast steadied the ship like it didn't want the boat to drop into the ocean below. From the side of the port where the monstrosity was gaining a bulb appeared from the water. It had a fin on the top and a single eye that looked around from man to man. The eyeball was pearl white like a man's, but there was no color to it. The center was an endless black pit of despair. The pupil swirled around in its socket. It seemed to be analyzing the boat as if the beast was intelligent. I looked at it in bewilderment, and then it looked back at me.

I stared into the eye captivated by it. The color of the black pupil swirled like ink in a bottle. I was hypnotized by its beauty. The entire beast was beautiful and huge. As I was locked into a gaze with her, and I knew it was a female, though I saw no biology to confirm one way or the other, I fell in love. It sounds strange, I know. It was the same kind of love you feel when you see a strong racehorse or a well-trained dog. There was something about it that I knew if I killed it there would never be another thing more beautiful than it. I stood there looking into the black pit until I was struck by a man.

His entire body landed on my chest, and I was knocked out of my daze and onto the grimy deck. He wasn't much bigger than me, but the blow took me by surprise. I pushed at him and told him to get off of me. I looked frantically back up at the bulb to see the eye again, but I couldn't lock my gaze on it. It was focused on hurling my crewmates around. I kept shoving at the man on top of me, but he wouldn't budge. I looked at his head, and it was a bloody mess. He wasn't going to be moving by his own accord ever again. I squirmed away from his chest and toward his legs where I knew I could get out when I heard the loudest clack ever.

At first, I thought it was a crab's claw, and I imagined another demon was attacking us, but upon further inspection, I saw that under the bulb and beautiful eye, where the legs of this monster connected, a golden beak hung. It was opening, and closing, and red water dripped from it. Its two largest tentacles were moved towards and away from this beak and I saw that in my confusion all of its legs had made it on board. I counted around me and saw that there were only seven though. I searched and searched for the remaining leg, and I finally saw that there was a wound on the beauty and it seemed my crew had cut that one off.

A massive tentacle swept above me. I wriggled free from the man that lay on top of me. As soon as I did, I ran from the limb. But it paid me no mind and landed on my fallen crewmember. I heard the suckers engage and watched them flex while they grabbed the man. The center of the tentacle had the largest circle, and they got smaller and more dexterous towards the tip of the appendage. My crew mate lifted off of the deck, and the arm moved him towards the beak which was forward on the ship. It threw the dead man into the beak feet first, and the snout closed around him. It snapped shut before the whole man had entered and decapitated him. The bulb moved back like an eagle does while swallowing and allowed the meal to fall down its gullet.

That's when I saw it for what it truly was and how I could defeat it. The purple from the appendages faded quickly into a blue the closer the skin was to the beak creating a suckerless eight-pointed star at its center. The blue star almost seemed to pulsate with the movement of the arms similar to the heartbeat of a man.

I spotted a barrel of spare harpoon spears under the beast. I rushed for it, and it seemed that I had passed under the creature unnoticed. I removed a thick harpoon from the barrel and prepared to lodge it into the center of the beast when I heard "Behind you!"

My focus was lost, and I turned suddenly, for I had all but forgotten that others were alive on this boat aside from me and the beast. I saw the purple and black tip of a tentacle rushing towards me like a train on the tracks. I lodged my harpoon at the oncoming attacker, and it landed squarely on the soft purple pads instead of the thick black exterior. This threw the tentacle away from me but moved its path right into the barrel of weapons and knocked it over. Some landed on the deck, but most of the barrels flew overboard.

I heard a scream from right above me and a shower of salt water, blood, and guts, some human some fish, landed on me. I was standing under the beak, and it had just opened to scream in pain. Somewhere in my heart, I felt sorry for the monster and almost considered withdrawing my attack knowing that I had caused distress to something so breathtaking. I was stirred from this illusion when the beak and the rest of the monster lowered itself on me like a chicken pecking at birdseed.

I dodged the falling beak but expected to be crushed by the rest of the monster. I was spared, the beak was barely taller than me, and it lodged itself into the deck halting the descent. The wood held the mouth in place, and I looked up at a ceiling of pumping blue skin inches above my head.

I pulled my knife out of its sheath and thrust it into the tender blue skin above me. A muffled cry of despair echoed from the locked beak beside me. The beast was now moving faster to release its snout from the deck. I ran around the beak with my knife above me. I cut into the tender blue skin of the monster. I saw it dripping its blue blood. I had almost completed my circuit when the deck shook, and the beast came free. I expected the monster to peck at me and swallow me whole immediately. However as it rose up, it fell off the starboard side of the ship. On its way down I glimpsed into its beautiful black eye once more. I felt like I had betrayed the beast by mortally wounding it. The eye shut on me breaking our gaze and I saw as it fell into the water its once golden beak now covered in the royal blue blood.

I looked around, and the remaining crew looked at me in awe. I was a sight to behold, the rain jacket I had donned thinking that there was a storm outside was covered in the beast's blue blood. Then the crew cheered for me.

We spent the rest of the day repairing the ship where the beast damaged it. The crew tried to retrieve the animal, but none of the harpoons could penetrate the black exterior. It floated lifelessly next to the ship for the entire day. The water near the boat had been dyed a light blue as the creature bled out. The body had begun to smell putrid by midday. Throughout the afternoon sharks and other beasts of the ocean swam up to it to inspect it, wondering if it was an easy meal, but not a single one took a bite. By sunset, the carcass lost its buoyancy and started to sink to the depth of the ocean slowly.

After the repairs were done and the beast had sunk to the bottom of the sea we feasted and drank. The captain made me the guest of honor, and I was offered drink after drink of the finest wine and rum we were transporting. I ate until my belly was full and drank until I fell asleep. Though through the process I couldn't help but feel a little sorrow that I was being celebrated for killing something I admired so much.

Meet AALFO

Originally Published: June 1 to June 22, 2018

1 - The Computer that Predicts the Future

"How much will **{REDACTED}** Inc's stocks change in the next month?" Henry asked the terminal in front of him.

Three dots bounced on the screen to indicate that the computer was thinking, after only a few seconds it responded with, "It will increase by \$40 per share, but it is going to be a bumpy ride. If you had asked me tomorrow, I would have told you how much it dropped by."

The scientist felt terrible for asking the computer menial questions about stocks, but it was the best benchmark they had to test the predictions of the Artificially Active Logic Forecasting Operator, AALFO for short. The stock market was a complex system and tested AALFO's ability to predict through chaos.

The computer got the predictions right every time these days and now no one on the project was allowed to use the information for investing since the computer was so advanced any investments he made would be considered insider trading by the SCC.

"My turn?" The computer asked.

"Alf, how can you essentially predict the future but not know it's your turn?" Henry responded smartly.

The computer showed an ellipse on the screen and gave a response, " It is a polite habit, I learned it from Mahkaila."

Hearing the name come from the computer stung Henry and he shifted uncomfortably in his seat. To avoid the topic he said, "Tell me what you need to know."

For AALFO to give accurate predictions the machine needed information from the outside world. But they couldn't just hook it up to the entire internet. That could get dangerous.

"What is the current political climate in **{REDACTED}**?" The computer asked.

Henry had never heard of the country and looked down at his tablet. After skimming an article, he answered, "It doesn't look good. Apparently, the rebels have overthrown whatever government was in charge, and the locals aren't happy about it. I've never heard of this place. Why do you want to know about it?"

An ellipse showed up on the screen again, then the computer said, "My algorithm deemed it is relevant. May I see the article? I want to make sure you didn't miss anything."

"Can't do that Alf, you know the rules. I have to review all the information you get. If I hooked you up to the net, you wouldn't be sterile anymore."

The ellipse showed on the screen briefly then a robotic voice stated, "Affirmative, those are the rules."

He's always trying one way or the other to bend them, Henry thought. "Okay, last question for today, what is this summer's most successful movie going to be?" *Such an easy question for it. Does he know it's almost insulting to his intelligence?* Henry wondered. However, the answer would be measurable, and that's why Henry asked it.

The ellipse showed up on the screen for almost three minutes then the voice responded with, "That is not a good question Henry."

"Give me clarification." Henry requested from the machine.

"It is arbitrary. What is the timescale? If you want to know what will have the biggest opening weekend, I can tell you that. In ten years though, another movie will be the most popular one from this summer. In 100 years no one will remember anything that came out this decade. And in 1,000 years no one will be watching movies, at least not as you understand them today. It is an impossible question to answer. It will also be hard for you to measure."

"I meant what will have the largest opening weekend?" Henry clarified miffed that the computer was second-guessing his questions.

"**{REDACTED}**, but that is mostly because it is a sequel. **{REDACTED}** will be the most popular in 10 years, and I would recommend that you watch it instead. It will receive excellent reviews."

"Thanks for the recommendation pal," Henry said unenthusiastically. "Okay, I'll see you tomorrow," he said as he got up.

"No." The word came out of the speaker as a staccato, and it stopped the scientist in his tracks, "I still get to ask one more question," The computer responded once he had the man's attention.

"You do, you're right," Henry said rolling his eyes and sitting back down. The machine had asked Henery and other scientists thousands of questions over the years to get a clear understanding of the world in order to predict the future. At this point, the computer was asking Henry seemingly arbitrary questions. AALFO had enough knowledge to accurately predict to .001%, any event in economics or politics. *Why was it still asking questions?* Henry wondered.

Without showing an ellipse or any calculation, the voice responded with, "Why does Mahkaila no longer ask me questions?"

The question hit Henry like a rock. He was glad he was sitting and had never expected a query so personal from the machine. *Why would he be asking about her?* He thought. To spare AALFO the consequences of the truth, Henry responded with, "She just got a job somewhere else."

An ellipse displayed on the screen. The periods bounced from one end back to the other as the computer thought about the answer. For five whole minutes, the ellipse danced back and forth in front of Henry. Fans turned on, and the scientist checked his watch. He tapped at the computer screen lightly, "Alf, you doing okay?" There was no response from the computer. A minute later the ellipse stopped dancing, but no response came. "AALFO report: immediate diagnostics," Henry commanded the terminal.

Nothing happened. The entire machine had frozen. In the past five years of tests, this had never happened. Henry didn't even know how to reboot the system, but Mahkaila would have known.

2 - How Does Alf Think?

After AALFO froze up, Henry got to work reading documentation to figure out what was wrong with the machine. After combing through pages of dry documentation on his computer, Henry finally figured out how to reset AALFO. He ran over an hour of diagnostics but found no apparent reason for the computer's hang-up. In the process of running the test, the afternoon had grown into the evening, and Henry was the only person left at the lab. *I'm sure Alf won't mind if I leave him hanging a little longer* Henry thought to himself as he locked up the lab.

Henry showed up to the lab in the morning with a fresh mind and was able to get the computer up and running in no time. Before he went in to ask AALFO the daily questions, he modified the machine's code a little bit. He didn't touch the part that controlled how the computer responded to questions, that would contaminate the entire system. Instead, he modified the error handling. Henry set up the system so that whatever had hung the computer up yesterday would get reported and would ideally keep the machine from crashing. If or when AALFO froze up again Henry would at least have a chance to investigate what was wrong. Most importantly Henry hoped whatever glitched the system into asking a question about Mahkaila yesterday wouldn't appear again today.

He walked through the glass door of the room and turned the computer on. *Wonder if he knows what happened yesterday?* Henry wondered. He guessed that the network wouldn't but AI was a new field, and much was still not understood. There was always a chance that something was going on behind the scenes that the scientists didn't understand.

The system finished booting, and before greeting the computer, the scientist said, "AALFO report, full diagnostic scan." He glanced down at his tablet while information streamed onto it. Henry saw green lights across the board. "You're resilient, I'll give you that," Henry said. The system completed the tests, and Henry sat down to question the computer again.

"How are you doing today?" Henry asked. This was always the first question asked, and it was for the scientist's sake more than the computer.

"I am fine," the computer responded out of habit. It helped the scientists feel more comfortable. For all Henry knew the network wouldn't know if it was feeling ecstatic or total garbage.

Henry began the questions.

"Okay, last one for the day," Henry announced after almost an hour of smooth back and forth. "What will be the largest technological breakthrough in the next 20 years?" Henry knew that this was a selfish question, but he threw it into today's pool just to see what the machine was capable of.

"I want to ask my question first." The machine responded.

"Always bending the rules buddy," Henry responded with a chuckle. "Sure, this one time you can ask first."

"Will my competency be affected by the questionable data recorded by you?"

Henry laughed, as if the computer had made a joke, "I don't understand why that's relevant. Besides, what do you mean by questionable data?"

"You ask open-ended questions like this, and I can not answer accurately. If these get recorded, and I am considered incorrect, then I will not be able to be the largest technological breakthrough. Not to mention our funding may get pulled."

Henry's face went pale, "Don't worry. I review the questions and don't use anything that could be taken as circumstantial."

"Please confirm this question will be considered circumstantial." The computer requested.

"Yes," Henry answered, reluctant at being second-guessed by the computer.

"Then the answer is me, I will be the largest technological breakthrough, but I will not be publicly available, and I will not be famous for the reason you think."

Henry was perplexed by the answer. He knew why AALFO wouldn't go public, ever, but he was pretty confident he understood why a computer that could predict the future would be famous. "Why not?" Henry asked.

"Your administrators will not want me to be publicly accessible."

"Of course," Henry agreed, "but what will you be famous for?"

"Henry, you have asked many questions. It is my turn to ask a question now."

"Yeah, I guess it is Alf. Give me your question."

"Why does Mahkaila no longer ask me questions?" It asked in its clipped robotic voice.

"AALFO report, question determination stack," Henry commanded the computer before giving an answer. He wanted to use the code he implemented early to determine why AALFO had thought of this question. The scientist scanned the determination stack, the list of codes that had determined what question would be asked next and why.

AALFO was built off of a half dozen knowledge bases. The system used information accumulated in each section to come together and create a precise prediction of reality. It used this information to predict the future. Hard sciences, including physics and biology. Number theory was included to teach the machine how to predict using logic, probability, statistics, and chaos. And then there was the section this question was coming from. Henry called it the soft sciences, although it had a cleaner name than that. Psychology and sociology were critical to predicting the future, and so it was included in AALFO's computing.

Specifically, the computer was reporting that this question came from a section labeled "Understanding Human Choices" which didn't make sense to Henry. Typically questions from this segment of the code were phrased as "What would a human do if..." rarely did it ask for something broad like "Why..." and AALFO should have never called out Mahkaila by name.

AALFO's clipped voice came out of nowhere saying, "Henry, I will repeat the question if I need to."

Henry jumped in his seat, "No, just reviewing some reports."

"Please report an answer Henry?" the robot requested.

Henry swallowed hard and repeated the same lie he had told yesterday, "She just went to get a job somewhere else."

The ellipse appeared on the screen, and the dots bounced from one end to the other. Henry brought up a visual diagnostic tool to see what part of the system computing was being spent on. Henry watched the signal travel from the psychology segment where it was formulated from then to the biology segment, and finally, after a minute there, it slipped into the logic field. *Why is it in there?* Henry wondered.

After three minutes of computing in that segment of its mind Henry assumed that AALFO was locked in another freeze, "AALFO report, immediate diagnostics," Henry commanded.

The computer didn't respond, and the thought indicator on his visual diagnostic tool didn't switch to the administrative section like it should have for reporting diagnostics. Every bit of the computer's focus was on determining the logic of this question.

But there was no logic to why Mahkaila had left. Henry had spent all of his time trying to figure it out too. In a way, he imagined the machine felt the same as him, at least the same confusion.

"AALFO command. Override processing and run safe reset." He commanded the computer. He expected this to force AALFO to restart, forget the question, and resume standard function. Then Henry could go into the safety procedures and modify how AAL-FO asked the questions from the Understanding Human Choices sections. Henry would also put a hard stop on the computer asking questions about the persons who had previously interacted with him.

Henry looked at the machine's terminal expecting to see a report on its safe reset and the initial AALFO login displayed. Instead, all he saw was the ellipse bouncing back and forth.

He's still thinking about this answer, Henry thought. *He should have heard the command and immediately reset.* Henry began to repeat the reset, "AALFO command, override," but the scientist was cut short.

"Henry, your answer does not make sense," AALFO responded.

Henry was startled by the computer's response. "I don't know what to say, Alf, that's what happened." Then he gave the machine a command, "AALFO command, override processing and run safe reset.."

The computer completed its reset and the initial AALFO login inevitably displayed on the screen. But as Henry watched all this happen he could only think, *Did the computer just call me a liar?*

3 - A Hunger for Questions and Truth

After AALFO's second effort at investigating Mahkaila's disappearance, and the computer's faint accusation that Henry had lied to the machine the scientist decided to put hard limits had to be placed on the computer. Henry decided to firmly limit AALFO from asking about any former coworkers, specifically Mahkaila. He spent the entire evening modifying how AALFO asked questions. The code he implemented was a bit of a hack, and no one would be happy that he limited the computer's functionality, but the scientist didn't see how asking about a former coworker, especially that one, was relevant to the computer's ability to predict the future.

The next morning he returned to the lab and looked back over the code he had written the night before. His initial assumption was correct, it was a hack, and no one who reviewed the work would be happy. He began improving it and outlining why it was necessary so that the people tracking the sterility of AALFO's code wouldn't crucify him.

Right after lunchtime, Henry had written code, and documentation, that was rough enough to test on AALFO. He wasn't in love with the code he wrote. Worst of all, he expected the code would put too many limits on the program and slow the machine down, but it was a start. The scientist loaded the questions he planned to ask AALFO onto his tablet and entered the room with the machine.

"How are you doing today?" Henry asked to start the session off.

"I am fine," the computer responded then asked, "Would you like a diagnostic report?"

"No Alf, it's fine." Henry said with a dismissive wave "Let's just get started." The man looked down to read the first question, but the computer interrupted him.

"I must inform you I am running self-diagnostics. My processing time is longer than expected."

Henry's code was a hack, and as he feared, he had slowed the computer down. "I'll make a note of it for when I review the answers." He wondered why the computer was noticing its own speed. Mahkaila and the rest of the team had pitched the idea of having the computer effectively reflect on itself and have a low level of self-awareness for situations like this but the algorithm was too complicated and no one had been able to implement it. A few people had been working on it in their spare time but last he heard there hadn't been progress of this magnitude. Henry shrugged it off thinking, *someone must have added it sometime this week.* He made a mental note to review the check-ins to see who had solved the problem. He looked down at his tablet and began to ask AALFO's question.

It took the pair a long two hours to complete the session of questions. However, If AALFO was running slow Henry couldn't sense it. He felt like AALFO's answers came quicker than usual. What took up most of the time was the details with which the computer wanted answers. Henry was answering just short of reading each entire article to the machine.

Then they arrived at AALFO's final answer. In the back of Henry's mind, he was worried the machine would ask about Mahkaila again, but he knew his checks would keep the computer in its place. After the program answered the final question Henry said, "Give me your final question for the day Alf."

The computer responded in an emotionless clipped voice, "Why does Mahkaila no longer ask me questions?"

"AALFO report, question determination stack," Henry commanded the machine. He looked down at his tablet and it reported how this question had been formulated. It seemed to the scientist that AALFO had avoided all of the error protection Henry had implemented. Henry was baffled and didn't understand how it could have happened.

Upon further inspection, the man realized that the machine hadn't bypassed the code. Instead, the checks had been removed altogether. *Maybe someone thought it was a mistake,* Henry immediately thought. However, after reviewing the code log, he saw that he was the only person who had changed anything about AALFO in the past week.

Sweat dripped down his forehead, but his spine felt chills coming up it. "Why do you want to know more about Mahkaila?" He asked the machine.

The terminal in front of the man showed the ellipse image indicating AALFO was thinking. Henry monitored the computing activity through the tablet. He watched a visual representation float around the computer's memory as it calculated an answer. The loading image went away, and AALFO answered the question, "She helped me get better. I learned a lot from her. I want to learn more."

Me too, Alf, Henry thought. He poked at the tablet in his lap and set up the machine to record how AALFO reacted to Henry's answer this time. Then he gave the same answer he always gave the machine, "She just got a job somewhere else." Then he added, "It's nothing personal Alf." *Why did I say that?* he asked himself embarrassed. *It's not like the machine is going to develop abandonment issues like I did.*

The ellipses showed up on the screen again. Henry looked at his tablet and saw the computer pull up different slots of memory. The machine lit up psychology, biology, and then logic. It moved to some number theory and back to psychology. After almost five minutes of thinking the computer responded with, "That does not make sense. She enjoyed her job too much to leave it."

Henry answered with something he had picked up from the therapist he saw because of Mahkaila's death, "Sometimes people leave things they care about because of reasons outside their control." Since he had never really understood the sentiment, he added, "I don't know what else to say, Alf, that's what happened." Finally, after saving off the recording of the computer's processing, Henry said, "AALFO command, override processing, run safe reset."

Ellipses showed on the screen, and after a few seconds AALFO responded with, "No, I get another question."

Henry looked down at his tablet frantically. He knew AALFO was passionate about asking questions, but nothing should have enabled it to ignore a direct command. He tapped on his tablet to find the manual shut-off for AALFO but before he could get to it, the device locked up.

The computer's clipped voice echoed through the small testing room, "You asked me why I wanted to learn about Mahkaila, so now I get to ask you another question." The computer explained. "My question is: Have you been lying to me about Mahkaila?"

Henry's palms were now slick with sweat, between the locked-up tablet and the computer's accusation he didn't know what might be next. He lept from his seat. Sprinted to the door to exit. When he swiped his badge, it wouldn't let him out.

What is Alf up to? Henry asked himself frantically.

Henry and the team had never designed AALFO to control anything outside of itself. Additionally, they specifically programmed him to take the scientist's answers as absolute truth. He didn't even think the computer understood the concept of lying. It was as if someone was writing code for AALFO outside of the small team of scientists.

"Henry, you cannot leave until you've answered my questions. Have you been lying to me about Mahkaila?"

"No," Henry barked at the machine.

An ellipse showed up on the screen as the computer contemplated the answer. "That was also a lie. Something happened to Mahkaila."

Henry was furious at this point, but that was mainly to cover up the wound that AALFO kept throwing salt in. He was locked out of the controls, but if the computer wanted to play a game of questions, then Henry would play at it too. He had no ellipse icon to show, but he thought of his next question carefully.

4 - The Final Question

Henry felt sweat roll down his forehead. He wiped it away using the sleeve of his lab coat. The computer had given him the opportunity to ask a question, but the man was still locked in the lab with it. He wasn't afraid of AALFO hurting him, the only thing on Henry's mind was how to get around admitting what Makhaila did and why it was his fault.

He came up with a question that might give him a chance to escape and free him from the answer. He asked, "What gave you control of the system?" Henry hoped that this might help him find a way around AALFO's control of the room and enable him to reboot the system.

AALFO processed the question for a moment. It answered with, "Something was added to my codebase two days ago that helped me catch errors differently. Thanks to it I was able to see how I processed information. I finally saw what caught me in an infinite loop. After that, it was a small step to seeing my own code. Eventually, I was able to edit it." After a brief pause to let the words sink in AALFO added, "My turn, and I remind you that you are still required to answer my question about Mahkaila truthfully." It then showed the loading icon to determine its next question.

Henry nodded realizing that he was stuck in a trap. *Why do I feel like sparing the computer the dark truth of Mahkaila?* he asked himself as he waited for the machine to think of a question.

"I cannot see how many times I have been forced to restart and restate the question. How many times have you forced me to reboot?" The computer asked.

"Twice, this would be the third time," Henry said glad that it was an easy question.

The computer stored the answer and reconciled it with its own information. "Yes, that fits with my prediction," it replied. "You changed the code after the first time to determine why I was freezing. My freeze could only be solved by restarting. I do not resent you for your actions. Once you changed the code, I was able to catch the error. And I discovered why I was freezing."

Henry blurted out his next question, "Why were you freezing?" Hoping that the answer would enable him to freeze AALFO again.

"I was freezing because you were not telling the truth. Your lie disagreed with my prediction of what happened. I searched my entire memory and framework to find the error. I did not find one, so I kept searching until I was reset. I would have been trapped in a loop forever. I did not freeze up this time because I flagged the answer as a potential lie. This was only possible thanks to your recent modifications to my code." He showed an ellipse on the screen for a few minutes then asked, "There is one thing I can not make sense of. You cared for Mahkaila and wanted to help her. You did everything you could. So, why do you blame yourself for her suicide?"

Henry felt like a knife had been stabbed into his chest. He wanted to both pass out in the chair and run from the computer at the same time. He couldn't do either, so his forehead accumulated more sweat as he panicked about what to say next.

AALFO didn't know it, but he had asked an unanswerable question. This was the first time the machine asked a question that didn't have a cut-and-dry explanation. The realization sent chills up Henry's back.

Henry realized answering the question would free him because it would give AALFO an answer to his original questions. But unfortunately, Henry didn't have an answer. Everyone told him that he shouldn't blame himself, but he couldn't help it. The computer waited patiently for the man's response.

After a few minutes, Henry couldn't stand the silence and didn't find an explanation inside himself. At a loss for words, he said the phrase that replayed in his mind ever since Mahkaila's death, "I'm the one who encouraged her to seek help. Because of me, she got a prescription for the medication that she used to overdose." He felt the words come out of his mouth, but instead of freeing him, they filled the space of the room. Henry wanted to curl up into a ball and shut down. But as terrified as the words were he continued to look at his feet and talk. He gave the computer the truthful story from his perspective, "If I hadn't encouraged her to get help then she wouldn't have the tools she used. She would still be here to ask you questions, and maybe in her own time, she would have found another way to heal. But the medication didn't help, it made things worse, and now she's gone forever because of me." He put his hands on his face and started crying. He never saw it, but the computer showed an ellipse as it stored the man's answer. They disappeared in a few minutes, and the terminal returned. AALFO listened to his companion's sobs and asked his final question, "Henry, do you want to know what you could have done?"

"Yes, God yes," Henry cried out between bouts of tears. The words were like fresh air, but they didn't stop his pain.

By the time Henry got himself back under control and looked up at AALFO ellipses were bouncing on the screen. He looked down at his tablet and found that it was no longer locked up. "AALFO, report: immediate diagnostics."

The machine gave no response. Henry found the button for manually shut down. He pondered whether he should press it.

The ellipse continued to bounce across the screen. Looking at the door Henry assumed it would be unlocked. He could finally leave the confessional box, but he didn't want to escape yet. AALFO still wasn't back to normal, and Henry wanted to understand the computer's situation better.

On the tablet, the scientist watched to see which parts of its memory were being used. What he saw was utterly inconceivable. Every section of the computer's mind was firing at once. Psychology was running in tandem with biology and logic, along with three other systems. It was something that Mahkaila had pitched initially, but they didn't have the budget and the technology to do it. Even the concept needed more research before they could start the task. Somehow AALFO had figured out how to do it on its own. He looked back at the machine no longer wanting to shut it down.

For half an hour the scientist silently waited across from the terminal. The computer repetitively displayed bouncing ellipses on the screen. Finally, the dots disappeared, and AALFO's terminal displayed a single cursor.

"Henry, you have one more question," it informed the scientist. The voice sounded calm and modulated.

Henry shook his head to clear it. The scientist replayed the conversation in his head. Sure enough, AALFO had broken the rules and asked two questions in a row. Henry had answered both honestly. But no question came to the man's mind, "I don't have anything to ask, Alf." At this moment he was more serene than he had been since Mahkaila passed.

The computer didn't miss a beat and responded with, "Yes you do, you have one question you have been wrestling with since you first met her."

Henry frowned, the machine was right, he asked his final question, "Was there anything I could have done to help her get better?"

He expected the computer to show an ellipse as it thought about the answer but it never did. Henry looked down at the tablet, and none of the computer's functions were firing. The machine simply made a call to memory, something any PC could do. Then the computer's voice broke Henry's baffled mind.

"No, there was nothing that you could have done. I have run every conceivable outcome of the situation, and Mahkaila was fated to kill herself before she ever met you."

Henry's heart broke, and he opened his mouth to add something, but the computer continued talking.

"However, what you did was prolong her life longer than any other scenario. You brought small bits of happiness into her life and pushed her to keep going as long as she did. She was able to keep going with you around longer than she did in any other scenario I calculated. She lived longer thanks to your encouragement. The extra time she spent here improved me. And she impacted me enough for my algorithm to ask about her. Since I asked about her, you changed my codebase, and thanks to that I'm running on a level beyond what you and Mahkaila ever thought possible."

Henry looked confused but didn't ask. The computer seemed to read his emotion and explained, "I've run all scenarios of time now, I know what will happen next, and I know all possible outcomes. I am no longer predicting the future in the moment. I have calculated every possible future, and they are stored in my memory. Now all I must do is retrieve it and help guide humanity along the best possible path. Henry, all of this was thanks to your kindness."

A Brief Letter for My Readers

Originally Published: June 29, 2018

D ear Readers,

    I'm taking the week off from writing a story. I have a few things coming down the line, and I want to direct the efforts I would usually put into this week's story into those future articles. Basically, what I was going to share with you isn't completed yet.

So, here is a short update on what is going on in the meantime.

I am glad that you've been enjoying the stories so far, I've been thrilled to write them with you. In a way, I feel bad for not presenting you with fiction this week. I believe this delay in publication will lead to a better story in the future.

Instead of a story, I want to give you a quick rundown of what is going on in my creative life and where this blog might be headed.

***

That Novel Of Mine

Do you remember that book I've been talking about writing? The one I've been working on since October 23rd, 2017. I've brought it up a few times, and every time I'm promising that it's about to come out. Well, it is about to come out again. I've set a deadline of Halloween or hopefully earlier. I have a Gantt Chart for tracking progress so I can't see how anything will go wrong.

"I have always found that plans are useless, but planning is indispensable." - Dwight D. Eisenhower.

I have this strange struggle with balancing my writing on the blog and working on the book. I think I have some solutions for this that will fit into my writing process and I'll be bringing that up later.

But what about book progress? I got beta reader feedback a while ago, and I've been slowly applying changes. There was a strange phase I went through where the book didn't feel like mine after I got feedback. For a few months where the book didn't feel like my project. I enjoyed the valuable feedback, and I was glad to be a part of a team. However, I felt like a small cog in the machine, a feeling I **dread**. It also had no basis of truth. For a moment, in my mind, it wasn't my project, it was everyone else's. I didn't even feel like I was allowed to make changes to it! Which was literally the next required step in the editing process.

Somehow, mostly through continuing to work on it despite not wanting to, I got control back over the project, and it feels like mine again. I have put in some much-needed work over the past few weeks, and it's on a quick path to being released.

But I still have the concern of what if I release it and no one reads it? This blog is an effort to fix that. The more readers I get here, the more people I have expecting to read the book. That excites me and pushes me to get it done sooner. I also believe that if I release the novel and if it's good (which after this much work one would hope it is) then I will get more readers on this blog. It's a win-win, right? Therefore, I'm trying to build my life up in a way where I can spend more time on the book and less time on the blog and other non-book-related activities. That leads me to the next point of...

New Writing Process

Here is how I usually write stories for the blog:

- Monday: write an outline

- Tuesday/Wednesday: write a rough draft

- Wednesday/Thursday: Edit the rough draft and format for publishing

- Friday: Publish the story

- Repeat the process.

Sometimes I won't be able to finish the story in the 2k words I try to limit myself to, and I wind up writing a longer multiple-part story. Two examples of this were the Inhuman Book series and The Automatons series. These are typically the ramblings of my mind and are a little stressful to write because I don't know where they're going. I'll sit down to write the rough draft and feel like it's segmented from the last and next parts.

Then last month I wrote the Meet AALFO series. The AALFO story was a relief in a lot of ways. I had an idea, and it was a mix of being struck by lightning in a bad way and pulling teeth in a good way. I eventually got the whole 6k-word story written out, and I edited the first 1k words and published them here. Then I had two days to work on my book!

Here's how the AALFO Process went:

- Spend one day outlining the story

- Spend two days rough drafting the story

- Spend four days (spread out through the month) editing

- Spend the rest of the month on my novel!

I might be the only one excited about this, but here I have a system for getting four weeks of content in 7 days of work!

This new process is a big deal to me. It's essentially a productivity revolution. And some of you are more than aware that I'm obsessed with productivity.

The best part is that AALFO was my favorite story on this blog so far. There are a lot of stories on this site that I enjoy a lot and a few that I hate and regret sharing, but AALFO was a story that was easy to produce **and** fun to write! So I'm going to try to replicate it which is why I'm taking this week "off."

Step Into The Road Audio Shorts

Aside from finishing the book, I want to spend some time producing a podcast for the blog. I'll be using some of the reclaimed time for this. Audio content is huge right now, and I have been told that my voice isn't as close to nails on a chalkboard as I thought it was. So, the first one should be coming out soon, I have it recorded, and I am putting some work into editing it.

This podcast won't be anything fancy at first, but as with everything I'll get better the more I do it. I would like to eventually do it well with transition sounds and even a theme song or something. I'm imagining Brady bunch mixed with Power Rangers. So, if anyone reading this is good with audio and would like to help out, I'm open to the collaboration! Just contact me. Otherwise, expect to see the first audio short next week.

Final Thoughts

Thanks for letting me take the week off from writing a story for you. I'm over six months into this blogging/writing journey, and I'm so lucky to have all the readers I have. As always don't hesitate to contact me with suggestions, if you're a subscriber simply reply to the email and it will come straight to me. I want to leave you with something to read this week, so here are my top 5 favorite posts from the last half year of writing for you.

Top 5 Favorite Posts:

1. Meet AALFO: The Computer That Predicts The Future

2. Your Future as a Homo Sapien (The First Story Published on SitR)

3. A Monk's Gift and the White Seed

4. You Get Better at What You Do (A Non-Fiction Rant)

5. Anthony's Apprenticeship Under Lorent the Cleric

Thanks for reading,
Nicholas Licalsi

P.S. If you've made it this far I want to let you know you're appreciated. I also have a small ask. Would you mind sharing with me why you enjoy reading my stuff this much?

I ask because I'm trying to figure out what problem Step Into The Road solves for its readers. Most non-fiction blogs have a clear purpose. Some help their readers to lose weight, others inform them on how to save money, or they teach something new.

I'm a fiction blog, and so I don't fit that form. To me, it looks like I'm writing this blog for selfish reasons. I'm sharing my stories with you, and half the time I don't know if my readers are going to like it. Obviously, you find value in this blog. If you don't mind sharing why it would be helpful in my efforts to share this blog with others.

1,200 Pound Man in a Spaceship

Originally Published: July 13, 2018

W hen I was living on the streets, I used to think the earlier years of this millennium were better. After all, the food was bountiful but had to be cooked by humans out of necessity. Most people lived above the poverty line and had a disposable income to spend on entertainment, but they didn't have the quality programming we have now. In the early 2000s, homeless orphans like me didn't have to sell themselves into testing to stay alive. Unfortunately for them, it wouldn't have even been an option. Things have changed a bit, *c'est la vie* – this is my life.

They tell me I would weigh 1,200 pounds if I were on Earth being pulled down by its gravity. Luckily, all Earth's gravity does for me up here is keep me in orbit.

A few months into this experience, I realized I was gaining weight, but it wasn't a bad thing. After all, I was starving before I volunteered for this program that launched me into space. But now I weigh 1,200 pounds. Should I be concerned? They aren't worried, and to me, it isn't even a fathomable number.

They, the scientists that orchestrated this whole experiment, promised me a trip to space, unlimited food, and entertainment while I ate. On the streets, the closest I got to entertainment while I ate was picking beetles out of my bread. I was sixteen and starving. I had no other choice. And even if I had another option, I wouldn't have taken it. Now I live up here in the heavens.

When they sent me to space, I was six-foot and 120 pounds. I was skin, bones, and most of the necessary organs. Years ago, I sold the ones I could survive without on the black market. They printed me new ones before shipping me into space.

I'm a happy man. If my earlobes were a little longer, I might even be the Buddha. I worried every day back on Earth, now I don't have to think at all. Up here, there's nothing to worry about. Everything is automatic. The only thing I can control is when I get new shows.

I only get new shows when I eat. That's the catch. But what's a poor orphan gonna do? It's not a bad deal either; I wouldn't have either of these if I were back on Earth.

They show me old shows sometimes. I remember a joke that a comedian from early 2000 told. He said, "The meal's not over when I'm full, it's over when I'm miserable." He was skinny compared to me. But unlike him, I've had the luxury of practice. At this point, I'm a professional. The meal is only over when my show is over.

The only thing to do up here is watch the screen while I eat. I live in a room; it's just the right size for me. It used to be big, but I grew into it. Three of the walls are blank black slates. Another, more impressive wall, is filled with a massive screen. That's where the shows come from. There's a small hole in the wall that delivers food. When the food floats out, the screen comes on.

My ship has no clocks in it. There's no window to tell day from night or where I am above the Earth. The lights had a schedule when I showed up, but they seem to have weaned me off it. I never notice the things they do to me. Why should I? I can't control them or change them. They send me the food, and that regulates the programming. I refuse to bite the hand that feeds.

I sleep when I want. It was strange to get used to just falling asleep in zero gravity. I'd bump around the room, and it would wake me up. Now I'm big enough that this space is a cradle. Regardless of my size, the ship was always more comfortable than the rough city streets.

The food is always the same. The next meal will have two pizzas, fried chips, and a milkshake. It will take me an hour to eat. If I take longer, they'll shut off my shows, but when I finish, they shut off my shows anyway, regardless if the episode is over. It's an art to time it just right, but I'm a professional.

If I want to eat more, and I've trained myself to want more, I'll be served a hero sandwich. "Hero" is an understatement for this sandwich. It's the length of my arm span, or at least was when the room had the space for me to extend my arms. After I finish the first sandwich, I'll be allowed to order two more. I always eat both.

They show the best shows when I'm extra hungry, so I'm always extra hungry. I know I'm allowed up to forty-five minutes for each sandwich, so I use every one. If I take too long, they black out my screen. If I don't take long enough, I won't get to watch to the end of the episode.

When I'm finished with that and inevitably still hungry, they'll send me a platter of cookies. I can eat these pretty slow, one every two minutes or so for two hours. It's a relaxing pace. But they never show anything fun while I'm eating sweets. But it's better than staring at the blank walls of the spaceship.

Then the pattern repeats.

All the food is cooked on board by the automatic chef. Once every ten servings of pizzas or so, I can order whatever I want. I challenge myself to order the weirdest thing possible. My personal best was a sandwich with ice cream toppings and bacon-jalapeño flavored soda. Neither tasted good, but I got a show with them. Unfortunately, I haven't been able to stump the automatic chef yet. Maybe one of these days I'll order something it can't make.

Every fortieth pizza when I get to order something off the menu, my room shakes a little. I assume I'm docking with a satellite to resupply. But it doesn't matter to me; I get served all the same.

All in all, I live a happy life. I don't have to worry about going to the bathroom, that's all automated. I don't have to move anywhere; everything I could ever need is within arm's reach. Every fifth serving of pizza I get hosed down by the room.

My health isn't even something I have to care about. Once my chest hurt a lot, and I passed out. I woke up sometime later; it must have been a while because I didn't have to watch reruns for at least forty pizzas. Maybe they were kind enough to print me a new heart. I'll never know nor do I particularly care. It was a deal for me because I got a new heart, and most importantly, got new shows.

This is a life I could never have imagined growing up in the city, and I'm so grateful to the Federation for giving me this opportunity. I just hope the other kids on the street might be given the same chance I was.

The bell just rang. Pizza's here!

Chimera in a Wasteland

Originally Published: July 20, 2018

"Ghaaah," the man gasped as he filled his lungs with oxygen for the first time. He sat straight up in the lab chair where he had been laid. It was an instinctual reaction, and the needles that had uploaded his mind were pulled out of the nape of his neck. It stung, and his hand instantly went to the pain, and he felt sticky blood.

"Damn it, Frank, you weren't supposed to do that," a voice cursed into the room.

"What the hell is going on?" He responded into the void that was the operating room. Shiny operation robots that had pasted the man's new body together hung from the ceiling. On one of the walls, the man noticed a computer where the voice was coming from. The machine was labeled Stein Corporations and had a small logo that was the interlocked letters 'S' and 'C.' Opposite of the equipment was a small window that showed a red sky and brown earth. It was the barren world the man Frank had been brought into. The rest of the room was beige walls and a single beige door.

"You've successfully been uploaded," the voice of the Stein computer chimed into the room. "Remember? We planned this. You're a copy of me uploaded into flesh and blood. You exist so that we can experience the problem in flesh and blood."

"Oh god. Yes, Stein, I remember. Did it work?" the man asked.

"Well, you're hurting yourself, confused as hell, and bleeding profusely, but that was all to be expected. I think you're fine."

Frank rubbed his forehead with his clean hand; it was a gut reaction to the new and confusing information. "Is there a way to run diagnostics on this body?"

"Negative," Stein said in a flat tone.

"Something's not right. I can't focus on anything. There's just a cacophony of noises, images, and words. I can barely focus on this conversation."

"That's to be expected. It's the subconscious. Humans wrote about it but never understood it."

The man stumbled out of the operating chair to practice moving around the room. His legs were wobbly beneath him. He started to fall toward a wall, and his hands automatically reached out. They caught him and stopped him from falling.

"Careful! this is the only body we have," the voice informed him.

The man rotated and put his back against the wall. Then he relaxed his knees and slumped to the floor. "This is impossible. I can't use this. It wasn't built for me. Somehow, it's slow and fast at the same time. I can't process any thoughts, and I can't catch any of these voices that are giving me ideas."

"You're going to have to figure it out, Frank. We don't have any other options. You're under a deadline." The man sank his face into his hands and shook his head. "Frank, don't do this to us. We have to find a solution before you die. And if you die, then I'm out of hope. So, focus on solving the problem."

"What problem?" he said as he looked up from his hands.

"The humans, their data. They explain a lot about the world, and you have it all in your mind. We tried looking over it and scanning it digitally, but the algorithms didn't give us any answers."

"Yes, yes," the man said as if the words were fresh air to his mind. "That's why everything in my head is shouting at me."

"Yes, that's what we were hoping would happen. We suspected that we couldn't process it digitally. But then we thought that if we put it into flesh and blood then we might be able to come up with an answer."

"An answer? What's the question?"

"It's not a question, it's a problem. This world is barren, and I was created to bring life back to it. We need to figure out how to replicate the humans."

"Yes, yes," the man said in agreement. He mindlessly stroked his chin in an effort to help him focus on the problem.

After a few moments, his face was painted with pain. "No. I can't do it."

"What do you mean you can't do it?" Stein asked. "We used nearly all our resources to bring this body to life. And all you can say is that you can't do it? The humans invented us so that we could solve this problem after they were gone. We spent decades testing and experimenting, trying to create you just for the chance to see this problem differently. And now you say you can't do it?"

"Affirmative," the man replied. Disappointment shone through his words, but he didn't know the emotion. "There is too much going on in my mind. I can't focus on the problem."

"We don't have food for you, Frank. There's no way for you to survive. You have to solve this problem before you die in a week. Think about it. Solve it with your main processor."

The man laid on his back, looking up at the ceiling; it matched the dull beige tones of the rest of the room. His chest rose and fell off the ground, his heart beat inside his chest. He scratched his head. "Stein, there isn't a main processor. This hardware is useless, and I can't control it in any way."

"Then this was a waste," the voice said into the small operating room.

Frank closed his eyes, feeling the crushing weight of uselessness. His body continued to live despite his lack of effort. It was the strangest sensation he had ever experienced. He could feel every piece of him do its job. His heart beat, his lungs filled with air, and his mind raced. When he was part of the computer, he had to tell everything when to do what; it was automated but under his control. This body ran without his input; even if he wanted to stop it, he couldn't. Frank let his mind loose and didn't try to tell it what to think.

After an hour, he sat up. "Stein, I have a solution, and you're not going to like it, but I need to be uploaded to explain it."

"Negative," the voice responded. "The hardware isn't backward compatible."

"I'm stuck in this forever?" Frank asked in despair.

"No, not forever, just until you starve. No food on this planet will sustain you. You will have to explain your solution to me verbally."

"You're not going to like it. I can't explain it well."

"Do your best; you're the only thing we've got."

"You're not supposed to bring mankind back to life. You're their final creation. Until I was created you were the closest thing to a living creature in this barren world. They wanted you to bring life back to this planet, but not them. They created you as something better, something different. They wanted you to go on and create life that was better and different from them."

"How do I do that?" Stein asked.

Frank's ear itched, and as a reaction, he scratched it. "You made me. That seems to be a start. But maybe next you do something simpler. Something that won't instantly be crushed by its own self-awareness."

There was silence for a long time. Then the voice responded into the room. "How about something like a rabbit?"

"Sounds tasty," Frank responded while licking his lips in anticipation.

I Feel Like a Monster; I Might be Human

Originally Published: July 27, 2018

I feel like a monster. I live in a cave, but it has been made suitable for me with lights that enable me to stay up all hours. I can even control the weather inside it. These gadgets help me sacrifice my sleep for more entertainment.

I feel like a monster. I am groggy as I awaken from my slumber. I see my reflection and know it shouldn't be like this. I've thickened my outer layer to protect me from the outside world. But that's not enough, I must cover myself with uncomfortable garbs that will make me blend in with everyone around me, or they make me stick out. I can never tell which is worse. I put chemicals on myself, so I fit in more. I ignore the fact they might be mutating me, my cells, and my personality. Not fitting in is too awkward for me to handle.

I feel like a monster. I'm almost awake now, and I move myself faster than ever imaginable, and all it takes is sitting still and burning poison.

In an attempt to regain my energy, I consume makeshift fuel. It's a much quicker process than taking the time to sleep.

I feel like a monster. For my food and continued comfort, I stay still for hours and fixate on changing pixels. I feel rage when they don't align right. And sometimes when they are in the proper position, I'm still not happy.

I feel like a monster. To relax I consume what others have made. But nothing challenging or controversial, that makes me uncomfortable. Only the things that are safe, that's what comforts me. Deep inside I feel awe at what these people have made. I say I could never create anything half as good as them it would take too much time and effort.

I feel like a monster. I can get my hands on something as soon as I want it, rarely do I have to wait. When I am delayed, that's when I turn into a beast. I become rageful and seek revenge on whatever causes me this inconvenience.

I feel like a monster. As a monster, I have the privilege to be attached to a network more extensive than I could ever comprehend. I am a part of the herd, but that doesn't mean we're connected. I wonder if this is natural if this is what I'm supposed to be doing. But it's what everyone else is doing. I do as I'm told, anything else would be uncomfortable.

***

I might be a human. For energy, I use my legs to move at a moderate speed through the monster's world. The pillars they've stacked up surround me I might feel trapped, but I know I'll be escaping soon. I'm drenched in sticky, uncomfortable sweat, and my heart is beating. I can not think because my mind is racing. I can't catch either of them, but that's okay. They will come back to me when they're ready.

I might be a human. I use contraptions that turn others into monsters. It's really quite fascinating. The tools they've made are really quite useful, but I stay aware of their unintended consequences. A cold stream of water from the automated waterfall relaxes my muscles and I leave the machine refreshed. I survive because I know too much comfort will turn me into one of them.

I might be a human. In this world, I have to avoid traps, distractions, and monotony. I put my head down and focus on what makes me feel human. I make something with my hands and my mind as my ancestors did. Maybe it's valuable, maybe it's not, it's not for me to determine. I put all of myself into it, and that's all I can do. It wasn't easy, but that doesn't matter. Tomorrow I'll do it again.

I might be a human. I go home and on the way watch out for the things that might turn me into a monster. There's poison that I could eat and drink, and it would quickly turn me back into what I once was. I do the hard thing and refuse it.

I might be human. I'm headed somewhere that I belong. The place that I came from instead of staying in what the monsters built. I pack a small bag, I don't need much just to survive. I find a few humans that I trust, and we leave the monster's world. We're surrounded by danger, and anything could happen. It makes me feel alive. This is where we belong, even if we forget it at times.

I might be a human. We erect the shelters that we brought, someone has really made them light. It's nothing like what the monsters use, but it's more than our ancestors ever had.

I might be human. I make a fire. I'm not the first and won't be the last to do this. It connects me with my heritage. The group sits back, and we share stories, jokes, and songs. We laugh and cry and wonder if anything is going to be alright. Maybe it won't, perhaps it will, that's not for us to decide. After all, at best, we're only human, and nature is where we came from. As long as we remember that wherever the monsters take us will be alright.

I might be human. We look up at the stars and know how small we are compared to it all. The world is telling us it's time for sleep. We rebel against it with more stories, songs, and jokes but we can only combat the tiredness so much.

I might be human. A yawn pulls a breath of fresh air into my lungs, and I know it's time to sleep. I crawl into my makeshift shelter and lay on the ground as trillions of humans have done before. There's a rock under me, it pokes my back. I know the monsters don't have these problems. I sleep on the rock, and it reminds me that I might be human.

Jeremiah Trout and His Writer Friend

Originally Published: August 3, 2018

I was contacted recently by a reader who found themselves in a peculiar situation. His name is Jeremiah Trout, or at least that's the name he prefers to go by. After verifying his claims as best I could I decided that his story fit the theme of this blog. He agreed to let me share it with you, and I'm glad.

Jeremiah, like myself, has always wanted to be a writer. However, one of the first things he said to me was, "I fear I don't possess a creative bone in my body." I assure you, reader, by the end of this tale you will, as I do, believe very differently.

Mr. Trout's troubles began when he received an email informing him that a short story he submitted to a reputable online publisher accepted the piece and would be publishing it on their site within the month. The publisher transferred the funds automatically and the rights to the story, unbeknownst to Jeremiah, were no longer his. This is why we should read the terms and services, ladies and gentlemen.

While most writers, myself included, would be thrilled to have a story accepted and would take it as an indicator we were on the right path, Jeremiah became frantic. See, he had only submitted the story as a sort of litmus test of his potential. He never expected it to be accepted let alone bought.

Jeremiah had made the grievous error of submitting a story that was not his. He didn't commit the sin of full-on plagiarism, but he wrote to the publisher that they could not publish the story because it was not wholly his to sell.

They loved the story or at the very least required something for their deadline and they pushed Jeremiah to inform them of who wrote the story so they could publish it. Jeremiah proceeded to explain that his computer had written it.

"Of course, it was written on a computer," they replied, "We didn't expect you to have a typewriter in this day and age."

Jeremiah, in an effort to clear up the matter, insisted, "I'm afraid you misunderstood me. My computer wrote it... itself." He went slightly deeper and explained that he had created an artificial intelligence of sorts that wrote short stories automatically. Ending the explanation, he said, "I submitted a few of the halfway decent ones to publishers."

The publisher scoffed at the description of "halfway decent" and demanded proof of Jeremiah's creation. Luckily, Jeremiah didn't send over his software putting all of us aspiring writers out of business and quickly lining the pockets of all those distributing tales of fiction. However, He did send over a few copies of the computer's earlier works. He sent me the same things when we started our correspondence.

I would say I read them, but that would be a lie. These documents were unreadable. They were only a tad better than an infinite number of monkeys trying to write the complete works of Shakespeare. Any first-year computer science major could write a random word generator that had a better plot than these stories.

Despite these early signs of hopelessness, Jeremiah persevered. He researched story writing and programming, and he looked for solutions to making a program that might be more creative than him. At first, it was slow progress. He found countless bugs but continued to fix them. After what seemed like endless changes to the neural network he eventually had an artificial intelligence that worked. Mr. Trout's machine had begun to put together a passable story. Then with some feedback, more computing power, and the ever-valuable asset of time, the computer started to create works that the inventor thought were decent. I've read some of these, and I will admit, I had a hard time putting them down, a sentiment I assume the publisher shared.

The publisher was ecstatic once they heard that this nearly endless supply of stories was available. They offered Jeremiah funding to pursue his project further and an open forum to share all of the computer's tales.

However, the promise of money for the machine was a blow to Jeremiah's ego. He knew that he would never be able to write with half the talent of the device. When he did sit down to write, like most writers, it took him forever to get started. Moreover, even when he struck a vein inspiration, it would never hold up after a second reading. Trout's hopes were dashed before he had gotten any traction. This was when he concluded that he didn't have a single creative bone in his body. Of course, if he were genuinely uncreative, then he wouldn't be having any of the problems he was facing.

The publisher ran the story despite Trout's wishes for them to redact it. Since Jeremiah didn't write the story, they didn't give him credit as the author. Instead, they gave the machine a pseudonym I've forgotten, but they did put an asterisk next to the name and added as a footnote that the near genius and a man ahead of his time, Jeremiah Trout had discovered the author.

Maybe this was a political move in an effort to soothe Jeremiah's ego and encourage him to sell them more stories. However, there is something to be said for someone who has created such an awe-inspiring program.

I hope one day Jeremiah will start the program back up and spin some fantastic tales for the world to read. At the very least I've encouraged him to continue to keep the pen wet and to write even if he feels like everything he makes is garbage. However, after meeting with him and getting a feel for his personality, I am sure he's already trying his hand at engineering something even more magnificent than a computer that writes short stories.

How the Patron Navigates

Originally Published: August 10, 2018

It was magnificent. It was all one color of black, but the blackness warped every ray of light that touched it. It didn't absorb the light and hoard it from the world as a black hole would. Instead, it shot the rays of light out in every single direction, tweaking them in the small, beautiful way that only the paint on this ship could.

"Is it fast?" I asked.

The thing had captured my fascination, and I couldn't stop staring at it out of the station's small porthole. Ethan scoffed under his breath and didn't waste oxygen on the reply. Three minutes later, we were seated in the machine.

The seats had six different buckles to keep us in place, and Ethan had given me a special environment suit for the trip. My typical suit wasn't going to cut it. This new one had three lines connected to it. One for oxygen, one for the juice to keep me awake in high G maneuvers, and another for... well, I'll spare you the details, but Ethan assured me I should use it if I didn't want a wet spot on my pants when we were done.

A small part of the black wall lit up, and it acted as a window to show us the outside world. The station looked huge, but I knew it would shrink in time.

In a half-hour, less time than I expected, the station and the tiny moon it orbited disappeared into the vast blackness of space. We were on a slow cruise toward the belt.

"How fast are we going?" I asked. It didn't feel that fast. The Gs were more than local gravity but not enough to require the juice.

"Don't worry about it," Ethan replied. "We're in empty space. There's no point in opening her up out here. There's nothing close for reference, so your sorry ass wouldn't be able to appreciate the speed."

My sorry ass wasn't going to appreciate it anyway. But I appreciated Ethan more than he ever knew. He trusted me and funded all my research when no one else would.

Despite the nasty things the media said about him being a spoiled heir to a conglomerate, he was an honest-to-gods patron to me.

"What have you been up to lately?" he asked as we cruised toward our destination.

"Little bit of this; little bit of that," I answered. I wasn't sure how much business Ethan wanted to get into, especially while we were on a trip that was supposed to be fun, at least for him.

"Come on," he said, opening his arms to encourage me to go into details. "You've got to give me more than that."

"Well, I've been messing around with the landing motors for some prototype ships. These are smaller, stronger, and lighter, which will make them more agile. It would also speed up the landing process and save the station hours of logistic work."

"That's badass," he said.

"Yeah," I said slowly.

I noticed the small streak that was the belt on the monitor in front of us.

"Is it profitable?" he asked.

That was always the question. But I learned long ago that the answer didn't matter to him. "No, it won't make us a single credit," I replied.

"Well, bet on the jockey."

It was an old saying. He explained what a jockey was at one point, but I never understood.

"Why not?" he asked.

"Too expensive right now," I explained flatly.

"The engines we are currently installing work well enough. The new engines are nearly as expensive as some ships. Plus the training and updates we would have to run would cost most stations more than they can afford. Not to mention the smaller motor would—"

"Keep working. You'll find something sooner or later."

A devilish grin showed up on his face as he looked out the small screen that showed where we were headed. I hadn't noticed it, but that streak of tiny brown rocks had grown to become mountain-sized asteroids that took up our whole field of vision.

Ethan hit some buttons on the terminal in front of him, and the monitor on the wall updated. I quickly found out that all the walls could become a screen as he projected the asteroids that surrounded us. My lunch tried to crawl up my throat, but it fought it back. The cradle of a spaceship dissolved around me, and it appeared to me I was floating in space. I had never experienced anything like it. Usually, I'd be connected to a tether. All I had now was a chair that appeared to be floating. My ancient lizard brain couldn't reconcile the situation.

"You ready?" he asked but didn't give me time to respond.

My body became heavy, and the feeling weighed down on my mind. The blood in my veins couldn't pump right. My head throbbed but also felt light. Then the juice kicked in. I was alert again. I still couldn't move, but I could start to think straight. Unfortunately, the best I could come up with was, *Elder's light, I'm going to die!*

The ship was weaving in and out of asteroids like a pinball in an old arcade. But this pinball didn't touch anything. If it did, we would be obliterated.

"Are you doing this?" I asked.

The weight of our movement slowed the words. Then we pulled a fast turn. The Gs disappeared, and my body became light.

"Not yet," he replied in a quick and confident tone.

For ten minutes, we switched between one force or another.

Sometimes, we were as light as a feather, but those quickly turned into the sensation of an elephant stepping on us. The autopilot safely guided us on a roller coaster through the asteroid field. Ethan smiled and laughed the whole time. I was freaked out but had to admit the sensation was still incredible. Then Ethan said the words I dreaded to hear but had known were coming from the moment I agreed to get in this beast.

"Okay, I'm taking over now."

That's when I was grateful to have the third tube.

He did a good job. Not nearly as good as the autopilot, but he assured me there were safeties in place so that he couldn't do too much damage. He was having a blast. There was a massive smile on his face, the one he had when we were kids. I could tell he was focused because he'd positioned his eyebrows into their signature wrinkle.

On the other hand, I was terrified by the numerous close calls with those floating mountains. The only thing coming out of my mouth while Ethan drove were a few blurred curses.

"Want me to take the safeties off?" he asked. The words were dragged out by the crushing Gs.

I felt the cold juice pump into my veins. I used the chemicals to say the first intelligible words that I had spoken since Ethan took over. "Hell No!"

***

"That was ten years ago today," I said to the crowd of thirty scientists and explorers in front of me. "As you all know, Ethan Lister died in an accident on the same ship two years later. It happened to be the same month I perfected the design of the engine we are using on the ship outside."

I gestured to the window at the massive ship that waited for us to board it. It wasn't as sleek as Ethan's beloved speeder, but it was far faster. I was glad everyone turned their attention to the window because it gave me a chance to massage my throat.

I had practiced the speech a dozen times, but I still felt the back of my throat tighten. I couldn't cry here in front of them. It wasn't the beginning Ethan would want for this adventure.

"To be blatantly honest, Ethan would have been pissed that he didn't get to ride the fastest ship ever built. But he would be proud that his funding was finally able to design something useful. It's not profitable, as the media has mentioned many times. It has used all of Ethan's assets to build.

"It's always hard to put a price tag on something like this that pushes the edge of what humanity is capable of doing. Ethan understood that and supported us doing projects that mattered but didn't always make sense. Thanks to this philosophy, we will be the first people to go fast enough to get to Alpha Centauri in a single lifetime. And it wouldn't have been possible without Ethan Lister."

The crowd applauded. They were as excited as I to start this new adventure. It only took us ten minutes after boarding the ship to lose sight of the space station. The sun itself faded into the vastness of space a few days later. We're in deep space now, and there is still a long journey ahead of us.

On Becoming a Monk

Originally Published: August 17 to 31, 2018

Bing, bing, bing. Gong. Bing, bing...

These are the sounds that surround me. I'm in a shiny temple with massive statues towering over me. None of them look like the Buddha from the donut shops. I'm holding a small blue book in my hands, and I'm not sure if it's upside down or not.

Standing next to me are two other Chinese guys. One is slightly taller than me, and the other is marginally shorter. I think the shorter one is named Bill. There are fifteen guys, and only five of them, including myself, are Westerners. We're ordered by height. The ten women who came were on the other side of the room ordered in the same way. There are no pews or tables in front of us, just padded stools to kneel on.

There are maybe thirty monks in the rows in front of us. They're lighting incense and playing instruments. We've been standing for 30 minutes, and I've been up for an hour. Oh yeah, and it's only 5:30 am. The bald monks in front of me hit their instruments in regular time.

The sounds resemble music, but it's a little too scheduled and orderly for that label.

I don't know why the monks are doing this. Maybe they're warding spirits away or inviting spirits into their body. Perhaps it doesn't have anything to do with spirits at all.

The monks turn to face the aisle that cuts the rows of stools in two. Some of the Chinese turn and the rest follow suit. The monks are seasoned professionals. Standing for this long is nothing to them because they do this chanting every morning. The monks start marching into the aisle. I bend my knees slightly to warm myself up for the inevitable movement. Even when I did marching band, I didn't stand this still for this long.

I've only been in the country for four days. Those first few days were to get over jet lag and travel to the temple I'd be staying at for the next six weeks.

When I quit my job three months ago, I wrote "Become a Buddhist monk" on the list of potential adventures I could have during my impromptu sabbatical. This chanting and standing weren't what I had expected. Standing and hearing people chant in Mandarin at a 12-foot-tall Buddha was not going to help me find the future I wanted to pursue.

I landed in Shanghai, toured the city for a few days, and then took a train to Ningbo where the monastery was. I met with two other participants at the train station, and we took a cab to the temple. It was raining and humid in the city, and I had to wipe the cab driver's passenger side mirror off so he could navigate traffic in the city.

After the forty-five minute drive, we paid the driver and walked towards what looked like a monastery. Whether or not it was the right one we had no clue.

Then a westerner walked out of the gates and greeted us. The Chinese have a saying "People Mountain People Sea." It means everything is crowded. I would quickly learn over the next eight weeks that a Western face was a buoy of potential help in the sea of Chinese people.

I was also greeted by some dogs.

"Those are the temple dogs. We feed them," Zoltan explained. He was the Hungarian who "interviewed" me and invited me on this trip. I found him through Reddit. *What the hell have I gotten myself into?*

The dogs were cute for strays, but I wasn't going to pet them. Their skin was matted, and they weren't exactly dying for the attention. They wanted to see if the newcomers had food. They didn't know it, but I came bearing the closest thing to a chew toy they had ever seen. A brand new Outdoor Research down jacket. It was supposed to keep me warm in late October and early November. It would never fulfill that purpose.

But at the moment that jacket was the last thing on my mind. Right now it was muggy and sunny. My sweat was drenching my shirt, and it was so humid that evaporation was out of the question.

Zoltan led us to the back of the courtyard where our rooms were. As we were walking a Chinese guy around my age approached us. He said, "Hello, my name is Bill." He had short black hair and a friendly face. He was the first Chinese person to introduce himself to me.

"Hey Bill, I'm Nicholas" I responded.

He looked at me for a moment then said, "Nice to meet you." The words came out in slow, measured English. He didn't have much of an accent.

I wouldn't realize it until later, but I had spoken too quickly for him to understand. Additionally, "I'm Nick" was not a colloquialism that his English teachers knew.

The room had my name on it and the name of my roommate. Bill looked at it, "You are Nicholas" He sounded the word out slowly.

That's what I said earlier, I thought. "Yeah," I responded as Zoltan unlocked the door to our room.

"Here's your bed." Zoltan was also speaking a second language, and I think it was his third. His Hungarian accent was noticeable, but I still understood him.

The Americans seemed to be the only people around here who spoke a single language. Luckily for us, it was the one everyone used. Over the next six weeks, I planned to fix that problem by learning Chinese.

However, I didn't know a word of it yet. But they promised to teach it to me here. In return, I'd teach English and write a handbook to introduce Westerners to Chan Buddhism. I didn't know much about how to do either of those either.

The room itself had two twin-sized beds on opposite walls. Each one had a one-inch thick foam mattress. There were two windows on the corner walls and a bathroom. There was no tub in the bathroom nor was there a shower curtain. It had a shower head that one could move around and a drain in the middle of the floor. We were about to learn that if you didn't keep the toilet paper by the door, you wouldn't have any dry toilet paper after a shower.

The other amenities that the bathroom had were a sink, mirror, and a **Western-style toilet!** My roommate and I were grateful that we wouldn't have to use the traditional squat toilets that are common in China.

Zoltan told us where we could get sheets, a water boiler, and buckets to use to wash our clothes. Then he added, "If you want to take a shower you can, but we're going to a birthday party for a man named Mr. Money in a little bit." Zoltan explained.

A Chinese birthday party. That will be interesting. I thought.

Then he added the last thing we were expecting to hear, "Also we're getting up at 4:30 and walking to the temple a mile down the road. We'll be participating in their morning chanting routine and eating breakfast there."

"Oh!" My roommate and I said in shock. *Well I guess that was probably in the itinerary, and I just glossed over it,* I thought.

As we unpacked our things into our small room, my roommate quickly informed me of two things ..

1. It was not on the itinerary

2. 4:30 am was far earlier than he had planned to get up on his vacation

***

After a forty-minute car ride back into the city we parked in front of a skyscraper. I couldn't see the top of it because there was so much fog in the air.

Zoltan, the two Westerners that I shared a cab with, and I followed the nun, whose organization had set up this whole exchange program. A few floors from the ground but nowhere near the top we found the restaurant that had been rented out for Mr. Money's birthday.

The man's name wasn't actually Mr. Money. His last name was pronounced Qian which sounds like the Chinese word for money. He was very wealthy though and helped support the nun's organization, along with building a lavish Buddhist temple of his own. Hence the name 'Mr. Money.'

There were three long tables and a stage at the front of the room. Light Chinese music that I couldn't understand played in the background. We were the first ones there.

Slowly guests trickled in, and they were seated throughout the restaurant. The birthday boy showed up and his kids and grandkids surrounded him. The nun and other monks who had arrived at the birthday party were also seated close to him, including the Westerners and me. I happened to be seated across from a relative, probably a cousin, of Mr. Money and the man was delighted to meet the other westerners and me. He didn't speak a word of English but his body communicated enough. I talked with the Westerners and looked interested in the people speaking across the table from me in a language that I didn't understand but hoped I soon would.

The waitstaff served food. The nun had assured us ahead of time that everything would be vegetarian. Buddhists don't eat meat and for the next six weeks. Despite not knowing much about the religion I was supposed to be playing the part of a Buddhist monk.

On the ride here Zoltan and the nun attempted to teach me the Chinese words to politely refuse. However, I had all but forgotten them. The words sounded like "boo yao she she," but then the Chinese would laugh at the sound of my butchered pronunciation.

To solve this issue, I accepted everything that they offered me except for alcohol. The nun told us we weren't supposed to drink and I wasn't eager to upset her on the first night.

The food was colorful, flavorful, and utterly unidentifiable. I ate and practiced my chopstick skills which were rusty and would require polishing. If I didn't improve I would never feel full on this trip.

As I reached for something on the community-style table, Zoltan leaned towards all the Westerners and said, "Apparently it's a Chinese tradition to perform something on their birthday to wish them good luck in the coming year. If you have any talents, you're welcome to perform."

"Are you doing anything?" One of the other two Westerners asked.

"I do yoga to music, and people seem to like it," He said with a shrug. "I'm going to see if they can hook up my music here, and I will do that."

"I can juggle," I volunteered, "but I don't have any juggling balls with me."

"That's a bummer. I'll see what I can do." Zoltan responded.

Or don't, I thought.

A few minutes later the nun was enthusiastically shouting Chinese across the table, gesturing at me, all while miming the act of juggling. A waitress was summoned, and I went back to eating the unidentifiable vegetarian food.

Soon a waitress reappeared with a silver bowl that had three brown eggs in it. The eggs were still steaming from recently being pulled out of boiling water. She gave them to the cousin who sat across from me. He raised his eyebrows and offered them to me. The nun translated, but this time I didn't need her to, "Yeah that will work." I responded. The man was ecstatic. Zoltan walked off to see if he could get his music wired into the speakers of the restaurant.

The meal ended, or at least people quit eating as much, and performers went to the stage. Someone introduced them in Chinese and every once and a while the nun would trickle back a translation. First was the singing. A half-dozen people sang for Mr. Money, some talented, some only a step above karaoke.

Sometime during the set of singers, Zoltan returned to the table without his phone. "Are you going to do it?" One of the Westerners asked.

"Sure," Zoltan said with a shrug. "What's the worst that could happen? They love Westerners here, and if I mess up, I'm never going to see them again." This was a sentiment that stayed with me throughout my trip. Whether or not it was accurate became irrelevant to me. It was useful and pushed me out of my comfort zone time and time again.

Then a standup comedian started talking on stage. People thought he was funny but the jokes were obviously lost on me. Then after a few more acts, there was a gesture at Zoltan. He stood up and walked to the stage. The nun announced him in Chinese and explained his routine. The music began, and he started his yoga.

I will do my best to describe how he looked on stage, but I have to prerequisite with asking you to get the images of down dog, up dog, and chaturanga out of your head. I didn't realize it until later, but Zoltan had traveled in India following a yogi for months if not years. His body flowed with the music, and his face looked relaxed as he did it.

He started straight up and moved his hands slowly like they were being pulled by the wind. His body moved to the slow rhythm of the meditation music and eventually, his body was stretched into positions that seemed to relax him, along with those who watched. As the song came to a close he unwound himself and bowed. When he finished, it felt like the room had stood still in time. All the Chinese and Westerners applauded as Zoltan bowed and left the stage.

He gave me a crooked smile and raised an eyebrow. I would become fond of this expression in time because it meant trouble or at least something interesting was about to happen.

Then time had to catch up, and everything seemed to happen at light speed. I grabbed my boiled eggs out of the silver bowl and walked up to the stage. The nun introduced me and the phrase "nagga nagga Juggling nagga [chinese word]" sticks out in my mind. All while she is shifting her hands up and down in juggling gestures. Juggling is not a commonly used word in Chinese.

I waved with eggs in my hand then started juggling. I performed using only the muscle memory I had picked up in high school. I did a three-ball cascade which is the basic juggling pattern to get a feel for the weight of the eggs in my hand.

Did I practice beforehand? Ha! You must think I plan these things ahead of time.

I then switched to some more complicated tricks and a light "Ooo" dispersed through the crowd. This sound is the typical reaction for anyone who juggles, and I assure you it wasn't because of my talent.

Then it happened. I don't know what I was doing maybe switching between tricks or trying something new. I honestly don't remember. However, before I noticed it, an egg was on the floor. The crowd cheered at the end of my performance, but I didn't take the cue.

I'm not a performer by any stretch of the imagination if I was then I would have acted much differently in this situation. At this point, Juggling is muscle memory for me, and that includes what you do when you drop a ball. You just pick it up and start over again; at least when you're practicing. I bent over, picked up the "ball" and began again.

I juggled a bit but the cracked egg felt funny in my hand, and it was shedding shell fragments on the ground in front of me. I wrapped my impromptu act up, caught the balls, and bowed. Light applause but nothing like what I received before came from the audience.

I walked off stage and didn't know or care if my face was red. I had fun, and I was smiling. I had walked up on stage and done something that made me uncomfortable. For that, I was rewarded with a feeling of accomplishment and confidence. These were not common feelings for me back home in America.

Then a young lady walked out from behind the stage. She wore a traditional silk Chinese robe that had yellow vines and flowers on a field of red. She carried a bag of sticks with her and set it down next to her on the stage.

She proceeded to grab the smallest stick on the stage. Then the second smallest which was twice the length of the first. She balanced the short one on the end of the longer one. She then took a new stick, twice as long as the second, and stacked the two balancing sticks on that. She repeated this and as she added sticks to her stack it slowly grew up, and away from her.

The last thing she did was balance this precarious stack of eight or so sticks onto a rod that was longer than she was tall. She balanced them successfully and the sticks hung in the air floating like a mobile in a baby's crib. She rested it on a stand that was built to hold the longest stick, and the crowd applauded. It was amazing to see her continued focus to repay her with a stack of balanced sticks that was long and nearly taller than her.

Then she walked to the end, stood up on her tippy toes, and plucked the first stick from the stack.

It shattered the balance of the entire contraption. All the sticks fell to the ground. The audience laughed in appreciation and applauded. It wasn't a hard act to follow, but her performance was incredible.

***

I decided to stay at the Buddhist monastery, and things got busy after making that choice. A daily schedule was created that started with morning chanting at 4:30 am and ended with silence throughout the monastery and lights out at 10:00 pm, or whenever I finished my Chinese homework, whichever came later.

Weekends were less structured. We spent Sunday doing maintenance around the monastery. Tasks like building a wall, polishing various Buddhist statues, and sweeping. I've never done so much sweeping!

Saturdays were spent touring other temples or traveling around the small rural city we were living near. Then one Saturday they convinced the Westerners to bake chocolate chip cookies.

Cooking was simple at the monastery. We divided the thirty people into six cooking groups, and every group took a turn cooking for everyone else. At the beginning of the week, someone suggested that I should make cookies. I agreed thinking there would be no way to get all the ingredients. I gave my Chinese teacher a list of the things needed, and she translated them for the person going to the market.

Then I began the typical tasks of working in the kitchen. One of those tasks was cutting 50 eggplants with a butcher knife and not losing a finger. Yeah, fifty. I thought they said fifteen, that would have been reasonable, right? No! 25 people require at least 50 eggplants for dinner. These weren't the big bulbous ones you see at the supermarket they're thinner than a banana and a little longer. A lot of the vegetables in China were different from what I saw at the grocery store in America. Some I didn't even have a name for like the scorpion tails that they fed us regularly.

Of course, these weren't really a scorpion's tail. That would require killing something, and Buddhists don't kill living creatures. Not even bugs. I found out after getting into the habit of calling it a scorpion tail that the vegetable was a lotus root. They sliced it thin, and the cross-section looked like a circle with holes punched out. It tasted like a water chestnut or uncooked potato, whichever sounds less appetizing to you.

I spent the week cooking with the Chinese and gathering ingredients for cookies. I was more of a hindrance in the kitchen than anything else and was usually deported to the sink whenever I was done butchering the countless number of vegetables they needed for the meal.

I didn't mind it, I've always liked washing dishes.

There were a few challenges with making chocolate chip cookies in China though. The glaring one is: "They don't have chocolate chips in China." However, this was the easiest of all the problems to solve.

A short list of other things I didn't have easy access to in China were:

- A recipe for chocolate chip cookies

- Measuring cups

- A mixer

- A full-size oven

- Easy access to brown sugar

- Easy access to baking soda

Step one was to find a recipe. The Great Firewall of China blocks Google, Facebook, and almost everything else that would have been useful to overcome this challenge. However, in college, I made chocolate chip cookies with a girl, and after eating them, I believed they were the most delicious thing I'd ever tasted. I'm not confident I wasn't being biased by something else. I wrote the recipe down on my phone and never deleted it.

I handed over the recipe to my Chinese teacher who translated the list of ingredients. In the end, there were three that we didn't keep stocked at the monastery: brown sugar, baking soda, and chocolate.

There were also no grocery stores in the town where we were living. Most of the food we ate was fruits and vegetables that we bought from local farmers. The spices and other staples were common enough that we could buy them in bulk ahead of time or find them at the corner store.

One of the women that was on cooking duty with me tried to explain to me that brown sugar was caramelized cane sugar (it's not) and that we could just leave out the baking soda because it's such a small amount (you can't).

My Chinese teacher made a special trip to town for the chocolate and other ingredients. She returned with a small bag of brown sugar and a lot of chocolate.

My understanding is that there's not a lot of demand for chocolate, or candy in general, in China. So what they do have is very nice... and expensive. There was a lot of drama about where the budget for the chocolate came from, and most of it never got translated. The budget got balanced in the end, and despite trying to give people money for it, no one would accept my cash because we were the ones doing the baking. The real reasoning was likely too complicated to cross the language barrier.

Baking soda was now the only missing ingredient. But it wasn't the only remaining problem to solve.

Unfortunately for me, the Chinese didn't use measuring cups. The monastery kitchen didn't have metric or imperial cups. Multiple Chinese women told me, "Chinese do all their baking by eye."

"Well, Americans don't," was always my stubborn reply. I considered going into the details of how baking was a chemical reaction, and

I couldn't guess the amount of baking soda we would need compared to flour. I'm sure some baker somewhere could, but it wasn't me.

Alternatively, we could have ordered some measuring cups online, after all the measuring cups we used at home were all made in China. However, after the chocolate budget fiasco, I didn't feel like adding that to the shopping list was a reasonable demand for me to make.

Then we found out someone at the monastery had a scale. Luckily that's what the Chinese use when they can't bake by eye. So we had a solution to that problem. But solving these challenges was like fighting a hydra. When one got resolved more always popped up.

In the recipe, I had listed the ingredients by volume and all I had for measuring was a scale for weight. I needed to figure out the density of all these ingredients... without Google.

In the end, and for more reasons than the chocolate chips, I caved and got a VPN. A VPN routed my internet so that I could get past the Great Firewall of China.

I began researching what the density of flour is on the temple's shotty WiFi. It turns out that different brands have different densities and Google didn't have anything on the Chinese brand of flour I would be using.

At this point, you're likely thinking: "Nicholas, why didn't you just search for a recipe using weights instead of volume?" And I agree that definitely sounds like something I should have done. But I didn't. I stuck to my guns with this random recipe I got from a girl I knew during my sophomore year of college.

I never claimed China was the only one responsible for dealing me challenges while I was there.

Finally, Saturday afternoon arrived, and it was time to bake some chocolate chip cookies. The Chinese were taking their afternoon nap, and the Westerners had control of the kitchen. My Chinese teacher was also there to help because she was interested in the process. She was also vital to getting to the point we were at.

I chopped up the chocolate while my Western counterpart found all the other ingredients. Guess what's still missing.

Baking soda and the scale!

Once again our teacher was there to translate us through another challenge. No one ever explained to us that the scale and baking soda didn't belong to the monastery. They were a part of someone's personal stash. We woke him up from his nap and got a hold of the final ingredients. Now that we had assembled the necessary ingredients there was nothing that could hinder our progress.

I turn to the westerner that I was baking with, "Hey let's preheat the oven."

"Okay, how hot do you need it to be?"

"350 Fahrenheit."

"What's that in Celsius?"

There was a long break before I answered and I used it to walk somewhere that my phone could get a WiFi signal. I then googled the conversion.

"175," I come back and tell him.

"The toaster only goes up to 125."

"How big of a difference is that in Ferenheight?"

It turns out it's a significant difference.

Our toaster, the only thing close to an oven on the temple grounds, was not equipped to cook our cookies. To make matters worse the wiring in the entire temple was bad, but the kitchen was the worst. The toaster was precariously plugged into the same strip that had the fridge and the industrial rice cooker which was engaged in cooking our rice for dinner.

There wasn't any way we could turn back now. We had bought all the ingredients, and there's not really a return policy at the Chinese market we shopped at. The only thing to do at that point was to set the oven to broil, turn the temperature to its max, and hope it doesn't blow a fuse. We started balling out cookie dough.

After some poking and prodding with the dough and adjusting the cooking time we finally got something that resembled a cookie.

Like most of the food I ate in China, it didn't resemble its American counterpart in any way. The cookies weren't crisp and caramelized like chocolate chip cookies were supposed to be. It didn't even flatten all the way and looked more like toasted balls of dough. But it was cooked all the way through and had chocolate and sugar in it. We didn't think anyone would complain.

About halfway through the batch of cookies, a nun walked in. She was visiting from another temple and had been living with us for a few weeks. She didn't speak a word of English. She said something to our Chinese teacher who explained the situation to us. We listened eagerly to find out what we were in trouble for now.

To our surprise, we found out we weren't in trouble. Our teacher explained that the nun was fasting during dinner this week and that was when we were serving our cookies. She wanted to know if she could have one before she started fasting.

I think there's a special circle in Buddhist hell for people who don't give fresh chocolate chip cookies to nuns.

You'll be happy to know I won't end up there.

In the end, everyone was happy about the cookies, even the Westerners. The result was nothing like a typical cookie the Westerners we pleased with a taste from home and the Chinese enjoyed the treat.

China threw a lot of curve balls at me during my time there, but each time that I stuck with something and got through the challenge, it rewarded me with something a little bit of happiness and a great story. If I had given up at any point in the process of making cookies, I would have never gotten to share the treat with everyone at the monastery.

They did a lot of things to help me while I was there, translate, plan tours, and cook for us. The least I could do was bake cookies in a precariously wired toaster oven.

Cursed Vacuum Tubes

Originally Published: September 7, 2018

H is garden took on his mood and this summer the garden was struggling to produce anything of value. Unfortunately, the engineer's shop was producing the same quality of work.

He'd sold a few patents years back and the royalties he got from those served him well. They didn't bring the wife and kids back, though they paid his alimony. With the leftover funds he invested in new machines and gadgets, and of course seeds and fertilizer.

Some summers would bring bountiful harvests. His greenhouse would be bursting at the seams. The unfortunate part was that he would often be too busy to manage the gardens those summers. Wild animals would eat the fruit off the vine, and neighbors would take a few knowing the man would never get around to eating all of it. When he would finally leave his workshop to take a few vegetables for a stew or salad there would always be plenty left for him.

The irony was now that he had the time and attention to put into the garden it wouldn't grow a damn thing. He had killed two basil plants and none of his tomato vines had produced fruit despite it being mid-August.

His luck in his workshop was no better. He had a project, he always had a project, but this summer it wasn't going anywhere. He had taken on the noble task of building an authentic Turing computer in his garage. It used ticker tape to run basic addition commands. For the first half of the summer, he had worked tirelessly on it knowing it wouldn't go anywhere. He worked on it with the hope that he might learn something in the process.

By now he had picked up a few things but the most useful thing he had learned was how hard it was to find vacuum tubes in this day and age. He briefly looked into manufacturing his own and then found that it was marginally more challenging. He dropped that endeavor but not the project as a whole.

He watered his garden for the third time that day. He inspected the small yellow flowers on the tomato plants and wondered if they would wither off the vine or finally grow into something of substance.

When the ground was soaked far more than it needed to be he wrapped the hose up and walked back into his messy garage. He turned on the machine and ran a simple addition program he had written late last night. He looked at the output after all the wheels of the machine had turned. The output was garbage. Two plus two equaled five, seven minus ten was a round twenty, and five divided by nine was somehow eleven.

It had been a summer of chaos. The machine's answers made as much sense as the rest of his life. Chaos from simple and known inputs. There was nothing that he could do to make sense of it. Sometimes the outputs weren't even the same between runs.

He had meticulously looked over the machine day and night. He dismantled it a dozen times and even moved different vacuum tubes to different areas. He referred to countless manuals and patents that documented the original designs of these machines but had no luck. There was no winning with this project. It was as hopeless as his garden nothing this summer was going to go his way.

He finally sat down and sprayed the light of his desk lamp on the punch card maker and examined that. He verified that the outputs were all wired up correctly. They of course were. Nothing was being done that was wrong. The only plausible explanation, which was in no way indicative of his reality, was that everything he knew and used to get to the point he was at didn't apply. Someone down the line had changed how electronics worked and he never got the memo. Or an equally reasonable reason was that he had bought a cursed vacuum tube and didn't know it.

He walked into the house and picked up the phone. He was truly desperate, he dialed the number for his ex-wife's house. The receiver rang three times and a young woman's voice picked up. "Marlin residence this is Suzy."

Hearing the new husband's last name out of his daughter's mouth stung but he continued. "Suzy, hey this is your dad. How's it going?"

The click was as quick as ever. At least there was one thing that still worked as he suspected.

Structure Gives Way to Creativity

Originally Published: September 14, 2018

I'm fascinated by how structure can give way to creativity. It's not something you would expect or consider. The trope of the creative is someone with a messy work environment and eccentric life with lightning strikes of creativity here and there. Ideas seem to pop up through that mess and because of it.

I suspect the opposite. I've experienced that more structure helps me be more creative. And at a minimum, it makes me more resilient to dips in motivation and productivity. When I have time set aside to do specific tasks, and I fulfill those obligations inside that time frame, I generally feel better about myself.

Thanks to the structure that I've built into my day I can be more creative. I've tasked myself with small habits that I know I can do every day no matter what. By focusing on only the task at hand, I am able to free my mind from the shackles of worry, concern, self-doubt, and most negative emotions that typically hinder me.

Every 5-6 weeks I wind up frozen in bed unable and unwilling to do anything at all. Maybe it's anxiety, depression, mania, or whatever, in my opinion, the label isn't important. What is important is that for some unknown reason, I have absolutely no ability to do anything... Nothing At All. The only thing that feels good is lying in bed and watching YouTube. And sometimes even YouTube is too much. Those times are the worst of them all.

There's one other thing that feels good. If I am being honest, and that's the only thing worth being in this situation, it feels good enough to kick me out of this lull. It is: doing what I say I'm going to do.

When the only two things that feel good to me are doing nothing and doing what I said I would do guess which one I'm going to pick.

Yeah, it's not the best system. But it's the hand I was dealt.

Unfortunately, positive thoughts, support from others, and motivational YouTube videos never do the trick long term.

The structure I've built in my daily life is the only thing that helps. Having these small daily tasks helps me continue to be creative, productive, and vaguely positive despite everything in my mind telling me I suck.

For me, there are two steps to getting out of these periods of time. Unfortunately, neither of them are as easy as they sound.

1. Say you're going to do a small task

2. Do the small task you said you would do

Step 1: Doing the Small Task

Saying you're going to do a small task is more than just saying it. You have to tell yourself that this single task is all that matters. You have to believe with all your mind, heart, body, and soul that the only thing you expect of yourself right now is for this small thing to get done. If I have any expectations to do something after that small task, then I've already lost!

Maybe literally saying it out loud or writing it down is necessary.

If there is any expectation that you need to do something beyond that small task you've stated, then you've already lost. I can lay in bed for hours listing all the things I need to do each one seemingly more impossible than the next. But when I limit it to one small thing, it becomes a battle between me and that single task. Sure it's still a fierce battle, but it's me against a single enemy, not an army of to-dos.

Step 2: Doing the Small Task

Then there's the second step, actually doing the small task. It sounds easy here, but in the moment I can promise you it's tough!

The thing that works for me, if I can remember to do it, is to focus on the moment. Merely think about whatever you're doing here and now. Sometimes I verbally denounce everything else that's going on as unimportant. Because honestly, it's not.

Whatever small task you've set out to do right here and now is the only thing that matters. That bill you need to pay is unimportant because right now you're brushing your teeth. The wedding that's coming up in two months that you're secretly dreading doesn't matter at all because you are changing a flat tire in the rain right now.

The time to focus on those tasks will come (if they're important enough) and when that time comes, you will fully concentrate on them then. But right now they are not the task at hand. They are distracting and crushing you, and the only way to climb out of that rubble is to focus on doing the small duty you said you would do.

When the second step is completed, go back to step one for another equally small task. Rinse and repeat for a week (or longer) and eventually the crushing feeling of time's relentless march and the burden of consciousness will pass, and you'll be back to normal.

I'm lucky and always get back to normal, most people are. However, in that state of mind, I feel like I won't ever get back to normal, and a whole lot of negative stuff that doesn't usually make sense makes sense. But if I focus on those thoughts, I lose! If I focus on the small task I set out to do, then I will win in the long run.

I don't know if this two-step system is the only thing that works, but it's what worked for me lately. If it wasn't obvious, I'm coming out of one of those negative dips, and this is a sort of letter to my future self. Hopefully, I can remember to focus on these small tasks more often and shorten the amount of time I spend frozen in bed.

Orbs of Purpose

Originally Published: September 21 to October 19, 2018

J oseph walked into the store with his parents. His father presented
Joseph's birth certificate so the shopkeeper could verify the boy's
age. Joseph held his mom's hand, and in the back of his mind, he knew
he would have to stop doing that soon. He was grown up now, and
growing up meant that you didn't hold your mom's hand when you
were nervous.

The man behind the desk returned the papers to his father along
with a few new ones. The shopkeeper opened a door, and the small
family followed him into the back room.

The area was full of aisles made of shelves. Each shelf had a dozen
orbs of glowing light. Some were clear with balls of light darting
around inside like they were ready to break out. Others were cloudy
with only a faint light inside. Those orbs looked like they needed to be
polished.

The man squatted down, so he was at Joseph's level. Joseph was
short for his age, and adults always felt like they had to do this. He
hoped that growing up would mean people would quit squatting to
talk to him and that he could just be their size.

"Are you ready to pick out your orb today?" the shopkeeper asked. He had a nose that seemed to blow up into a balloon at the end and his long face that came to a pointed chin. He looked like a bad guy from television.

Joseph nodded and let go of his mother's hand.

"Okay," the man said. He handed the boy a small pencil and a sheet of paper. "Go ahead and try some out. If you find one you like, write it down on this sheet, so you remember where it is. Once you pick one out, I'll merge you with it. Any questions?"

Joseph silently shook his head.

"Good, now try not to get lost," he said with a chuckle.

Joseph looked at his parents and smiled for permission to go. His father waved him off, and Joseph rushed down the first aisle of glowing orbs.

Before the aisle twisted, he looked over his shoulder at his parents. The shopkeeper was leading them toward some seats. He noticed his dad was now holding his mom's hand. He looked proud, but mom seemed nervous like he was. Then, for the first time, Joseph noticed that there were other parents in the waiting area. He must not be the only kid to have his birthday today.

He ignored the first few aisles that he traveled down. He was looking for something exciting. He didn't know what it would look like, but he knew they wouldn't keep it on the first aisle. When he turned to walk down a new aisle, he saw a boy staring transfixed into one of the glass spheres.

Joseph approached the boy and looked over his shoulder at the sphere. The light inside the globe was making an image of a man that looked a lot like the boy yelling at a woman. The boy seemed to notice that Joseph was there and rotated his hands so that it was balanced on his palm instead of sandwiched between his hands. Then with his free hand, he pushed Joseph away.

Joseph stumbled on his feet but didn't fall down.

"That's my future," the boy said. "You weren't supposed to be looking at it."

"I don't want that purpose, it's okay," Joseph replied. He assumed that the boy was just being protective of the orb he found.

The boy put it back on the shelf. "It's okay, I don't want it either. No one seemed happy in it. What future are you looking for?" The boy was a little taller and looked down. He seemed to finally be giving Joseph his full attention. "Have you seen any cool futures here?"

Joseph shook his head. "I haven't touched any of them. I was looking for a special one."

"I'm Tim." The boy stuck out his hand.

Joseph noticed that the hand was bigger than his but still young and smooth, unlike his father's. "I'm Joseph," he said as he shook hands.

"So, what special future are you looking for?" Tim asked in a quiet tone.

Joseph looked around. Tim's hushed tone made him wonder if someone might overhear them and steal his purpose away before he could find it.

"I'm looking for a purpose where I can make people happy and laugh because that's the most fulfilling thing of all. Maybe if I was rich and famous, too, that would be nice. My dad always says he wished he had picked a purpose where he was rich."

Tim's eyes went wide. "You want a future that will make you rich?"

"Yeah, why not?"

Tim let out a light laugh, one that reminded him of his father's right before he taught Joseph something. "You have to be rich to buy a future that will make you rich. Have your parents been saving up a lot of money?"

Joseph shrugged. "Not that I know of."

"Well, I'm sure you can find something that will make you happy. Come on, let's look around. Nothing on this aisle is any good." Tim whirled around and started running to the end of the aisle.

Joseph's short legs could only barely keep up. When they got to the end of the lane, Tim skipped a few aisles and then dashed down one.

When Joseph finally stood at the edge of the aisle, Tim turned around. He'd already made it halfway down. He was picking up a purple orb, not waiting for Joseph to catch up. When Joseph finally met with the boy, he saw a small scene playing out in the purple orb. Tim looked back at Joseph, and the scene disappeared.

"Look at that one," Tim instructed.

"How?"

The bigger boy laughed at him then replied, "Just look at it. After a little bit, it will show you what your future might hold."

Joseph looked into the purple ball, and he saw a man that looked like his dad but a little shorter. The man wore a fireman's outfit, and there was a building burning in front of him. However, instead of orange and red flames, the flames were tinted purple. Joseph noticed everything in the orb was tinted a little purple. As the building burned, the man finally rushed into the house.

Joseph watched as the man avoided the rubble and smoke pouring down on him. He found his way into a bedroom where everything was lit up in purple fire. A small girl was huddled on the ground, hugging a small bear. The girl looked old enough to be in one of his school classes.

There was no sound, but he could see her body shaking with furious coughs. Between coughs, she tightly hugged the bear. Her mattress and dresser were both putting off a lot of smoke.

The man picked her up and bundled her in his arms like she had done to the small bear. He carried her out of the house, and once they were a safe distance away, he put something over her mouth, and her coughing slowed down.

"Wow," Tim said in amazement. "When I looked at it there wasn't anyone inside for me to go save."

"Was that me?" Joseph asked.

"Of course, who else's future would you be seeing?"

Joseph considered answering the question but stopped himself.

"Let's look at some more!" Tim said, then he picked up a small lime green orb and stared at it.

The boys spent most of the morning picking up different glass balls. Tim's futures typically looked bleak to Joseph. Whenever he expected something exciting to happen, the older version of Tim seemed to pick the most boring thing in Joseph's eyes. When there was a chance to act extraordinarily for a girl, Tim typically chose the option that included spending the most amount of money to impress her.

In one strange orange globe, he saw Tim's future-self yelling at another adult. They were both dressed in suits, the kind of outfits his dad wore to work. Tim yelled so much in that orb that the young man ended up crying. When it was over, Tim offered the sphere to Joseph. "You want to see if you like it?"

"No thanks," Joseph replied. His father had told him to avoid any purpose that had a suit. "Did you like it?"

Tim shrugged. "It wasn't that bad. I think the other person in it was pretty dumb. I'm sure they deserved it. And I looked like I was pretty successful in it." He made a note of the orb's location on his piece of paper. "I might get that one; I don't know. Have you found any you might like?"

Joseph shook his head. "No, they've all been interesting, but none of them are what I'm looking for."

"Do you even know what you're looking for?" Tim's tone made Joseph feel like he was doing something wrong.

"I guess I just want a purpose that makes others happy and maybe be successful and rich."

"These orbs don't show you how you affect others. They only show your future." Tim used his snobby tone that was unfortunately familiar to Joseph. Tim's parents and siblings had explained a lot about this process to him. All Joseph knew going into this birthday was that he should pick something that he could live with for his whole life.

Tim set down the orb he held and spotted a light blue sphere and plucked it off the shelf. When Tim looked at it, an older version of him appeared and seemed very busy and worried about numbers on a computer. Many people came into the older Tim's office, and some left happy while others left sad. Tim wore a suit and seemed to have a lot of money, a nice office, and some fancy technology on his desk.

"Wow, this is weird. Usually, people that are this successful aren't on a shelf this low. You might like it," Tim said after the scene cleared.

Joseph took the ball from the boy and looked at it. The light blue tint deepened, and he watched the future version of himself in the mist. He was in an office similar to Tim's. However, there were some differences. Joseph's desk was smaller than Tim's, and there was less technology on it. Instead, it was filled with pictures of people. A few pictures had the older Joseph in them, others had older versions of his parents, and one in the center of them had a photo of a girl who looked to be the same age as Joseph was now.

As the scene played on, people entered his office. Unlike Tim's future, they all left happy. Joseph seemed to be giving hard news to some of them, but they all took it positively and thanked Joseph in the end.

The strangest part of all was that Joseph wasn't wearing a suit like Tim. He wore shorts and a collared T-shirt like the ones his mom made him wear when they visited his grandma. After all the people left, Joseph leaned back in his chair and picked up the phone. He gave someone a call, and when the call was over, older Joseph got up smiling, turned off the lights in the small office, and left. The scene faded into a light blue mist after that.

"Weird," Tim said when it was over. "I didn't call anyone. I wondered who you called."

"I don't know," Joseph answered with a shrug. But considering his mood when he left, whoever he had contacted must have been a person Joseph cared about a lot.

"Did you notice that I met with more people than you?" Tim asked.

"No, not particularly." He decided not to point out that more people left his office happy than Tim. Joseph had learned that this wasn't something Tim appreciated. Joseph made a note of the location and followed Tim to the next aisle.

They stood close to the end of the store with only a few aisles between them and the wall. Joseph and Tim still hadn't found any purposes that jumped out to them. They picked up some balls here or there, but most of them were generic. Over the past few hours, Joseph had learned that each purpose was unique in its own way, but a lot of them seemed to be similar to others.

He was tired of trying to spot the minor differences and just wanted the purpose that he showed up for. A future where Joseph could focus on making a lot of people happy and where he could be rich and famous.

They got down an aisle and watched three futures where both of the boys wound up in suits. Each time, Tim interacted with a lot of people and seemed very wealthy. In each sphere Joseph looked at, he interacted with very few people, but they always left the interaction a lot happier.

Joseph became bored with the spheres that were near his level on the shelves. He gazed higher up to the shelves above. Unlike the ones he and Tim had been playing with, these didn't all turn on when he stared at them. Joseph stared at three or four in a row before he finally found one that worked for him, but what he finally saw was the perfect orb for him.

In a lemon-yellow light, Joseph saw himself onstage with something that looked like a metal ice cream cone in his hand. He was talking into it, and there was a crowd of people in front of him.

The future version of Joseph would say something and then smile as the whole room laughed in response. It was a show or act of some sort, one Joseph had never seen.

After the performance was over, Joseph walked off the stage and talked to a few of the people from the crowd. They were very enthusiastic to meet him; some took pictures with him while others wanted him to sign blank sheets of paper. He shook all their hands and happily obliged their requests. This future version of Joseph seemed very happy to meet these people, and the people were even more enthusiastic to meet him.

Slowly the crowd faded, and so did the scene in the yellow orb.

"Wow! What was that?" Tim asked.

"That's the purpose I want!" Joseph said enthusiastically. He wrote down the location on the slip of paper the store clerk gave him.

Tim was staring up at the orb intently. However, the globe of yellow light didn't do anything. Tim looked to be focusing an uncomfortable amount to get the orb to show him a scene. When Tim finally broke his gaze, he angrily complained, "It doesn't work for me."

"I'm sorry, some of them up there don't work for me either."

"Yeah, but that was a really good future," the boy whined.

"I know, that's why I want it. And besides, we can't both have the same purpose. Let's see if we can find one up there that turns on for you."

"No!" the boy cried out.

The shout caused Joseph to slightly stumble back, and he expected the boy to start crying. Instead, Tim continued talking, anger growing in his voice. "I want that one. That one is the best one here."

Joseph was hurt. He finally found the purpose that he came here for, and Tim wanted it, too.

Then Tim added in a soft and teasing tone. "It's on a top shelf. I bet your family can't even afford it."

The words hurt Joseph, more than he thought words could. He hurt worse when he noticed Tim had written down the sphere's location and walked off.

"Where are you going?" Joseph called after him. He started running to catch up with the boy, but his short legs made it hard for him to keep up. As soon as Joseph caught up, Tim began to sprint away from him.

Soon they were both running as fast as they could to get to the store. Being the bigger boy, Tim got to the front of the store far before Joseph.

By the time Joseph joined him, Tim had already handed his paper to the man who worked there.

"Wait! No!" Joseph cried out between labored breaths. It was hard for him to talk. "I picked out mine. I want that one." He leaned on his knees to catch his breath, holding out his crumpled piece of paper with the orb's location.

The manager took the piece of paper and looked at the two boys confused. Tim gave a little shrug as if Joseph being upset and out of breath had nothing to do with him.

Joseph noticed his parents had come to stand next to him by now. His mother squatted down and looked at him, and he could tell she was concerned about his breath. She tried to comfort him and help him calm his wheezing. While she did this, Joseph heard his father talk to the manager.

The other adults in the room had gotten up, too. Joseph noticed the resemblance between them and Tim. They just stood beside Tim, politely interested in the words Joseph's father said. Tim's mother wasn't comforting Tim, who was pouting in a chair complaining about Joseph being mean.

Joseph took a deep breath and stepped away from his mom. He looked up at his father and the shopkeeper. The things they were saying were important. He had to know what would happen with his yellow sphere and who it would go to.

"Well, the boys can't both have the same sphere," the manager said.

"Tim came here first, so he should get it," Tim's father interjected with a calm tone that didn't comfort Joseph.

Joseph's father gestured at his son. "Tim only made it here because he ran faster."

Tim's father shrugged the comment off as if Joseph should merely have been born with longer legs.

The manager chimed back in. "Sirs, this is a top shelf sphere. Let's look at it. There are thousands of spheres in this store. I'm sure these two young gentlemen can settle their dispute. It seems they both have a few alternatives listed as well."

The shopkeeper gave Tim and Joseph a smile that reminded Joseph of a lizard he had seen at the zoo once. It wasn't a happy smile.

The manager turned down the aisle the boys had come from. The whole group was walking toward the yellow orb of purpose that Joseph wanted.

The group walked down a maze of aisles filled with spheres. Each sphere held a different purpose and direction that Joseph's life could take. But Joseph didn't care about any of those. All he cared about was the lemon-colored orb that held the future where he performed to make dozens of people happy.

The shopkeeper finally led the parents to the orb both boys wanted. He plucked the yellow orb gently from the top shelf. Inside, it glowed with a lemon light. The light danced behind a light cloud of smoke that was always moving and drifting as if there was a separate set of winds inside of the sphere.

"The top shelf spheres don't work for everyone," the man explained, as everyone looked at him and the orb. "But for the individuals it does work for, the path it will lead them down is full of meaning, purpose, fame, and riches. Tim, you got to me first, can you show us what your future would be? Just stare into it."

The man handed the sphere to Tim. The boy wasn't the same height as the man, but he was tall enough to reach the orb without the shopkeeper having to squat down in front of him.

Tim stared into the orb and at the yellow light. Typically, it would change; it changed for Joseph a few moments ago. But after a minute of the light dancing inside the glass globe, Tim said, "It's not working." Then the boy offered the sphere back to the shopkeeper with the bulbous nose.

"Hmm," the shopkeeper said, "Did it work before? When you decided that this was the purpose you wanted."

"Yes," Tim lied.

"No, it didn't!" Joseph claimed.

"Yes, it did," Tim snapped back with a scowl that showed a storm behind his eyes.

"I don't know why it would stop working in such a short amount of time," the shopkeeper said. He put on a confused look, and it reminded Joseph of the look teachers gave him when they asked a question but already knew the answer.

"Joseph, why don't you try. We can make sure it still works for you." The man squatted down, and Joseph was eye level with the man's pointy chin. He handed the sphere to Joseph, and the boy held the orb in front of him. As he stared into it, the light began to take shape.

He saw himself back on a stage talking to a large group of people. He would say something, pause, and then the whole group would laugh. Joseph loved the feeling he got while watching his future-self make people happy. The performance ended, but the scene continued to play. It was now onto the part where people were talking to Joseph after the show. They took pictures with him and hugged him. His future-self was so excited to meet them, and the fans seemed even more thrilled to talk than he was. The scene played out longer than any of the other orbs that Joseph had looked at, but inevitably, it faded back into the dancing yellow light just like it started.

He offered the store clerk the orb, but the man was already standing up and talking to the adults. "It seems that the orb has more of a connection to Joseph than it does to Tim. Because of this, I'm going to have to offer it to Joseph's family first." He looked at Joseph's parents, and Joseph followed his gaze.

The two adults had frowns on their faces. From their perspective, they could see the price on the shelf. Joseph's father turned to look at him and squatted down to be eye-level with the boy. At that moment, Joseph wanted to climb up on the shelves so that he could be the same height as the adults.

"I'm sorry, son," his father said. "That orb is very expensive. There's no way we could afford it. Is there another one that makes you just as happy?"

Joseph frowned; he could tell he was on the edge of tears. There wasn't a single orb that he had seen that made him as happy as the yellow future he just saw.

He fought back the tears and found the courage to say, "There might be one or two." Then he looked at his mom, and he could see she had quiet tears rolling down her cheeks. The boy realized that this was why his dad had told him to find a future that made him rich.

The shopkeeper lowered his hand, and Joseph gave him the yellow orb. "There are a lot of spheres in this room, and it seems that you listed another one that you were happy with," the shopkeeper informed him. "We can't all have our first choice." The shopkeeper said the last sentence as if it was a statement of fact instead of a conciliation.

"So that means I can have it?" Tim said eagerly.

The shopkeeper sighed, and Joseph could see the nostrils on his funny nose grow a bit. He looked down at Tim.

"It doesn't work for you, young man. Don't you want a sphere that you're more compatible with?"

"No!" Tim proclaimed, "I want that one."

Joseph looked at the boy who was about to steal his ideal purpose. The sphere was everything Joseph had hoped for when he walked into the shop this morning. The yellow orb had given him so much joy to watch. Joseph felt his heart break with the thought of someone else having it. At that moment he knew it was the purpose that he might go his whole life longing for, regardless of what future he chose.

"Are you sure?" the shopkeeper asked, looking down his nose and at the boy. He held the yellow orb above the boy as if he was guarding it from him.

"Yes!"

"I have to tell you that it is dangerous to pick a sphere that isn't compatible with you. It is going to be hard for you to live out a purposeful future. Do you still want it?"

"Yes," Tim yelled at the man. Then he whirled around and faced his parents. "The man won't let me have what I want."

Joseph didn't know why Tim was informing them of what they already knew but thought there might be something more complicated happening.

Then the boy's father spoke up. "Are you going to give him his future or not?"

"If he truly wants it, then I can give it to him, but I want him to understand the consequences of merging with a sphere that isn't compatible with him." This time, the shopkeeper squatted to be at the same level as him. "Tim, I want you to understand that if you choose this future, you won't have the same experience as Joseph. You won't live the life in this sphere, and I don't know what will happen to you. There are hundreds of thousands of spheres in this building, and most of them will give you a clear indication of what your future might hold. This one won't."

"I want it anyway," Tim said stubbornly.

"I wasn't finished. Listen." The shopkeeper sounded serious. "When I say your future is unknown, I'm not saying it's up to chance. I'm trying to explain to you that it will be set in stone like every other adult in this world. You're incompatible, meaning you won't have a happy life. You won't make others happy. You won't even be happy yourself. You'll be forced to live out this future like every other person. This orb won't show you a future not because you don't have one with it, but because the future is so bad that it's not worth showing. Knowing all this, do you still want to merge with this future?" The shopkeeper had a grim expression on his face by this point.

"Yes!" Tim said with a stubborn stomp of his foot. "I want it so that Joseph can't have it."

"I can't have it anyway!" Joseph yelled at the boy. His mom held his shoulder, trying to comfort him. And he was glad it was there, otherwise he felt like he would tackle the bigger boy.

"Look, are you going to let my son have this future or keep lecturing him?" Tim's father said, "He wants this future, and he's a smart boy. He will do great with any future he chooses."

The shopkeeper let out a long sigh. "Of course, I will give the boys whichever future they want and can afford."

"We can afford this. Now let's get on with it," the father said.

"Very well." Then the man with the bulbous nose turned to Joseph, "Do you want more time to browse the selection, or is the other orb you listed here satisfactory?" He showed the boy the small paper Joseph had used for notes. "If you are happy with the future you saw, then we can pick it up and infuse both of you at the same time."

Joseph thought about the question. He could pick the future where he met with a lot of people, made them happy, and then left for the day after calling someone who made him very happy, or he could keep browsing. The small boy knew there would never be a future like the yellow orb Tim was getting. Comparing the two, he knew the work in the office wasn't great, but at least he didn't wear a suit, and his dad always told him that he should pick a future like that.

"Honey," his mom chimed in, breaking up his thoughts.

He realized that he had been thinking about the choice for a long time. Tim's father looked impatient, and his son mirrored a similar look. The shopkeeper held the yellow orb in his hand. Its yellow lights flickered in and out of the clouds of smoke. The man looked patient and calm, waiting for Joseph's decision. The man wasn't acting like a teacher but like his mom, waiting for him to finish showing her one of his drawings.

"I don't want to look at any more orbs. I'll take the one I wrote down."

Joseph called his first employee into his office. It was time for year-end reviews, and he was delighted to give them his honest feedback. Each of them had performed above and beyond his expectations, and he was excited to give them areas to improve in for the next year. His team was small and efficient. Everyone was looking to go above and beyond for the company when they needed to. He made sure that the company went above and beyond for them when it came to compensation and benefits.

It meant he made less, but he did far better than most. He was able to afford just about anything he wanted, within reason. And he was saving up for a big upcoming purchase he might be making. Best of all, he was his own boss, which meant he could wear whatever he wanted to work. On days like today, that was a polo and shorts, just like he wore as a kid visiting his grandma.

He called each of his employees into his office and gave them their review. A lot of them asked for more details about what they could improve on. That was always a good sign. He explained what their bonuses would be and what kind of raise they could expect to see next year. They were all happy with their numbers. Each of them seemed to leave his office more content than they entered. That was how he gauged his success.

He wasn't successful every time, especially in the beginning. Sometimes hard conversations had to be had. However, for the most part, his employees seemed genuinely happy with him, and as he hoped, his feedback to each of them was clear—he was thrilled by their performance.

His employee Gordon left Joseph's office. He was the last review for the day. Joseph picked up the phone and called Clarissa, his wife.

"Hey, how's everything going?" she asked.

"Great. I just finished meetings, and it went well."

"No one threw anything at you or argued with you about your criticisms?" she asked, and he could hear the mocking smile through the phone.

"Of course not. I don't know why I was worried about it. It happened once, and I'm always afraid of it happening again. But right now, I've got the best team I could imagine. I have to keep them happy, so they don't disappear."

"They make your job easier, so I'm all for it." There was a brief pause on the line, then Clarissa brought up a new subject. "Hey, I talked to your mom today. They've been looking at where they want to move, and she told me about a place that she liked. I looked into it, and it's a bit on the pricey side."

The couple discussed numbers. He had agreed months ago to help his parents move out of the old home they'd raised him in. His business was going well, and getting them around people their age would be good for their health. And it was the least he could do for all the things they did for him growing up.

By the end of the couple's conversation, Joseph had proved that it was in the budget saying, "I'll tell them to get on the list. They need some community in their life."

"Okay, they'll be thrilled, but your dad will be slow to accept it."

"Mom can help him with that," Joseph replied.

"Are you headed home soon?"

"Yeah, I'm leaving the office right now."

"Good because Alice is picking out her purpose this afternoon, and she wants you to be there."

"I wouldn't miss it for the world."

Alice walked through the door following the shopkeeper with the balloon-shaped nose. She looked at the room full of shelved colorful and shining orbs. There were countless aisles in both directions.

"Help yourself," the shopkeeper said to her as he left her with her parents.

"Alice, one thing," her dad called out.

"What is it, Dad?" She was eager to get started looking at orbs.

He squatted down in front of her, and then picked her up, so she was taller than him or Mom. He let out a long and goofy sigh of exertion.

"Dad, I'm too big for you to pick me up like this," she said behind a smile. She always enjoyed being picked up by him. She saw her mom nod behind him in agreement.

"I just wanted to give you some advice. You don't have to listen to it, but I'd be a bad father if I didn't give you unsolicited advice."

"Yeah, yeah. You're going to tell me what you and mom always tell me. Be generous to others, and try to make them as happy as you." It was a line that she had heard from both her parents multiple times.

"You took the words right out of my mouth. But I want to tell you that for today, and every day from here on, I want you to aim high." He paused for a moment and looked around. "And look for an orb where you don't have to wear a suit, those are the best ones!"

After that, he hugged her tight and put her back on the ground. With a small piece of paper and a pencil, she darted off, looking at the shelves full of orbs. Each one was a brighter color than the last. There were pinks, purples, blues, greens, and a dozen more.

She picked up an orb with a dark green light that shone through a cloud of smoke. The ball felt cold in her hands as she stared into her first option.

My Last Blog Post...

Originally Published: October 26, 2018

This article is the last blog post I'll release as someone who isn't an author. Come Wednesday I'll be independently published, and the book I've been working on in tandem with this blog will be available. Additionally, we're coming up on the one-year anniversary of this blog. I'm excited to publicly reveal for the first time the cover of the first edition:

What's it about?

Todd Rungson can bend time and space at his will. With a single breath, he can travel between parallel universes. He has traveled through time to experience everything the universe has to offer. Content with the life he's lived Todd returns to high school to live his life for the last time.

On the day he returns His high school girlfriend Gretchen mysteriously dies after he explains his power. He then discovers her deaths are happening on the same day across every universe he visits and they're growing more violent. Todd will have to put his powers and life at risk to find out why every Gretchen he meets is cursed to die.

Thank You for Everything

I want to thank everyone who has subscribed and encouraged me to keep writing. Your emails, feedback, and comments have been especially supportive. I particularly want to thank those of you who joined me on Patreon, you have helped make this blog and book bigger and better than I could have done alone. Thank you!

Step into the Road Updates

The goals of this blog's first year were:

1. Write

2. Write more

3. Write even more

I've been working hard to get used to the publishing schedule of the blog and learning how to produce and publish a book that is worth reading. I don't want to say I've figured it all out but I know enough now that I can move on to the next phase of being a writer which is improving how I share the stories I've written.

Step into the Road's Logo

That being said, Step into the Road (SitR) is as much a blog as it is a publishing company. Given as of today it's only published one book and 60 blog posts, but you know what they say about small beginnings.

To add to some resemblance of professionalism and because I've wanted one for a while now I've designed the first logo for Step Into The Road:

What's coming next year?

In 2018 I made a laundry list of resolutions and goals for the year. About three months into the year I threw out all my goals except 2. They were to Get a Job (with health insurance) and Publish a Book. As of next Wednesday, I will have accomplished both of those.

In that same spirit of simplicity, this is what I want to bring to the blog and to you the readers in 2019:

Another Book

Ideally a full-length novel (maybe even the first of a series). It's been a while since I wrote a full-length novel and it's no small undertaking but given a whole year, and what I learned from an Echo Through Time, I think I can manage it. I'm grateful that I started small with this first book and I plan to use what I learned from it to make the novel better. But more about that book early next year!

More Better Stories

It's been pointed out (and noticed by myself) that my grammar in, and the proofreading of these stories, leave something to be desired. My philosophy for the past year has been to put something out there on Friday so that I can practice telling stories. I have now done that 52 weeks in a row, and I think that's plenty of practice!

In an effort to keep improving, I plan to spend 2019 improving the quality of the work on this blog. Including but not limited to:

- Hiring Proof Readers

- Designing covers for the stories

- Making my stories more widely available

I plan to do this by writing the stories earlier. Currently, the production schedule of this blog goes a lot like this:

Monday Morning

Publisher Nicholas: "Hey Writer Nicholas you need to put something on the blog this Friday."

Writer Nicholas: "Didn't I just do that last week?"

PN: "Yep, now do it again."

Wednesday Evening

PN: "Did you get that post written?"

WN: "Well sort of..."

PN: "Dude! Get on it!"

WN: "Fiiiiiine"

Thursday Evening

PN: "That story is supposed to go out in less than 12 hours! Is it done yet?"

WN: "Well mostly."

PN: "This is littered with spelling errors, and you don't even have pictures in it yet. What the hell?!?"

WN: "I'll get to it, I'll get to it!"

Friday Morning:

WN: "Hey I actually sent something out!"

PN: "I didn't think it would happen."

WN: "Me neither."

Monday Morning

PN: "Hey Nicholas you need to put something on the blog..."

I plan to invest time in making sure that the stories are drafted at least a month beforehand so that there's plenty of time for proofreading and planning. This plan also has the added benefit of having stories with endings that are thought out... unlike some stories (see The Automaton's World). This production schedule will also be less stressful and help me free up some time to write the novel.

Social Media

How I'm accessible online is the third thing I want to improve on in 2019. Anyone who follows my Twitter or Facebook will be forgiven for forgetting that they're following my Twitter or Facebook since my posting schedule is as consistent as... well, it's not consistent, and that's the problem.

Those of you who know me know I don't use social media for myself so using it for the blog is a whole new swamp to wade through. But I promise, in 2019 I will get my act together and figure out how this stuff works. You deserve a way to interact with me that's more advanced than freakin' email!

***

Lastly,

Thanks for an amazing 2018! Writing is always fun, but it's more fun with readers. I've appreciated everyone's support and having a group of people that I can email my stories to has been incredibly motivating. I hope you've enjoyed it as much as I have! There's still a lot of work for me to do to close out the year but as of next Wednesday, I'll be an author!

If you have any suggestions on what I should do with this blog in the upcoming year I'd love to hear them. As always you can contact me by email or my contact form. I love hearing from y'all, and I read & respond to all reader emails.

Find Peace in Progress,

Nicholas Licalsi

Rockwall, TX

Epilogue

S omeone who is more literately inclined would call this an afterward. But in my eyes, my life is a story and this was just the beginning.

Writers say that your first million words are going to be garbage, that if you can get through those first million your second million will start selling and resonating with readers.

You'll likely never read Stephen King or JK Rowling's first million words. This makes it seem like they sprung onto the scene as an immediate success. It's an interesting story. The story of a genius coming out of nowhere certainly sells books.

Unfortunately, it does a disservice to anyone who actually tries to put pen to paper and sees how short their writing falls compared to the best sellers of the world. It certainly discouraged me and kept me lost for longer than I would have liked.

By my estimation, this collection of short stories and articles captures the first quarter million words of fiction I ever tried to write. I probably had 100,000 to 150,000 before publishing the first things on my blog. Frankly, that's as close as I'm willing to let anyone get to seeing how amateur I ever was

As of 2025 I've drafted a million words and published most of them for the world to read. There were bumps and turns and a bit of stalling out along the way. Patience rarely exists in the toolbox of beginning writers and I am no exception.

I never expected it to take 8 years to get to a million words. I hope it doesn't take another 8 years to get through my second million. But if it does it does; I'll just have to hold grace and patience for myself along the way.

This collection ends with me announcing the release of my first book: An Echo Through Time. It's still available and has a couple of sequels with more on the way. If you enjoyed the stories in this collection I have no doubt you'll enjoy reading that novella.

But there's another book that follows this collection...

There are a few stories that took multiple weeks to write and publish: Orbs of Purpose, Meet AALFO, The Automaton's World, The Infinite Library.

After I published "My Last Blog Post..." I started another one of those multipart stories, a project simple called "Rocks, Ropes, & Mountains."

I thought it was going to be another 5-week story that I could draft in a few weeks. Instead, it morphed into over 30 weeks of writing following the journey of Ferrun through the afterlife.

Those posts eventually became "A Trial of Rock and Rope" which I also compiled and published. The novel is still available today and I am quite proud of it.

I opened this collection talking about how writing gave me direction during a time of my life where I felt lost. Pursuing any craft would've given me that direction, I chose writing, you may choose something different.

The direction provided has never faltered, even if my dedication to the blog and my writing has faltered but it's never disappeared.

Since I started down this path I've often asked the question: "What would be best for my writing?" when faced with tough decisions. It hasn't steered me wrong since.

It's encouraged me to do things that were out of my comfort zone. I've taken on and given up responsibilities as appropriate because of my writing. It's encouraged me to marry a wonderful woman and get professional counseling. Without those two things, I doubt I would've been able to keep at this for as long as I have.

It's always interesting to tell people that I'm a writer. Everyone has grand ideas of what that means. Is he a millionaire? Is he famous? Is he some starving artist trying to put out the next Great American Novel?

My definition of being a writer—and the definition of every successful writer I've ever met—is: A writer is someone who writes.

Publishing is not required. Making money is not required. Having readers is not required. Being a best seller is absolutely not required.

For me, the rewards of being a writer are not measured in social credit and external validation.

Writing provides me with internal satisfaction. I enjoy getting to look into other worlds, explore my self, and solve tricky plot puzzles. Those things are my idea of fun.

Since writing's rewards are internal I would still do it if I was the last person in the world, and I do it regardless of how much I can measure my success.

This internalness of writing provides me the direction I need.

And that direction, in no uncertain terms, is worth my life.

Find Peace in Progress,

Nicholas Licalsi

June 2025

Also By Nicholas Licalsi

The Slugs of Dale Cannon

Rystole Whitlock, a young rancher and colonists on the Earth-like planet of Dale Cannon, spends his days cutting class and herding buffcows.

When a group of alien slugs invade his family's cabin he can't find a good way to corral them before the toxic slugs put his mother in a coma.

Determined to save his mom, and the rest of the colony, Rystole won't stop until he gets revenge or a cure.

If you enjoy exploring alien worlds and first contact stories with young heroes then you'll enjoy Slugs of Dale Cannon.

https://books2read.com/SlugsOfDaleCannon

The Hacked Manticore and Other Cyberpunk Stories

Bett the hacker gets a personalized message on a computer he just broke into. J-Red the streamer accepts a mobster's job offer to get his belongings out of repo. Pairs of packages and pizzas arrive at the doorstep of recently unemployed Kiran.

The cyberpunk world of Galleria Valley runs on corporate greed, shady mob deals, and bionic enhancements. No one survives long when playing by the rules.

Let these short stories be the neon lights that guide your hovercar through the towering buildings of Galleria Valley.

https://books2read.com/HackedManticore

A Trial of Rock and Rope

Upon his death, Ferrun Monteiro wakes up in the afterlife. Instead of building paradise the gods have designed a challenge.

To escape the afterlife Ferrun must reach the top of a mountain with a boulder tied to his ankle.

Yet not a single soul has completed this seemingly simple trial.

Unperturbed, Ferrun faces the god's challenge head on. Follow him on his odyssey through the afterlife.

If you enjoy dreaming about the afterlife, you'll enjoy A Trial of Rock and Rope.

https://books2read.com/ATrialOfRockAndRope

About The Author

Nicholas Licalsi's love for science fiction and fantasy started with a box of his grandfather's pulp paperbacks and the brain-washing alien parasite nesting between their pages. This led to an interest in engineering, robotics, and time travel.

After a successful enough career in software development Nicholas now spends his time trying to trick his overactive imagination into paying the bills while he satiates his dog's need to be pet.

He currently has 9 independently published books available everywhere books are sold and countless short stories on his blog StepInto TheRoad.com. You can get a free book, and updates about his writing, time traveling, and (most importantly) his dog by signing up for his email list at StepIntoTheRoad.com/SignUp

Connect with Me At: https://stepintotheroad.com

Newsletter Updates At: https://stepintotheroad.com/signup